WHILE YOU SLEEP

SHERILEE GRAY

Content Warnings

Obsessive/predatory hero, stalking, dubious consent, consensual non-consent, explicit sex including an instance of somnophilia, what some will consider an unhealthy or toxic relationship, child abuse (emotional and physical, off-page), murder, guns, violence.

Chapter One

Cillian

She was a heavy sleeper.

Sophia didn't wake when I let myself into her apartment, or when I slid the book from under her hand to see what she was reading this week.

I put the book back carefully and picked up the bottle of body lotion that sat on the bedside table, then twisted off the lid and breathed it in. Vanilla and cinnamon. Her favorite. I put it back and studied her lying there.

My mother had read fairy tales to my brother when he was little. I used to sit outside his room and listen. I hadn't really understood them. I wasn't one for whimsy. I wasn't one for anything at all when it came to the finer nuances of emotion, but I'd come to think of Sophia Brennan as my very own little Sleeping Beauty.

When Seamus asked me to find out everything there was to know about her, I did the usual: her address, details of her building's security, the places she regularly went to, the people she spent time with. She worked from home as a graphic designer, so that kept her list of in-person acquaintances short. I'd also bribed the receptionist at her doctor's office and gotten a copy of her medical records.

I'd handed all the information over to Seamus. Job done.

But then, I'd come back—repeatedly—only these times while she was here. While she slept.

She whimpered in her sleep now, her leg kicking out, her arm jerking back. The sound gripped me low in the gut, my body reacting as if she'd made the sound just for me.

Sophia suffered from REM sleep behavior disorder, which meant she often physically acted out her dreams and nightmares—thrashing, screaming, talking, crying, moaning in her sleep. All that restlessness had resulted in a secondary disorder: hypersomnolence. She needed more sleep than others, slept for longer periods, sometimes needed naps, and, in Sophia's case, very heavily.

She whimpered again, and I stepped closer.

I didn't know why I kept returning to her bedroom week after week. I didn't do things like this. I studied her face, like I always did, as if she could somehow give me the answers. Her head was to the side, her cheeks pink, flushed. The blond hair at her temples was damp. She always had too many covers on. I peeled one back, like I did every time I came here. The nights I didn't visit, I wondered if she was too hot or if she'd thrashed so much she'd hurt herself. Why? I had no idea. I didn't know why I thought about her at all.

Yes, she was beautiful—you didn't need to be in possession of a wide variety of emotions to see that—but there were lots of beautiful women in this city. She had a good body; nice tits, a round ass that jiggled when she walked, and a tight waist I imagined wrapping my hands around while I fucked her from behind.

But I wasn't desperate. If I wanted to fuck, there were plenty of women who would offer themselves to me. Even if they looked at me with fear, I had status and money, and that was enough to get them to spread their legs for me. And others just wanted to know what it was like to fuck a monster. I didn't think about them, though, about any woman until I had use for one. When I was done, I didn't give them a second thought.

So why did Sophia Brennan keep entering my head at random times of the day and night?

Her lashes rested on her cheeks, her eyes moving behind her lids as whatever dream she was having played out. Her lips were full and a little puffy in sleep. I wondered, not for the first time, how soft they'd feel against mine. I didn't think about a woman's lips, except for how they'd look stretched around my cock.

Sophia stilled suddenly, so much so, I couldn't hear her breathing. She did that sometimes as well, becoming so still, so quiet, she could be dead. I held the back of my hand in front of her mouth until I felt her warm breath brush over my knuckles. My heart rate increased instantly.

There were only three things that made my heart beat faster: working out, fucking, and Sophia Brennan. My pulse didn't even elevate when I blew the top of someone's head off.

So what was it about her that had that effect on me? There was no logical explanation for this obsession, but I'd found a word for it online. Limerence: a state of involuntary obsession for another person. Symptoms included obsessive thoughts about that person, a strong desire for reciprocation, and an idealized image of the object of one's obsession—I had them all.

She rolled over, making a little noise that lifted goose bumps across my arms, then she stiffened, her body bowing before she opened her mouth and screamed. Her arms flew out, her legs kicking under the covers. She barely missed the bedside table. The cushion she'd put there before going to bed had fallen. If she hit the table hard enough, she could break her arm or hand; if she fell out of bed, she could knock her head, despite the extra cushions and quilts she'd scattered around the bed for protection.

I stepped forward and did what I had to, what she needed me to do, even though she had no idea that I regularly did it. I climbed onto her bed and wrapped my arms around her, restraining her so she didn't hurt herself, holding her tightly until the dream passed and she settled down.

I lay there as she thrashed in my arms, until her cries and whimpers finally stopped, then I buried my nose against her neck, in her hair, and listened as her breathing evened out, breathing in her addictive scent.

Once, I'd walked in to her apartment to find her moaning and rocking. Someone had been fucking her in her dreams, I was sure of it. I'd never seen anything like it, and I'd had the irrational urge to murder whoever she was dreaming about. Then and now, I thought about how easy it would be to slip under the covers with her, to stay right here—she'd never know. But I wanted more. I wanted her to look in my eyes as the O'Rourke monster claimed her as his.

For now, this had to be enough.

Whatever this feeling was inside me, the logic I lived by didn't apply, and, apparently, I was okay with that.

Chapter Two

Sophia

Eight months later

Brian's gaze sliced down my body and back up. My face heated. I really wish I didn't blush so easily. He'd been texting while I was home with my family this weekend, and we'd talked about going out on a date.

"Soph, hey." He gave me a hug, pressing me tight to him.

"Hey." I squeezed him back.

He sat in the booth, moving along for me, and slid a drink my way. "Got you a vodka and Coke."

"Thanks." I took a sip and looked around. The bar was packed and the music loud. This was exactly what I needed. After the weekend I'd had, I was in the mood to dance, to shake off the weight that going home always left me with.

Tommy was the only good thing in that house. My baby brother was the only thing I missed when I wasn't there. My father was always busy, but he'd been more distracted and irritable than usual. Celeste, his wife, had been just as awful as she always was. I'd tried to help out around the house, and with Tommy, as much as I could to make things easier on both of them, but I couldn't seem to do anything right.

It's not like we'd been spending quality family time together, I don't even know why Dad insisted...no, demanded that I come home for the weekend. I shuddered. Seamus O'Rourke and his slimy son Adam had come by the house on Saturday, and my father's mood had deteriorated even more. But then Dad hadn't been himself since my uncle died and he became head of the family. He never said it out loud, what our family was, but all you had to do was search our name online and it was all there, speculation at least, about both our family and the O'Rourkes.

He was obviously struggling with his new responsibilities. Not great when you were in charge of one of the biggest crime families in Chicago.

Fiona plopped down in the seat opposite me, beside Steve, and he slung an arm around her shoulders. She'd met him on a dating app, and they'd been seeing each other for about a month. I glanced at Brian. I'd met him at the cafe I took my laptop to when I needed a break from my apartment. We kept running into each other, and he'd eventually asked me out and I'd turned him down. Dating when you came from a family like mine wasn't easy. Add in my sleep disorders, and I'd given up on ever having a relationship at all. He hadn't gotten pissed off though, when I turned him down, and we'd become friends. We started hanging out, and he and Steve had struck up a friend-ship, which made it fun when we all went out like tonight.

But recently, Brian had been pushing for more, and this weekend, while we'd been texting, I'd kind of caved. I was a twenty-four-year-old virgin for fuck's sake and seriously sick of being alone.

Brian gave my leg a squeeze under the table, and my face

heated. "Missed you," he said and moistened his lips when he looked down at me. "So...when are we going out?"

My belly fluttered. "Am I hallucinating...or are we not, in fact, out right now."

He chuckled. "Smart-ass. I meant just the two of us. A real date."

"Fine. If you insist on having me all to yourself, I'm free later this week." Was I supposed to play it cool? Not seem too eager? How the hell would I know? I was far from cool. Brian was cute, and nice, and we had lots in common. We were friends first, and that was a good basis for a relationship. Though, once he found out about my family, he'd probably run for the hills.

He grinned and gave my leg another squeeze. "Cool. How about Thursday night? Dinner and a movie?"

More belly flutters. "Sounds good."

A song Fiona loved came on, and my best friend jumped up, grabbed my hand, and yanked me out of my seat. Brian waggled his fingers in a silly wave as she tugged me out to the dance floor.

"Damn, girl, Brian wants you bad," she yelled over the music.

I laughed, feeling light and happy for the first time in a long time. "You think?"

"I saw him wipe drool off his chin."

I chuckled, shaking my head as she spun me around, then we were singing the chorus of the song at the top of our lungs. The music was so good, we stayed out there for the next song as well.

Fiona leaned in. "You have an admirer." She bit her lip. "He hasn't taken his eyes off you since we got out here."

She did a little spin so we switched places, and I looked over her shoulder, expecting to see Brian.

Not Brian.

A guy leaned against one of the pillars that bordered the edge of the room. He was tall and built, but not in a bulky gym-body way. He wore jeans and a dark tee. His tattooed arms were folded over his chest, and his biceps stretched the sleeves. His gaze caught mine, and I sucked in a breath. His eyes were the brightest green I'd ever seen. My gaze dipped. His beard was trimmed close, surrounding a mouth that looked as if it'd been sculpted by the gods. Goose bumps broke out all over me.

Fi was right, he was definitely watching me, and when my eyes met his again, he gave me a chin lift.

Heat bolted through my veins so fast that my limbs went weak. Fiona twirled me again, and I laughed breathlessly. I tried not to look back, and succeeded for a few minutes, but when I finally gave in, he was gone.

Brian and Steve joined us then, dancing around like goofs to the next song, and I made myself stop searching the room for Mr. Green Eyes.

We danced and drank for the next few hours, and Brian pulled me close for two songs and we slow danced, something I'd never done before, which was embarrassing, but with how controlling my father was, there'd never been an opportunity. Even after he'd allowed me to move into my own place a year ago, I'd followed the rules, his rules, as if I were still in his home. It'd taken six months for Fiona to get me to come out with her, and a full year to finally agree to going on a date and slow dance with a good-looking guy.

Brian smiled down at me and pulled me close, and I instantly wrapped my arms around his neck, feeling bolder now, thanks to several vodka and Cokes. More than once tonight, I thought he might kiss me, but so far he hadn't.

"You're really fucking beautiful, Soph," he said, looking down at me.

"You think so?"

He nodded, his gaze dipping to my lips.

I called on all my courage. "Then why haven't you kissed me?"

His gaze sliced back up to mine. "I wasn't sure you'd want—"

"Kiss me," I said.

His lips curled in a cocky grin, then he cupped the side of my face and pressed his lips to mine. I'd been kissed twice before. Both times had been at parties my father had thrown. My first kiss was with Ethan McGory, the son of one of Dad's friends. The other had been with a guy he'd hired to work the bar a couple years later, his name was Luke. Those kisses had been okay, nothing exceptional. I'd had high hopes for Brian, but as his lips moved over mine, there were no tingles or sparks —then I felt guilty for thinking it.

I tightened my arms around his neck and slid my tongue over the seam of his lips. He groaned, his tongue thrusting into my mouth like a dart aiming for my tonsils, then it was tangling with mine, but it was too wet and way too sloppy.

I pulled back, and he stared down at me hotly before pressing another soft kiss to my lips.

It took everything I had not to drag the back of my hand over my mouth right in front of him. "I'll be right back," I called over the music. "Ladies' room."

I turned to grab Fi, but she and Steve were sucking face, and the way my friend was basically climbing him, the building could come down around us and neither of them would notice.

I strode across the room, and as soon as I was sure I was out of Brian's view, I wiped my mouth with my sleeve and rushed into the bathroom.

Disappointment filled me. *Don't panic.* Maybe he was drunker than I thought? We're a good fit. We had all this stuff in common: movies, books, and we both loved to cook. I just had to give him a chance. We were going out on Thursday. I'd let him kiss me again then, and I was sure it'd be better. I'd finally found my courage; this couldn't all be for nothing. It couldn't. What if I never found the courage again? What if I never met anyone else who could take me away, take me from my life.

What if...

I slammed the door on those thoughts. I was spiraling, going places I didn't need or want to go.

Quickly using the bathroom, I washed my hands and was fixing my hair when Fiona's text dinged on my phone, telling me to hurry up, that a good song was playing. I grinned. I needed to be more like my best friend. Fun and free. *But you're not free, you'll never be free.* Shaking my head and those thoughts out of my mind, I shoved the door open and rushed back out—and slammed right into a wall.

No, not a wall—a man. And I didn't just bump into him, my front literally smashed against his. I tried to scramble back and, *oh my god,* my hand brushed his junk. I tilted my head back, my face aflame. *Shit.* Not just any man, it was the guy with the tattoos and the pretty green eyes.

"Um, I...sorry."

He flashed a grin that made my insides melt. "No worries."

His voice was deep and had a raspy quality that lifted tingles across my head and down my arms.

"I ah...saw you...before."

He studied me for several long seconds. "Yeah."

He was still close, really close. Nerves exploded in my belly, and when I got nervous, that's when the verbal diarrhea happened. I knew it, I hated it, but there was no stopping it, and the alcohol wasn't helping. "I'm just here with friends. I needed to dance, have a drink. I spent the weekend with my family, and well, you know what family can be like?" My face was so hot now, I had to stop myself from fanning my cheeks. "I mean, if you have a family, I shouldn't have just assumed. Sorry, that was...god, sorry..." I cringed and slammed my mouth shut.

"Family can be tough," he said, those green eyes studying me in a way that set off little sparks all over my skin.

I nodded. I'd been right, his lips were sculpted perfection. "Sorry, I have a habit of babbling when I'm nervous."

"And apologizing."

"What? Oh, yeah. I do that too."

"Why are you nervous?" he asked.

"Um..." *Because you're so incredibly hot I'm having trouble standing upright.*

His gaze kind of darkened. "That guy you're with, you know him well?"

I blinked up at him. "Yes," I whispered. Why did he ask me that? And why was I whispering? Probably because this suddenly felt weirdly intimate.

"You left your glass with him." His dark gaze moved over my face, and I shivered, visibly. "You shouldn't do that. You need to be more careful."

He'd been watching me, not just while I danced? I opened my mouth—

"Soph!" Fiona rushed up. "We're leaving..." Her head tilted back, looking up at the guy standing beside me. "Hey there."

He nodded.

"I have to go," I said to Mr. Green Eyes and inwardly cringed again. The guy was most likely just trying to get back to the bar after using the men's room, or god, trying to *go* to the men's room, and I was acting as if we were in some Shake-spearian tragedy. *Parting is such sweet sorrow!*

His mouth curled up on one side. "Okay," he said.

My face erupted again, the flames burning my cheeks.

Thankfully, Fiona saved me, grabbing my hand and tugging me away.

Steve and Brian were waiting by our table, and Brian took my hand when we reached them, but I couldn't stop myself from turning back as he led me from the bar.

Mr. Green Eyes was right there. He'd followed after us—and he was still watching me.

———

Cillian

Sophia walked away with the preppy-looking fuck who'd kissed her earlier, and the urge to stop them, to grab him by the throat and gut him in the middle of the pub was harder to resist than it should be.

I walked out onto the street as her friend and the other guy split off, getting into an Uber. Sophia lived close, a couple blocks away, and I wasn't surprised when she and her date headed off together in that direction. I followed, hanging back, sticking to the shadows.

The floppy-haired fuck still held Sophia's hand like she belonged to him.

That wouldn't do. Not at all.

The beard had worked. I'd grown it when talks of an alliance had heated up, in case she recognized me. She hadn't. Not surprising. The few times I'd been in the same vicinity as her, she hadn't noticed me among all the men in the room, it was like I was part of the furniture. Probably because she kept her gaze averted and her head down. Wise in a room full of preda-tors. I didn't mind, it was the way I liked it. I stood back, preferred to observe. If people didn't see you, they didn't see you coming.

My gaze slid over Sophia. She was short, hips rounded, belly soft, natural tits, you could tell when she moved they were all her. Her body, the imprint of it, how it felt pressed into mine while I held her sleeping, thrashing body, was a constant. Her blond hair was a little wild from dancing. I knew how soft it was, and my hand curled, imagining thrusting my fingers into it and fisting it tight.

When she moved out of her family home twelve months ago and Seamus asked me to get intel on her, it didn't set off any alarm bells. He liked to have that kind of info at his disposal, especially since her father was the new head of the Brennan family. It made sense. The Brennan and O'Rourke families had conducted business alongside each other for over thirty years, each backing the other's endeavors when necessary, while carefully not stepping on toes or tipping the balance of power. Each had their own particular business interests, and with the two families working as closely as we did, the Irish owned half of Chicago.

But Seamus had grown wary of sharing—he'd been looking for a way to tie the families together in case Callum Brennan got any ideas to fuck us over. Seamus had finally gotten his opportunity when Brennan fucked up, encroaching on our territory, and the end goal was now pushing him out and taking over completely. Brennan owed Seamus, and Seamus had made his move this weekend.

I'd had to stand by and do nothing while a deal was struck. Sophia didn't know it, but if things went the way Seamus and her father planned, my piece of shit half brother, Adam, would be marrying Sophia Brennan, my precious sleeping beauty, in six weeks' time.

I was older than him by eight months and had just as much

of Seamus's poisonous blood in my veins as he did—only my mother had been the mistress and Adam's had been the wife. No one spoke of it, and the old man had never claimed me or my brother Declan as his, but we did share a surname—my mother had been canny enough to put his name on our birth certificates. Seamus told everyone we were the poor cousins from Ireland, but everyone knew the truth.

I was the oldest son.

Sophia should be mine.

When they reached her building, her date was definitely hoping she'd invite him up, but she stopped at the door. Of course she did. She wouldn't trust preppy yet, not enough to fall asleep beside him, to be that vulnerable. I couldn't hear what they were saying, but he leaned in and kissed her again.

Cold steel touched my hand. I'd gone for my gun without even realizing it.

Sophia's eyes were squeezed shut, and she was kind of pulling back, but he leaned into her more, his hand roving up her side, going for his target, her chest. I gripped my gun tighter.

She pushed at him and lifted her head, a shy laugh bubbling from her lips. The asshole was panting, thimble dick stiff behind the zipper of his trousers, eyes wild. I understood his reaction. He wanted to fuck her, badly, but good girl that Sophia was, she'd make him wait. Either that or she just wasn't that into the desperate gobshite.

They exchanged a few more words, and he loped off.

She watched him go for several seconds, looking flushed, then turned and rushed inside, shutting the door firmly behind her.

I pulled her wallet from my pocket. I'd lifted it when she'd collided with me. I'd waited for her outside the restroom, and she'd done exactly what I expected—apart from the babbling.

Adam wasn't much for talkers, he liked his women quiet and obedient, mainly because he was weak.

Sophia was naive, detrimentally so. Starved of affection, desperate for approval. Her father was a piece of shit and her stepmother was a bitch—she wasn't getting any love or kindness from either of them—and her best friend, Fiona, was self-absorbed and more interested in the guy she was fucking than her supposed best friend. Sophia would be eager to please, desperate for a kind word, for affection. Adam would eat her alive. He'd break her within a week. That light in her blue eyes would be dull and faded by the time he was finished with her.

Watching her tonight, I got the feeling my wee beauty was looking to get fucked so badly, she was considering letting some preppy asshole do the honors. I wasn't going to let that happen.

None of it.

I wasn't the best at reading people, but I knew interest when I saw it, and Sophia had looked at me with a good amount of it. A lot more than the man she'd been kissing on that dance floor. I knew every facet in those eyes, every facial expression, I'd studied them like it was my full-time job.

Usually, when a woman looked at me like that, she wanted me to get her off, and if she made my dick hard, I gave her what she wanted. But I'd never had a woman look at me the way Sophia had. She'd stared up at me, babbling, about fuck knew what, all flushed and trembly, eyes big, silently asking me for something she couldn't even fucking describe.

But I knew.

I knew what she wanted from me, even if she didn't.

Because I knew her.

I'd killed more people than I could remember, taking a life was easy. Meaningless. For most of my life I'd been numb, felt nothing, and I'd wanted nothing but for Declan and I to take the positions in the O'Rourke family that were owed to us —until now.

I pulled my phone from my pocket and hit Declan's number.

"What's up?" my younger brother answered.

"I'm done waiting."

There was a beat of silence. "Then so are we."

I disconnected and looked up at the second-floor corner apartment.

No, Adam wasn't getting one more fucking thing that was meant to be mine.

Chapter Three

Sophia

My phone dinged as I walked out of the cafe, then someone called my name from across the street before I could pull it from my pocket.

Brian jogged toward me.

I hitched my bag higher, fighting my nerves as heat rushed to my face. "Hey." Being shy sucked, I blushed all the time, even when there wasn't anything to freaking blush about. "How did you know I was here?"

"I didn't." He grinned. "Fate seems to like throwing us together."

If I believed in that kind of thing, I'd say he was right. I seemed to bump into him all the time.

"You excited for tonight?" he asked.

"Yep." Well, kind of, but I was trying hard to get enthused. We'd had our movie-and-dinner date last Thursday, and I'd had a good time. Brian was a nice, normal guy. That's what I wanted, right? And it really was cool that we'd started off as friends, and now that he and Steve were tight, it meant we could double-date with him and Fiona, and that was fun. We had a good time when we all hung out.

Brian grinned and his dimple popped. "I'm really looking forward to it, Soph. Though, technically, it's our third date," he said.

"Oh, and how do you figure that?"

"The pub was kind of like our first. I mean we had our first kiss there, right? The dinner and movie last Thursday was our second, and, if I remember correctly, I kissed you good night then as well."

Where was he going with his? "You did," I said and my stupid face went hot again. He'd latched on to my boobs and jammed his tongue down my throat like it was a fist and my uvula was a punching bag.

He leaned in now and pressed his lips to mine, taking me by surprise. He'd done the same after our date last Thursday as well. Just when I was about to walk away, he swung me back to him and planted one on me before I realized it was going to happen. I wasn't a big fan of the sneak attack or making out on the street in front of everyone. His hand crept higher, and he swiped his tongue over my lips. I kept them firmly shut—because, good god, so much saliva—and grabbed his hand, stopping its steady progress.

His mouth went to my ear and he chuckled. "You don't have to be shy, Soph. Besides, I want everyone to know you're mine."

His? I wasn't so sure about that. We'd only been on two dates. Yes, I'd been trying to convince myself he and I should be a thing, but I wasn't quite there yet, despite how nice and normal he was—how different he was from my father and the men who surrounded him.

He lifted his head and looked down at me, a kind of wild look in his eyes. "You know what happens on the third date, don't you, baby?" he said, his voice all deep.

It took me a minute to work out his meaning, then the light bulb flicked on.

Oh shit. He thought we were going to have sex.

He winked and smirked at my dumbfounded expression. "I've gotta go, but I'll pick you up at seven." Then he sauntered off down the street.

I stood there, not completely sure how things had progressed this fast. We'd literally only kissed a couple of times and now he expected sex? A car horn blared, jolting me out of my stupor. I took off, speed walking in the other direction. Is that what I wanted? Did I want to have sex with Brian? Last week I would have said yes, now...I wasn't as sure.

And that's why you're still a freaking virgin.

Fiona said I was too picky, but she was wrong. It wasn't like I'd been saving myself for Mr. Right, it just hadn't happened yet. Yes, I was shy, but I'd been working on that. Backing out of this date would be taking a giant step backward, wouldn't it? It wasn't exactly my fault I was so inexperienced. It was hard to meet a guy you could get serious with when you had a family like mine. It wasn't like I could take him home to meet my father. Then there were my sleep issues. I'd have to tell whoever I slept with that I might give them a black eye in the night or scream suddenly or make some other weird noise. They'd have to put up with me napping or randomly falling asleep, and always sleeping in. The only other option was sending him packing as soon as the deed was done so as to never fall asleep around any guy I had sex with.

Would Brian run for the hills when he found out what my family was? When I told him about my sleep disorders? I wouldn't blame him.

I needed someone who loved me enough to see past all of it, someone who'd take me away from this city and start a new life. Failing that, someone strong enough to protect me from the world I was part of, but I wasn't sure a man like that existed.

I shook my head as I pulled my phone from my pocket. I

was way ahead of myself. It was just a few dates, we were so far from meeting the parents, if it ever even came to that. I checked the screen and smiled.

Dean: How was your day?

I'd dropped my wallet at the bar last weekend and was frantic when I realized I'd lost it. Dean had found it at the table we'd been sitting at, and he'd used my driver's license to look me up on Instagram, then messaged me, saving my ass completely. We'd struggled to find a time to meet up, so I'd asked Sharon, who owned the coffee shop, if he could leave it there. She'd happily agreed. It turned out Dean was a really cool guy and funny. We'd been talking most days for almost two weeks. I guess we were friends now.

Me: My client loved the web design. I'm starting to actually believe this could be a career for me.

Dean: Yeah, it could, and if anyone says different, I'll take them out.

There was a water gun, a bomb, and a snake emoji at the end. I laughed, shaking my head.

Me: Good to know. If I need anyone taken care of, you're my guy.

Dean: Don't you forget it. Customer just drove in. Talk later.

Dean was a mechanic. The garage had been his father's, and after he died, he and his brother had taken over. He'd shared that with me during one of our late-night texting sessions.

I got in my car and headed home. I had more work to do before I got ready for my date. I'd been designing websites and making graphics for people since I was in high school. I hadn't wanted to spend years in college, so I'd taken some design courses after graduation, building on what I already knew. It was important to me to be independent, to make my own money, to show Dad I could do it on my own.

I thought about Brian again and my belly churned, and not in a good way. What the hell was wrong with me? I had a good-looking, sweet guy interested in me. My virginity wasn't the freaking crown jewels. I didn't need to keep my hymen under lock and key for a special occasion. What I did...*who* I did, was my own freaking business. I needed to break the damn seal, grow the hell up, and get on with it.

———

Several hours later, I'd finished the graphics I'd been commissioned to do and stood in front of the mirror, studying my reflection.

I felt as if I were playing dress-up. Fiona loaned me one of her dresses. It was short and low cut, and I wasn't sure I could pull the look off, but Fi didn't think anything of mine was sexy enough for the date, and I knew she was right. My stomach gripped. Walking around like this would send my father into a rage.

He wouldn't know, though, how would he? Plus, I had a long coat to cover myself until we got to the restaurant.

Slipping on my sandals, I checked my lipstick, then popped it in my bag. I wasn't sure where we'd end up tonight, if he'd come back here or if we'd go to his place. I still wasn't completely convinced, but if things between us did progress, I planned to be safe. I took the unopened box of condoms from my drawer and tore one off. Would one be enough? I had no idea. I grabbed a strip instead and shoved them in my purse. I'd be honest, explain I had a sleep thing, and that I wasn't comfortable sleeping over yet. Though, I wondered if perhaps it'd gotten a bit better recently. It'd been a long time since I woke with an injury. It used to be most mornings I woke with bumps and bruises, occasionally a cut or two. In the last year, it'd only been maybe once a month.

My phone chimed.

Dean: My brother's having a party and some fucking amateur just puked outside my bedroom door. Gonna have to crack some skulls.

Me: Gross. I bet he feels terrible.

Dean: If he doesn't now, he will soon. What are your plans tonight?

Dean wasn't the kind of guy you fucked with, and he didn't sugarcoat it, but I like that he didn't pretend to be something he wasn't.

Me: I have a date. Not sure about my outfit, though.

Dean: This the same guy you went out with last week? Things getting serious?

Me: It's only our second date, even if he's insisting it's our third...

I finished the text with the rolling eyes and a laughing face emoji.

Dean: Show me the outfit.

I chewed my lip.

Should I? We'd been talking for two weeks, and he hadn't said anything weird. He'd been honest to the point of blunt. No, I hadn't known him long, but I trusted him. His social media profile picture was of him with his dog, not that you could see his face, he had his back to the camera, the pair of them looking out at a sunset. It was cute. Serial killers didn't have pictures with their dogs and sunsets as profile pictures, right? And he already knew who I was, he'd seen my driver's license.

I stood back and snapped a picture of myself in the mirror, then hit send, a weird little flurry of nerves zooming through my belly.

Me: What do you think? Too obvious?

His response came back almost immediately.

Dean: You look fucking hot, Soph.

I bit my lip as the little flurries turned to zaps of electricity. Yeah, I liked the way he said things. He just seemed so real— and he thought I was hot.

There was a knock at the door.

But Dean wasn't here. He hadn't asked me out, Brian had.

Me: Thanks! Gotta go! He's here!

———

Cillian

I stared down at the picture she'd just sent. I hadn't been able to stop staring at it since it came through five minutes ago.

I zoomed in on the counter. Condoms.

She was on a date, looking like that, and she had condoms in her purse. What I wanted to do was follow them, then shoot him in the head as soon as I could get him alone.

But that wasn't an option. I had to play this carefully.

I scanned what she'd said again. *He's insisting it's our third...*

I didn't have any personal knowledge when it came to dating. I didn't date. But I knew what a "third date" meant. I'd heard the reference and its meaning enough in movies and TV shows. Preppy was expecting to get his dick wet.

There was another bang outside my door, and I strode over and yanked it open. The guy who'd puked on the carpet was stumbling around fucking shit-faced. I grabbed him by the front of his shirt and slammed my fist into his face, once, twice, a third time. "You're a disgrace," I said, then tossed him aside.

Declan jogged up the stairs. "Jesus."

"He's fine."

My brother used his foot to roll the guy to his back. "Oh aye, he's just grand. At least he's still fucking breathing, I guess." Dec shook his head. "Why are you here again?"

"You know why." He knew as well as I did how important this deal going my way was. I needed to be close to Sophia while she had Brian sniffing around, and Dec's apartment was closer to her than my place. I grabbed my jacket. "I'm going out."

Declan leaned against the wall. "No, wait...please...stay."

I ignored his sarcasm and strode out, almost knocking over some woman who basically dove for my dick as I walked past. Knocking her down was an accident, but I didn't stop to help her up. I wasn't a fan of being pawed at by random strangers.

I pulled out my phone, texting as I walked.

Dean: Where's he taking you? So someone knows if this guy turns out to be a fucking psycho.

I got in my car and waited for Sophia to reply.

Sophia: Some Italian restaurant. It's fine, you don't need to worry. Have a good night. I'll talk to you later.

I gripped the steering wheel so tight it groaned, then started the car even though I wasn't sure where the hell I was going. I'd fucked up. I thought the insecurity she had about her sleep disorder would stop her from getting serious with anyone. I was wrong, and now she was out with this guy, with condoms in her purse.

I swung by several Italian restaurants, but I had to be careful. More than one in this area were frequented by Alto Leone and his men, and they wouldn't welcome Seamus's enforcer strolling into their territory unannounced. Things between us and the Italians had been tenuous for a while now—something I planned to change when I took over. But if I showed up now, they'd assume the worst, and we had enough to deal with among ourselves, let alone start something with someone else.

This was pointless.

I'd miscalculated. I hadn't seen this guy as a real threat. Not until she'd sent that picture. With nothing else to do, I headed back to Sophia's apartment and parked across the street. All I could do now was wait and hope he didn't take her back to his place.

Several hours later, I finally spotted them walking along the street. He was talking, and she had an odd look on her face. I clicked open the camera on my phone and snapped several pictures. I didn't know who this guy was, but there was something off about him. They stopped at the door, and he grinned down at her, saying something.

Sophia blushed, I could see it from here, it was something she did a lot. Then she chewed her lip, but not in some coy way, not trying to be sexy. She was uncomfortable. I'd been watching this girl for a year, and I'd seen this look on her face multiple times. She had the same expression when he'd walked her to her door after their date last week. I'd almost gotten out of the car that night. He'd fucking mauled her, and it wasn't hard to tell she wasn't into it. I thought she'd be done with him after that.

Fuck knew why she'd gone out with him again.

He tried to lead her to the door, motioning to the keypad for her to unlock it and take him upstairs. When she balked, he pulled her into his arms and kissed her. Her smaller frame stiffened before she pulled away, shaking her head. His hands fisted, and the look on his face set off alarm bells.

He thought he was getting a taste of her tonight, and he wasn't happy she'd turned him down. Sophia backed up and quickly keyed in the code. Brian said something else, and the uncertainty on her face slid away. Whatever he'd said she hadn't liked it. She yanked the door open, and he lunged to grab the handle, but she shoved it closed, locking him out.

He banged on the door as she took off.

Brian cursed several times, then punched the wall.

I looked at him more closely.

I was no expert, but that seemed like a big reaction over being rejected by someone you'd only been out with a few times.

He pulled his phone from his pocket, hit the screen, and walked off down the street. I looked up as Sophia's lights came on.

Two minutes later, my phone dinged.

Sophia: So my date was awful. Brian's a gargantuan creep. I'm staying single for the rest of my life.

I thought about what Dean would say, he'd want to play the hero. He was the good guy. I quickly typed out a reply.

Dean: What did the asshole do?

Sophia: He wanted to come up to my apartment. I wasn't into it. He didn't take it well.

Dean: What did he say, Soph?

Sophia: That I'm a cock tease, that he's looking for an adult relationship, and I'm obviously too frigid to give him what he needs.

I found this kind of interaction difficult. I didn't know how a woman's mind worked, or what Sophia would need to hear. I quickly typed out my reply and hoped I got it right.

Dean: Did he really think spouting some reverse psychology bullshit would convince you to fuck him? Fucking pencil dick.

Sophia: How is it you can make me laugh when I'm on the verge of tears?

She thought Dean was funny for some reason. I didn't know how to be funny, I was just observant, but mainly I channeled my brother. Women seemed to like him, found him humorous.

Dean: Don't cry over that douchebag. There's a reason you didn't invite him up, yeah? If you were into him, he'd be there with you now.

Sophia: You're right. I was trying to force something that wasn't there.

The lights in her apartment went off.

Dean: You gonna be okay?

Sophia: Yeah. Thanks. I think I'll just go to bed and pretend tonight never happened.

Dean: Night, Soph.

Sophia: Night, Dean.

I'd make sure she was okay. As soon as she fell asleep, I'd go to her, and if that fucker caused her nightmares, I'd be there to hold her down.

I quickly sent the picture of Brian to Declan, along with his name.

Me: I want to know what this fucker eats for breakfast.

Declan replied with a thumbs-up.

I had a bad feeling about this guy. He wasn't going to go away easily, I knew that much. He wanted Sophia, and he wanted her badly.

If he didn't take the hint after tonight, I'd make him go away. No, I didn't need a reason to put a bullet in his head, but I preferred there to be more than just being the idiot dumb enough to get a hard-on for Sophia Brennan.

If that was the criteria, I'd have to shoot half the guys who crossed her path.

Then turn the fucking gun on myself.

Chapter Four

Sophia

It was Saturday night, I was supposed to be out with Fiona, but I decided to stay home instead. I was avoiding Brian. He'd been calling constantly, and I didn't want to run into him, not yet. I'd texted him and told him as nicely as I could that we weren't a good fit, that I didn't want to see him anymore, and still I'd seen him waiting outside the cafe when I arrived earlier today to work. I'd actually hidden so I didn't have to talk to him. He'd freaked me out the other night. He'd kind of acted like one of the men my father surrounded himself with, instead of the mild-mannered guy I'd gotten to know. He'd become aggressive, and abusive, and honestly, I didn't want to be alone with him. We definitely had nothing more to talk about.

Lying back on the couch, I scrolled for something to watch.

My phone chimed and another text from Brian popped up on the screen.

Brian: Would you just meet with me? Give me a second chance, please.

I swiped it away trying to ignore him, but my phone started ringing a few seconds later. This was getting ridiculous. He wasn't taking no for an answer. I had no idea why he was so persistent. We'd been friends, yes, but only for a short time, and he'd destroyed that when he'd behaved the way he had. I didn't want to talk to him, but he obviously needed to hear me say it.

Taking a fortifying breath to ease the nerves rioting in my belly, I answered. "Brian..."

"Soph, fucking finally. What the fuck? Why are you ignoring me?"

If he thought snapping at me would help his cause, he was seriously mistaken. God, he even sounded different, like he'd been hiding an entire side of his personality. "I told you why. It's not going to work between us. I'm sorry, but I don't want to see you anymore."

"You're not thinking right. You don't want to take things between us further yet, fine. I'll give you more time, okay?"

"You're not going to change my mind. This is over—"

"For fuck's sake, Sophia! Why are you being such a fucking bitch?"

My breath locked in my lungs, dread filling me. I'd been around an angry man, an abusive man, my whole life, and at his raised voice, his anger, my flight instincts kicked in and it was hard not to shrivel in on myself. "Don't call me. Don't text me. We're done."

"Don't you fucking hang up on me!"

I quickly disconnected, confused, shaken. I thought he was a nice normal guy. I'd been so wrong.

I hadn't heard from Dean all afternoon. He said he had a family thing, but right then I needed to talk to someone, and I don't know why, but Dean made me feel safe. No, I'd never met him face-to-face, but something about him, the things he said, the way he said them, it was like he knew me. He wasn't fake or pretended to be some good guy because he wanted something from me. And he didn't judge me.

Maybe it was stupid, but I felt like Dean understood me more than anyone else in my life. I quickly typed out a message.

Me: Sorry, I know you're busy, but Brian just called and completely lost it with me.

His reply was almost instant.

Dean: Don't need to be sorry, Soph. Text any time, yeah. You okay?

Me: I guess. I just freaked out there for a minute.

Dean: Understandable. I'm driving, so can't text for a bit. You'll be okay till I get home?

Me: Yeah, thanks, Dean.

I instantly felt at ease. While I waited for him to get home, I changed into my pj's and washed my face, then poured myself a glass of wine to steady my nerves. Curling up on the couch again, I found a romantic comedy, one that looked light and fun and put it on.

I was fifteen minutes into the movie when my phone dinged again.

Dean: Home. You doing okay?"

Warmth filled me instantly.

Me: I'm a lot better now that I'm talking to you. And the glass of wine's helping as well.

Dean: You sure? If you're really worried, I could come over.

I blinked down at the message. We'd never talked about meeting in person. I didn't even know what he looked like. We'd grown so close, so fast, but neither one of us had suggested it. I felt safer just texting him, but inviting him over? I wasn't so sure.

Me: What if you're secretly some weirdo catfishing me?

I didn't believe that, not really, but you couldn't be too careful.

Dean: A catfish pretends he's someone else, using pics of

other people. I've never shown you a pic of me. What if you've been catfishing me?

I smirked.

Me: You saw my ID pic and one of my outfit the other night!

Dean: What if someone else picked up your wallet when I handed it in? That other photo could've been in there as well. You could be the old woman at the cafe.

I laughed.

Me: And she gave you her number instead?

Dean: Sure. Those catfishing types go to all kinds of lengths to fool their targets. Maybe you have Soph locked in a closet?

I snorted, then impulsively took a pic of myself. My hair was a little mussed, but in a kind of sexy way, and my eyes looked bright, and there was just the smallest peek of cleavage. Not that I was trying to be sexy. We were just friends. I mean, Dean could be some old dude for all I knew, but then he didn't really sound old in his texts.

Gah! I was overthinking it. I hit send on the picture.

Me: See, not in a closet.

I tried to watch the movie while I waited, but when my phone lit up, nervous excitement raced through me for some stupid reason.

Dean: Good to know. You're also seriously fucking stunning, Soph.

I was glad he couldn't see me because my face went hot. Dean thought I was stunning. My nerves increased as I typed out my reply.

Me: Your turn.

It doesn't matter what he looks like, you're just friends. I told myself that repeatedly, but when his reply came, nerves exploded in my belly. I squinted, too scared to look as I clicked the message open.

I sat up straight, sucking in a breath.

I stared down at his picture in shock and—awe. It was him. Dean was the guy from the bar. The one I'd walked into outside the ladies' room.

He was sitting back on a leather couch, wearing dark pants and no shirt. Tattoos covered most of his lean, muscled chest and arms, and his bright green eyes stared back at me, clear and gorgeous. He had a slight tilt to his sensual lips. The short beard was a little thicker now, his hair falling over one side of his brow.

Me: It's you.

Dean: It's me.

Me: We talked that night in the bar, and you've never said anything.

Dean: I don't think you missed I was checking you out that night, Soph. Didn't want you to think I was some stalker. We okay?

Were we? He'd kept who he was from me, yes. But he also hadn't been creepy or pushy. He'd been a friend to me and nothing more. Brian aside, I was usually a pretty good judge of character.

Me: We're okay.

My phone dinged again, but it wasn't Dean this time.

Brian: I'm here, let me up. We need to talk face-to-face.

Me: Go home.

Brian: Let me the fuck up now, Sophia. You don't let me up, I'll find my own way up, I promise you that. But I'll be a lot less pissed if you do it right the fuck now.

What the hell was going on? Why was he acting like this?

Brian: NOW!

Fear shot through me, and without thinking, I hit Dean's number. He answered instantly.

"Soph, hey."

"I'm sorry to call like this, but Brian's here. He's downstairs and he's really angry. Demanding that I let him up. I'm scared."

A normal person would call the police, but that wasn't done, not in my world. We were told from a young age never to call the cops, but there was no way in hell I could call my father, I'd be signing Brian's death warrant if I did.

"Barricade your door and don't open it to anyone but me. I'm on my way."

He didn't disconnect, he said something to someone else. It was muffled, and I didn't hear what it was. I put Dean on speaker as messages kept coming thick and fast from Brian. He was so angry, and the things he was saying were seriously fucked up.

"Talk to me, Soph," Dean said. "What's happening?"

"He's texting a lot of threats, but he's still on the street."

The sound of an engine revving came through the phone. "I'm not far away. Be there in five."

I walked to the window and peered down. Brian was pacing, his phone to his ear. He was trying to call me. His name kept coming up on my screen while I talked to Dean, and I kept rejecting it.

Mr. Blake from the floor below was walking toward the building, and I watched, horrified as the rage on Brian's face slipped away and what I now knew was a mask slid into place, hiding what a deranged creep he truly was. He smiled at the older man and said something to him, laughing. Mr. Blake laughed as well and opened the door letting him straight in.

"Oh god."

"What is it?"

"He got in. He's in the building."

"Fuck," Dean bit out. "Lock yourself in the bathroom, and don't come out until I call."

He disconnected, and a second later Brian was banging on my door. I ran for the bathroom, slamming it shut, and locked myself in. Dad owned this apartment and only let me live here because it was safe. The main door was steel, the bathroom door as well, with a hefty lock.

I shrieked when I heard the main door crash open. How the hell had he gotten in? A moment later he was banging on the bathroom door.

"Open the fucking door, Sophia!"

I sat on the floor, my back pressed to the door and my feet braced against the tub, while he kicked it, screaming at me to let him in.

———

Cillian

I ran up the stairs, pulling my gun from the holster at my back as I went.

The door was open. He'd shot out the lock using a silencer.

Brian spun to face me when I walked in and strode straight for him.

He pulled out his gun, and I knocked it from his hand. The kid was green, had no idea what he was doing, but he was determined. I'd watched him with Sophia, he wanted her and he would have hurt her if he'd gotten the chance. I slammed the butt of my gun into his head when he swung at me, then grabbing his skull, I smashed it into the door, once, twice, a third time, and lights out. Shoving my gun in the waistband of my pants, I fisted his hair and wrenched back his head, exposing his throat—

"Hall's clear, cameras are out," Declan said, striding into the apartment. "What the fuck are you doing? You can't kill him, Cillian."

I froze, staring down at the unconscious fuck on the floor. I barely remembered pulling my knife free, but it was gripped tight in my hand. I wanted to slit his throat, badly. Unfortunately, Dec was right. We were still in Sophia's apartment for one, but that wasn't the only reason I couldn't kill the prick.

"Cillian?"

I'd lost control.

I nodded and put away my knife. I couldn't let that happen again. We quickly wrapped him in the tarp Dec had brought with him and carried him down the stairwell. We needed to get him out before he regained consciousness. Con was waiting, trunk open. We tossed him in. "Find his car, deal with it, then take him to the warehouse. I'll be there soon as I can."

Declan nodded, and they took off. I headed back upstairs.

It turned out Sophia's boyfriend wasn't just some random asshole. No, he was Alto Leone's fucking nephew. Paolo Amato. It took us a minute to ID the kid because no one had seen him before.

He'd been living in New York until recently, and as far as I could tell, he hadn't had much to do with the family business —until now.

I strode back into the apartment. "Soph, it's me. Open up."

"How do I know it's you?" she called back.

I took a pic of me standing by the bathroom door and sent it. "He's gone. I promise."

The door cracked open a minute later, and she peered through the gap. As soon as she saw me, she threw the door wide and ran at me. I caught her on instinct, wrapping my arms around her in return because it's what she'd expect Dean to do. She hung on tight.

"I was so scared," she said, her voice muffled against my chest.

The last person to hug me had been my mother. I'd been

five years old. I remembered it because in those five years she'd never hugged me. Most of the time she ignored me, even avoided me. Seamus told me later that she'd hated me, that she thought I was evil. But that night, she'd kissed Declan good night like she always did, then she'd surprised me with a quick hug good night as well, before she'd put me to bed.

I'd been shaken awake an hour later. Seamus's hands had still been covered in her blood. Declan had only been two at the time, and I remembered one of Seamus's men carrying him, still sleeping, out to the car, while I stared at our dead mother, lying in a heap on the floor. I'd been shoved into the car as well, and we'd been shipped off to one of Seamus's cousins in Ireland that very night.

No, Seamus had never claimed us as his, not publicly, not even when he'd sent for us ten years later, but he had used it to manipulate us, to turn us into good little soldiers.

Sophia trembled against me, and I rubbed her back, not quite sure what to do. I'd never held a woman like this, but I'd seen my brother do it. Her body was pressed tightly against mine. Her tits and belly were soft and warm, and I knew if I dropped my hands to her ass, it'd be just as soft. I breathed her in, vanilla and cinnamon.

"I've got you," I said, not sure where the words came from, probably a movie I'd watched. I watched a lot of shows and movies—as a child I'd been fascinated by other families, the shows with kids that made snappy jokes and had deep conversations with their parents about right and wrong—they'd helped when I'd needed to be someone else, like now. And when I got older, I'd read a bunch of psychology books as well to try and understand why I was the way I was.

She nodded and stayed tucked against me for several more minutes.

Finally, she lifted her head. "Sorry for blubbering all over you."

She tried to step back, but I held fast for some reason, keeping her close. Yeah, I liked the way she felt pressed against me, but there was something else as well, something deep and foreign in my gut that had me holding her tighter. "Don't worry about it. You're okay, that's the main thing." In my line of work, pretending to be someone else was part of the job, and something I was good at. I'd been doing it so long, I easily slipped into whatever persona was necessary. Dean was the good guy. The nice, solid guy, and now Sophia's hero, and needy little thing she was, she was eating it up.

To a girl like her, fairly sheltered and innocent in a lot of ways, from a family as fucked up as hers, Dean was the dream guy. I knew she liked the way I looked—women seemed to like my body—add in the nice-guy routine, and she was putty in my hands.

I had her.

And right now, I was pretty sure, she'd let me do anything I wanted to her.

Chapter Five

Sophia

I stared up at Dean. His intense green gaze had my heart galloping in my chest. He'd saved me. He'd rushed straight in here and sent Brian away.

"Thank you," I whispered and impulsively lifted to my toes, pressing a kiss to his cheek when he dipped closer. Then I dropped my gaze, unable to hold his any longer. "I'm not sure what would've happened if you hadn't come."

He cupped the side of my face, the rough skin of his thumb brushing over my jaw. It sent shivers dancing through me. "You don't need to think about that. You're safe now."

He hadn't let me go, and I hadn't tried to step back again. I didn't want to. I liked being held by him. I looked back up. His head was still close, and his gaze dipped to my mouth.

"Do you think he'll come back?" I wasn't sure why I was whispering, but he was so close and I was finding it hard to breathe let alone speak.

He shook his head. "He won't bother you again."

I believed him. I wasn't sure why, but there was that feeling again—*safe*. He made me feel safe. God, he smelled good too.

There was something in the background, under his deodorant or whatever body wash he used, but I couldn't place it.

"You...ah, smell really good...somehow, familiar," I nervously blurted.

"Do I?"

I nodded, my cheeks warming. My gaze slid to his mouth without my say-so, and I quickly looked up. "Thank you," I said again, voice shaky this time, then I lifted up on my toes and kissed him on the cheek once more, because I was so incredibly thankful, and god, right then, I couldn't seem to get close enough to him. This was the first time we were in the same room since I'd briefly spoken to him at the bar, but all those texts, what he'd done for me tonight, I felt like I *knew him*, and I was scared that if I let him go, he'd leave. Embarrassingly, I thought I might fall to pieces if that happened.

His fingers flexed against my back. "Is that where you really wanted to kiss me, Soph?"

He hadn't missed it, and the way he said my name set off more little shivers across my skin. I shook my head, because there was no point lying, not to him or to myself. His darkened gaze saw right through me.

He made a gruff sound, then slid his fingers into my hair, gathering it in his hand before tilting my head back.

"Dean..."

He closed the space between us, his mouth covering mine without hesitation. The kiss was hard, demanding, and I, god, I melted in his arms. No one had ever kissed me like that. He'd taken full control, over my mouth, over my body, and I completely surrendered.

A gritty, growly sound escaped his lips, and with his other hand he gripped my ass and hauled me up his body, like my weight was nothing, and strode across the room. My back met the wall, his body trapping mine. He tilted his head, his tongue delving deeper. He nipped and sucked my lips, then kissed me deep again. My head swam as an ache grew deep in my core.

In that moment, he could have all of me. I wanted him to take whatever he wanted from me. I hooked my legs tight around his waist, and he ground his hips against me until I was panting. He was hard, everywhere, and I whimpered into his mouth, rocking my hips, trying to get closer. My pussy ached and my panties were embarrassingly soaked.

"You wanna come, Soph?" he said against my lips.

The way he said it, the way he held me, all of it was a turn-on. "Y-yes." If he didn't get me off, right now, right here in his arms, I might actually fucking perish.

His fingers stayed in my hair, controlling my movements, my mouth. His thigh held me in place as the hand on my butt slid around my waist and down the front of my pj shorts and into my underwear. I gasped in surprise, even as I rocked forward against his hand. I don't know what I was expecting, definitely slower, gentler, but he thrust two fingers deep inside me, then fucked me with them, hard and fast.

I cried out, my head dropping back, and it would have hit the wall if his hand hadn't already been there. My body trembled, and I felt utterly out of control. Dark pleasure spun around me, coiling in my belly.

Dean kept my head tilted back, my body where he wanted it, how he wanted it. He stared into my eyes, not letting me look away with nothing but his will.

"Fucking dripping, Soph," he said, roughly. "This tight-as-fuck little pussy needs to be fucked hard and often, doesn't it? But you knew no one could give you what you needed until now, isn't that right, pet?"

No one had ever spoken to me like that, and it confused me, scared me—yet turned me on even more. I groaned low, making a sound I'd never heard come out of my mouth before. I shook harder as that dark pleasure gripped me so tight I couldn't draw breath, sweeping me up and taking me so high I was spinning out of control.

Dean didn't let up, his fingers ruthlessly owning me, deep and punishing. His hand left my hair, and he curled his fingers around my throat, pinning me to the wall, applying light pressure. My inner walls contracted, hard. I gasped, trying to drag in a breath, to get some control, almost afraid of the feeling building inside me. It was too much, too earth-shattering.

Oh god.

His mouth went to my ear. "Let go. Let me feel it, Sophia, right the fuck now."

As soon as the demand left his mouth, I crashed, falling, tumbling over and over as if I'd left my body and was watching someone else shake and writhe against his hold, as if I were hearing someone else beg and scream for more.

There was a gush between my thighs, and there was nothing I could do to stop it. I bucked against him, my body not my own.

"Good girl," he said roughly.

I'd never done that before. I didn't even know I could do that. I was breathing hard, still shaking, not sure what just happened. How it happened. One minute we were kissing, the next, I was...a sobbing, shaking mess.

He carefully pulled his fingers free, and I blinked up at him, panting, my legs trembling with weakness. "That's never happened...I've never...and I got, um...it all on you..." I sucked in a shaky breath. "I'm sorry."

His nostrils flared. "Are you apologizing for squirting?"

I moistened my lips. "Um...yes?"

His gaze bore into me. "You don't apologize, you thank me, then you ask me to get you off again."

My heart pounded in my chest, and I studied him. Something about Dean seemed different, rougher, more...intense. "Thank you," I whispered, feeling shy all of a sudden.

"And the rest, pet," he said, an unyielding look in his green eyes.

Pet? I wasn't sure what I thought of that either. It felt weird, like he thought of me as some creature to order about as he wished, but it also made my belly swirl.

"I—I would, but I can never...ah, orgasm more than once. So..." My face was burning again.

He laughed, without humor, and it was a dark and scary sound that sent my pulse racing. "You'll come as many times as I want you to."

I blinked up at him in shock.

His phone rang, and he put it to his ear, still pressed against me, his eyes intent on my face. "Yeah?" He listened and his jaw tightened, but there was no other outward sign of emotion. "The Italians are trying to fuck us over."

The Italians? His voice was different. I knew an Irish accent when I heard one.

Fear slammed through me.

He listened some more, then his gaze dipped to my mouth and back up. "I have eyes on her." Another beat. "Done." Then he hung up.

No, this couldn't be happening. "Oh god, you work for my father, don't you?" My pulse sped faster, but for a different reason now.

"No. Now get changed, unless you want to leave here in your soaked pajamas."

"Dean—"

"Now, Sophia."

His voice was hard, emotionless, the Irish accent even stronger. It was like a wall had come up—no, like his facade had come tumbling down. "Who the hell are you?" I demanded.

Cillian

I didn't have time to be gentle with her. We needed to move. I'd already let her distract me. That had never happened to me before, but then from the moment I'd laid eyes on Sophia, she'd distracted me, testing my usually iron-clad control and smashing it to pieces. "Get dressed."

She shoved at me, and I stepped back, giving her the space she wanted but staying between her and the door. Her expression was confused, hurt. She'd get over it.

"Tell me who you are?" she demanded again.

The strength in her voice was a surprise. I had wondered if she had any backbone to speak of. This was good. She'd need it. "Dress, and then I'll tell you what you want to know."

When she didn't move straightaway, I took a step toward her and she darted to the other side of her bed. "Get out of my apartment. Now." She snatched up her phone.

"Who are you gonna call, pet?"

"Don't...don't call me that. I'm calling my father. You know him, don't you?"

I strode to her drawers and yanked the top one open. "Good idea. Call him."

She stared at me, her chest rising and falling fast, the vein at her throat fluttering wildly. "You are one of his men, aren't you?"

"I already said I wasn't." I dug around in her drawer and found underwear, pink with a matching bra. I tossed them on the bed. "Tell him you're with Cillian." I opened the next drawer and grabbed shorts and a shirt and tossed them down as well.

"Cillian?" She paled.

"Do it," I bit out.

She jumped, fumbling with her phone, and hit the number for her father.

"Put it on speaker."

Her gaze darted to me, then back down. The sound of the phone ringing filled the room. "I can't talk now, Sophia."

"Dad—"

"I said I'm busy—"

"Perhaps you'll find time for me, Brennan," I said.

There was a pause. "Who the fuck is this? Cillian?"

"Sophia's in danger."

"What? How?" he yelled.

"Leone."

There was another beat of silence. "Bring her to me, O'Rourke, do you hear me?"

His attempt to intimidate me would be laughable if I actually found things humorous. I strode over and snatched the phone from her, ending the call, and shoved it in my pocket. "Put the clothes on."

"I don't understand any of this," she choked out.

"Because your father is an idiot. He'll explain what's happening when I get you to him."

She was trembling again, but this time because she was afraid. "And you'll take me to him?"

"I will."

She snatched up her clothes and ran to the bathroom, shutting herself in. I sent Declan a text, letting him know what was happening and to stay with Paolo. I had no idea what Alto was up to, but it was looking like he'd heard of the upcoming marriage between Sophia and Adam and sent Paolo in to get to her first. The O'Rourkes and the Brennans cementing our alliance had to worry him. Maybe he wanted an alliance with Brennan and this was how he thought they'd get it? It didn't seem his style. Whatever this was, it wasn't good for any of us.

No wonder the kid was losing his shit and trying to get to Sophia. No one disappointed Alto and got away with it, not even family. What Paolo planned to do when he got up here, I'd find out later.

We had to move fast, Alto might already know his nephew was missing, and if he did, he'd assume Brennan was the one to discover the kid sniffing around his daughter, which was the way I wanted it. If his men weren't already here, they were on their way.

The bathroom door opened and Sophia walked out, looking pale.

"Shoes," I said.

She shoved her feet in a pair of runners and grabbed her purse. I took her arm and led her out of the apartment, ignoring her attempts to get free of my hold, and rushed her to the elevators.

"You're an asshole, you know that?" she said.

"Aye." Pulling my gun from my holster, I released her long enough to attach the silencer, then stood back as the doors slid open.

One of Leone's men stood there, gun raised.

I fired twice, head, heart. He landed mostly in the hall, and I kicked his legs out of the way and dragged a screaming Sophia into the elevator with me.

Pressing her into the wall, I covered her mouth with my hand. "There'll be more. Don't make it easy for them."

Her eyes were huge, and she nodded. I could smell her

pussy on my fingers, and if she licked her lips now, she'd be able to taste herself. I wanted more of her. I wanted to unravel her again, like I had in her apartment, over and over again.

I dragged my nose up the side of her throat, breathing her in. "You tell anyone what happened between us in your apartment, pet, and I'll kill your father. Nod if you understand?"

She whimpered against my hand but nodded.

"That's a good wee pet." The elevator dinged, and I shoved her behind me, taking out the two men waiting. Two shots, both between the eyes. A third appeared out of nowhere, rushing us, and grabbed my gun hand, trying to wrestle it from me. I pulled the knife from my boot and stabbed him in the throat, and he went down.

Sophia didn't scream this time, but she did look close to fainting. I hooked her around the waist. "Fire exit?" She pointed down the hall, and I practically dragged her along with me. I shoved open the heavy door and looked out into the alley. *Clear.* My car was around the back. I stopped where the alley opened at the back of the building and peered around the edge. Another of Leone's men was going in through the back. I watched as he climbed in through a window, disappearing, then kept going, taking Sophia with me.

The car was just ahead, the street quiet as I scanned our surroundings. Unlocking the passenger door, I opened it, and Sophia scrambled into the car. I jogged around, got in, started the engine, and got us the fuck out of there.

Sophia sat silent beside me for several minutes, the only sounds she made were her panted breaths. Her hands were fisted on her lap, every inch of her stiff, rigid. "You lied to me," she finally said.

"I did."

"And you just...you killed four men. You just *shot* three men and stabbed another," she whispered, horror, fear in her voice. "You're a...you're a psycho."

This time I didn't answer, I didn't need to, she already knew the answer to that as well.

Chapter Six

Sophia

I'd thought about opening the car door and jumping out several times, but that would only end in me getting badly injured or worse. The monster beside me was an O'Rourke, a criminal like my father. But worse, Cillian O'Rourke was the worst of them all. The realization of who he was hit me when Dad said his name. I'd heard my father's men talk about him. They called him an enforcer to his face, and the monster behind his back. He had no trouble killing—enjoyed it even—and had no conscience whatsoever. I curled my fingers into tight fists to stop my hands from shaking.

I should have realized something was up when I'd called him for help, and instead of calling the police like any sane person not part of our world would suggest, he'd taken charge as if he dealt with angry, unstable people all the time.

God, I still felt his mouth on mine, his fingers inside me. I glanced his way again, afraid he'd suddenly pull over and use that gun on me next, but he drove with ease, unhurried, calm and emotionless at my side. He'd pretended to be my friend, for some reason he'd wanted to get close to me, and like the needy, desperate idiot I was, I'd fallen for it.

We turned down the next street, heading to my father's house, and the sick grip on my stomach eased the tiniest bit. The sooner I was away from this fucking creep the better.

Then I thought about Tommy and spun to face him. "You won't...you won't hurt my family, will you?"

"I'm not the one you need to worry about," he said as he turned into the driveway, no longer hiding who he was or masking that strong lilting brogue.

There were several men standing at the gates, all of them armed. We always had security, but not like this. Dean...no, Cillian, slid his window down. They saw who he was and the gates opened for him instantly.

As soon as he pulled up outside the house, I shoved the door open and ran up the front steps, throwing the front door open. More men spun my way, all armed.

Cillian walked in behind me. His phone was to his ear, his expression blank, cold, unreadable. "I'll tell him," he said to whoever he was on the phone with, then disconnected.

My father strode out of his office, and I wanted to run to him, to throw my arms around him, but he wasn't the hugging type, no matter the circumstances. So, straightening my spine, I walked to his side.

"Brennan," Cillian said to my father.

Dad eyed him coolly. "Thank you for bringing her to me safely."

Cillian stood with his hands loose at his sides, but I knew how fast he could get to the gun under his jacket.

"What's going on?" I asked my father, trying to keep the anger, the fear, from my voice. He didn't like it when I questioned him, and he hated it even more if he thought I was being *overly emotional*. It made him angry.

"Best you talk to your daughter, Brennan. Tonight."

What the hell was going on? "Dad?"

He was flustered, sweaty, and his furious gaze sliced to Dean...*goddammit*, Cillian. "Don't tell me what to do with my own daughter."

Cillian's expression didn't change, not in the slightest. "Seamus is moving things forward."

My father bristled. "We had a deal."

Cillian kept his frigid gaze on my father. "Things change. Maybe if you were better at protecting what's yours, you wouldn't be losing it."

"Dad?" I said again as dread slithered through me. "What the hell is he talking about?"

He didn't look at me. "My office, Sophia. Now."

I knew that voice. When my father spoke in that tone, he was not to be disobeyed. I wanted to scream, to demand answers, to get the sight of Cillian stabbing a man in the throat and blowing holes through three others out of my head, but that wasn't going to happen. Ever.

I followed my father into his office and shut the door behind us, then watched as he paced back and forth, fury written on his face. My stomach churned. "Dad?" I choked.

"I'm sorry, Sophia," he said, and he was actually shaking. "I wouldn't put you through this if I didn't have to."

"You're scaring me."

He cursed and slammed his fist down on the desk.

I jumped and wrapped my arms around myself.

Finally, he looked up at me, his gaze so filled with rage that I took a step back. "You're not stupid. You know what we are."

I nodded, my palms growing sweaty.

"We don't follow the same rules...laws as other people. The Brennan family has influence in this city, and we earned it with blood and sweat. My father, your uncle, and now me, we will do whatever necessary to keep that influence, to maintain the power we've fought so hard for."

"We're criminals, you mean," I said, my voice trembling.

His jaw tightened. "We're entrepreneurs, businessmen, and we put our family ahead of everything and everyone. We play by our own rules, and because of that, the Brennans and the O'Rourkes, control half of Chicago."

"Did you get Cillian to follow me?"

Thunder filled his gaze. "No, I didn't, but it's a good thing he did." He shook his head. "Alto Leone made his move, he came after this family, and there's no going back from that."

This was bad, seriously bad. "What move?"

"He sent one of his men after you tonight."

I grabbed for the chair in front of me. "Why? Because of you?"

"Sit down, Sophia."

"No, I don't want any part of this—"

"Sit down."

I shook my head and took another step back, my mind spinning. I knew our world was fucked up, but I'd stupidly assumed it couldn't touch me, that despite his faults, my father would protect me. "I need air...I need to get the hell out of here." I yanked the door open and sprinted for the front door.

I only managed a few steps before a strong, unyielding arm locked around my waist, lifting me off my feet. *Cillian.* He carried me back to my father's office as I struggled and cursed against his hold.

Dad hadn't moved. He knew there was no escape for me.

Cillian put me down but didn't leave us alone. He shut the door and stood in front of it, his cold green gaze locked on my father. "You've told her?"

"Who the fuck do you think you're talking to?" Dad said, his voice raised.

Cillian didn't flinch. "While I'm here, I speak for Seamus. A slight to me, is a slight to him. So watch your mouth, old man."

"I'm head of the Brennan family. You will show me respect."

"When you earn it, I'll show it. It's happening tomorrow."

My father paled. "Tomorrow?"

"What the hell is going on?" I bit out.

Cillian's gaze sliced back to me. "Your father fucked up. He owes us, and with the Italians possibly readying for war against your family as we speak, he needs us even more. We need to maintain a united front."

I didn't like what he was saying, but at least he was telling me something. "What does that have to do with me?"

"Brian's real name is Paolo Amato. He's Alto's nephew. My guess, he was sent in to seduce you, to try to forge some kind of alliance with your father, but you turned him down, so Paolo moved to plan B, take you by force. As a result, I had to take out several of their men to get you here. They'll assume it was one of your father's men who killed them, which means you're all in serious danger. Your father's second fuckup? He didn't protect you. He left you exposed and vulnerable, and now he finds himself in a very tenuous situation."

My father stared at Cillian like he wanted to murder him, but he didn't correct him.

"Our alliance was with your uncle, and your father's actions have caused us to lose all trust in him."

"What actions? What did he do?"

Dad straightened. "That's none of your concern—"

"He was doing deals in our territory without telling us, and without offering Seamus his dues," Cillian said, talking over my father. "He's lucky Seamus didn't order me to put a bullet in his brain for the insult. I've done a lot worse, for a lot less."

I believed it. I tried to hide the shiver of fear that washed through me. He would have killed my father without a second thought or a lost night of sleep if Seamus ordered him to.

"Now this mess with the Italians." Cillian shook his head. "He's put your family in a very dangerous position." His gaze didn't falter from me. "And if your father wants the O'Rourkes' considerable manpower behind him when Leone comes for you and your family, we'll need to cement our alliance another way, and quickly."

I looked between them, ice trickling through my veins. "How?"

Cillian's gaze bore into mine. "You'll marry an O'Rourke, tomorrow, uniting the families by marriage, and then by blood when you have children."

A laugh of disbelief burst from me, and I turned to my father. But he said nothing, standing completely still and silent, watching the exchange between me and Cillian, and the truth of what the monster in front of me said was in my father's eyes.

"You've lost your damn minds," I said.

Cillian nodded slowly. "I understand your reservation," he said as if this was some normal everyday conversation, "but it is necessary."

I spun to my father, pointing at Cillian. "You can't make me marry that psycho. I won't do it."

"Not Cillian," he spat. "He's just an O'Rourke bastard. You'll be marrying Adam, Seamus's son and heir."

For some reason, that felt even worse. Adam terrified me. Whenever he looked at me, I felt like scrubbing myself clean afterward. "I won't do it. I won't marry a complete stranger—"

"Sophia," my father snapped.

I took a step back. "*No.* I won't do it."

"Yes, you will," my father roared, slamming his hand down on the desk again. "You will do as you're told."

"No," I said again, hating that it came out shaky and weak.

"Then our men will leave," Cillian said to me. "More than half of the armed men outside protecting your family are ours.

But know, the moment we go, Alto will move in. They will mow down your father's men, and then your family, like they are nothing, and that includes your little brother. And since your father will be dead, you'll no longer be needed, or important. Alto will either kill you, keep you as a whore for his men, or sell you. If you're still a virgin, he'll get a good price in some circles—"

"Enough," my father snapped.

"You did this," Cillian said, his calm voice sending an icy trickle down my spine. "You put your family in this position. Sophia needs to know the truth and the consequences of her decision."

My heart was pounding in my chest, visions of what Cillian had said playing through my mind in grisly detail. Of my brother, of him being so scared, of his little body still and covered in blood. I couldn't bear it. Despite all the lies Cillian had told me, about who he was, everything, I knew what he said now was the truth. He wasn't feeding me lies to get his way, not this time, and judging by his dead gaze, he didn't care either way.

"I'll do it," I choked out. "Just please, make sure Tommy's safe."

My father said nothing, but his relief was obvious.

I spun to the door, needing to get the hell out of there. Cillian blocked the way.

"Let me past."

"If you run—"

"Where would I go? If I leave, my family dies, right?"

He nodded.

"You know how much my brother means to me, don't you?" I said, somehow finding strength in the face of this lying monster, reminding him of the conversations we'd had over text. Talking back and forth for hours. This psychopath who'd played the role of someone warm and kind and funny and protective, so easily, knew all about me. I'd told him so much about myself, my hopes and dreams, everything. I thought he was my friend, when in truth I'd been sharing private details of my life with a man as cold and ruthless as a reptile.

His gaze searched mine, and when he saw whatever it was he was looking for, he finally stepped aside, but not all the way, forcing me to squeeze past him, my front to his side.

Another involuntary shiver raced through me, my traitorous body remembering what he'd done to me against my apartment wall, even though I was terrified of him, even though I hated him. He made a rough sound, and I knew he felt it too.

I ran upstairs, ignoring the looks from the men gathered around. In a matter of hours my world had been uprooted, torn away, and set ablaze, revealing the horror that lay beneath the facade I'd built for myself.

And there was no escape from it.

———

Cillian

An image of Sophia running up those stairs before I left Brennan's house earlier had played through my mind most of the night.

Running away with nowhere to go.

I understood betrayal. I knew how it felt to be thrown to the wolves. She was suffering now, but it'd make her stronger.

I drew in a deep breath as the sounds she'd made when she came apart for me filled my mind, settling in my gut.

You…ah, smell really good…somehow, familiar.

That was because I had a bottle of her vanilla and cinnamon body lotion at home, that I was working my way through. I'd used it to stroke my cock, thinking about her before she'd called. Because I wanted her all over me, and that was the only way I could have her. That's why I smelled familiar.

But I'd had her first. No matter what happened during my meeting tonight, I'd touched her before Adam. I'd claimed her as was my right. She was mine, and she always would be, no matter what happened tomorrow.

Declan and Conor were waiting near the restaurant when I arrived.

"Ready?" Dec asked.

I nodded. Until the deal was made, this meeting, what I was about to do, needed to stay between the three of us. If things went the way I hoped, I was sure the rest of our men would follow me. If not? Well, we'd deal with it if it came to that.

This could be a suicide mission, but I liked my odds. We had something Alto wanted. His nephew. I'd gone straight to the warehouse after leaving Brennan's place several hours ago, and questioned Paolo. I'd been right, Alto had been toying with the idea of an alliance with Brennan, the Italian never had liked Seamus, but hadn't been ready to make a move. Paolo decided to take that upon himself to impress his uncle, to play with the big boys. But then Sophia rejected him, so the little fuck decided to take her. The men I took out tonight at Sophia's apartment were Paolo's not his uncle's. Alto had no idea the position he'd been put in and neither Seamus nor Brennan were any the wiser, which meant this meeting between me and Alto needed to happen now, before shit got back to either of them. The more desperate Brennan was, the better.

Chances were good that Alto wouldn't want to go to war over Paolo's fuckup, but his nephew had made it impossible for him to walk away without looking weak. Despite what I told

Sophia, the Italians didn't kill children and, like me, were more interested in making money than wasting time and resources fighting among ourselves.

I was going to give him a way out that benefited us both and kept his pride intact. Unless, of course, he refused to listen.

Marco, one of Alto's enforcers, stood at the door to the restaurant and aimed his gun at me as I strode toward him.

I held my hands out at my sides. "We're not here to fight. I want a sit-down with Alto."

Marco scowled but pulled out his phone and muttered something into it in Italian.

I felt my brother brace on my right, Conor doing the same on my left, ready for whatever came next.

Still holding his gun on us, Marco shoved his phone in his pocket. "I'll take your weapons."

"We're not armed."

Two more men stepped forward and quickly patted us down, then Marco waved us inside.

We were either about to have a meeting with Alto Leone— or we had a night of torture and a slow brutal death ahead of us.

Only one way to find out.

Chapter Seven

Sophia

Celeste stood back, studying me from head to foot.

"I'm not wearing this. Why the hell would I wear a wedding dress—"

"Arranged marriages happen all the time, Sophia. Stop being dramatic. One day you'll want to look back on your big day, and won't want to be wearing shorts and a T-shirt. Your father loved my dress when we married. Don't you want to look nice for your new husband? Adam's a handsome man. If you don't grab his interest immediately, he'll start looking elsewhere."

"I hope he does. I hope after this sham of a ceremony is over, he forgets I exist. The kind of man who would marry someone against their will is deranged." I grabbed the zipper on the side of the *wedding dress* Celeste had stuffed me into. There'd been several here this morning for me to choose from. Celeste and my father had thought of everything it seemed, except of course, *telling me* that they were planning on destroying my life, at least until they were certain there was no escape.

If I had to marry this creep to protect my brother, I would, but I wouldn't pretend this was something it wasn't.

Celeste grabbed my hand, stopping me. Her eyes turned pleading. "Please, Soph, keep the dress on."

She never called me Soph. She hated me. "I'm not wearing a wedding dress. I'm not some blushing bride. This is the worst day of my life—"

"You go down there in anything other than a wedding dress, you'll offend Seamus and Adam O'Rourke. We don't want to do that, Sophia, we really don't. That wouldn't be good for you or your father."

The fear that filled her eyes was genuine. God, I wanted to scream. What kind of a father sold his daughter to the devil to save his own hide? Not much of one. If it wasn't for Tommy, I'd run the hell out of here and never look back. But Tommy was here, and he was the only person who mattered in this whole mess. I'd do anything to keep him safe, and they all knew it.

She patted the chair in front of her. "Now come sit so I can do your hair and makeup."

I wanted to argue, to run the hell out of there, but there was no point. Fighting was pointless.

Celeste fussed with my hair for far too long. I was restless and angry and terrified. I could hear voices downstairs. Had the O'Rourkes arrived? I wanted to fucking puke.

Would Cillian be here? He'd left after I ran upstairs. I saw him through the window, while I was contemplating throwing myself out of it, or at least shimmying down the drainpipe. I'd checked several times afterward, but he hadn't come back.

Part of me wanted him to be here, so he could watch. So he could see what he helped do to me. So he could watch me marry a complete stranger and witness the destruction of my life. But another part of me knew he wouldn't care. A man like that felt nothing. When he'd looked at me last night, after he'd let his Dean mask drop, there'd been...nothing.

Tommy poked his head around the door. "Dad said you have to come down now."

I forced a smile. For him, I'd be strong. I wouldn't let him see the horror that consumed every inch of me.

"Doesn't she look pretty, Tomo?" Celeste said.

He nodded and made a face. "She looks like a girly marshmallow." Then he cracked up and ran back downstairs.

"We better head down," she said, but when I didn't immediately follow, she turned back with a sigh. "Sophia, we don't have time for your tantrums."

"I'm doing this, I'm marrying that creep, giving up my life, for Tommy. Only him." Celeste had made my life a living hell when I lived here, and my father hadn't cared. He'd never cared. I held her narrowed gaze. "Dad's throwing me to the wolves today, throwing me away to save his own ass. You need to know, if anything happens to Tommy, if you fail him, if you don't protect him and something...happens to him, I will find a way to escape the O'Rourkes, and whatever it takes, I will destroy you and my father both."

"Sophia—"

"I don't want to hear it. Protect him, Celeste, with your life, because if you don't, yours won't be worth living. I'll make sure of it." My voice trembled with rage.

She stared at me, her shock obvious. I'd never spoken to her like that before. I'd never spoken to anyone like that before. She waited for me to retreat, to take it back, but when I didn't, the truth of my words clear in my eyes, her shock turned to fury. It rolled off her in waves. She didn't go on the attack, though, she didn't need to, she'd already won.

"Give me your word," I said, pushing, not backing down.

"Tommy's my son, of course I'll protect him," she said, as if it were obvious.

It wasn't. She put herself before everyone, always, even Tommy. I headed for the door. "Let's get this over with."

"Sophia?"

I turned back, and something glittered in her eyes. "I know you don't have much experience with men, but I want to warn you, Adam O'Rourke has a...reputation. He gets a little rough with his women." Faux concern transformed her plastic face. "I think...no, I'm sure, a few of them actually went missing. But I'm sure if you do as he says tonight, don't cry or make a fuss, you should get through it all right."

My heart slammed into my throat. "My father knows this?"

False sympathy rearranged her face. "Of course. Everyone knows." She strode toward me and fussed with my hair, then smiled like a shark. The real Celeste was now coming out in all her glory, the side of herself she hid more often than not when my father was around because he preferred his women to be soft and sweet and docile. "You'll be sore in the morning. A warm bath might help." Then she looped her arm through mine and said with a smile, "We better get going. We don't want to piss off your future husband. It could make for a very unpleasant wedding night."

Stunned, I let her lead me out the door and down the hall toward the stairs. I was on autopilot, too wounded to do anything else.

What would Adam do when he realized his new wife was broken? What would he do when I woke up screaming and thrashing, when I kicked and punched him in my sleep?

We stopped at the top of the staircase. My father stood at the bottom, waiting. I gripped the railing, straightened my spine, and headed down. "Where are we doing this?" I said when I reached the bottom.

Worry creased his brow. "They're not here yet. Seamus said

they'd be here at seven. I've tried calling, but Adam's not picking up."

They were an hour late. Maybe Adam didn't want to go through with this either. Had he refused to marry me? A kernel of hope bloomed. "Maybe they've changed their minds—"

The front door opened, and we all turned.

Cillian O'Rourke strode in like he owned the world and everyone in it. Tall, strong, handsome—and utterly twisted. He had a handful of men with him, all armed, and through the open door I could see there were more outside. He didn't so much as glance at me, his gaze was on my father.

"Where's Seamus? When's Adam getting here?" Dad demanded.

Cillian wore a black suit, a white shirt underneath. He stood tall, imposing. The suit should make him look more civilized, but the tattoos on his hands and above his collar told a different story. They let everyone know what he really was, and as much as I hated him, my body remembered all too well the way he'd made me feel.

"Seamus has taken a turn. He needed urgent medical care. As for Adam? He won't be coming," Cillian said.

I locked my knees, the force of my relief making them weak.

"He's calling off the wedding?" my father said, and he wasn't happy about it, worried only about what it meant for him.

"Called it off? No. Adam's dead," Cillian said without a trace of emotion. "But the wedding will still be going ahead."

"What?" I choked out. That's when I saw it, the blood spatter on the side of his throat, a fine spray of it on his white shirt.

"I'm in charge now," he said to my father. "You'll deal with me from now on." He turned to me. "I'll be marrying Sophia."

I turned to my father, not sure what I expected, a protest of some kind, anything but what I got—his acquiescence. Not even when the man standing in front of him, announcing he was marrying his only daughter, still had the blood of the last man he'd murdered on his skin. But then I shouldn't be surprised, we were just exchanging one monster for another.

"Let's get this over with," my father said and grabbed my elbow, towing me into the living room.

The priest turned to us with a smile as we walked in. "Shall we begin?"

———

Cillian

Sophia's fingers trembled as she slid the wide band on my finger. When I'd done the same, a feeling settled in my gut that I liked very much. She stared up at me wide-eyed as the priest told me I could kiss my bride. If I were a good man, I'd have let her off the hook—but I wasn't a good man, and I wanted to make sure everyone in this room understood that Sophia O'Rourke was mine. My wife.

So I stepped closer, curling my fingers around the back of her head, my thumb under her chin, and tilted her head back. I could see the debate in her eyes—should she take a step back or pull away from me. Sophia wasn't stupid, though. Yes, there was hatred in her pale blue eyes, but she was also smart enough not to test me, not then, not in front of my men or the kid she was so attached to.

I bent low, bringing my face close to hers. "Wife," I said to her, as if I were introducing myself for the first time. In a way I was, Dean was gone, I was here now. Her husband. And I wanted to make sure she understood what she was, who she was. She may always despise me, but she was my *wife*, and that meant in every way that the word implied.

I closed the space and kissed her, our second kiss. It was brief but firm, and I sucked her plump lips gently before I lifted my head, fighting the urge to devour her right here.

She tasted as good as I remembered. I didn't usually kiss the women I fucked, it created a false intimacy that I didn't want or need, but for Sophia I'd make an exception—I found I wanted to taste her again, and I could. I could do anything I liked, because she was mine.

After that first night, a year ago, I'd followed her, watched her sleep, searched every drawer in her place to try and quench my strange appetite for everything Sophia Brennan, but it hadn't worked. Nothing had worked. I didn't obsess over things, or people—until her. I wasn't like other men. The way I felt about my new wife confounded me, alarmed me...electrified me. I hadn't understood it then, the way she'd made me feel, and I still didn't, but I wanted to keep on feeling those things.

There'd been only one way to do that.

Make her mine.

Claim her.

The fact that tied in with me finally taking my rightful place in this family was the result of years of eating shit, luck, and perfect timing.

I forced myself to look away from her, her cheeks flushed and so incredibly tempting, before I pulled her closer, before I kissed her again—before I showed everyone here how Sophia tested my control. I knew she was my weakness, but I couldn't let anyone else know that.

Her father didn't congratulate us, and no one cheered. This wasn't a joyous occasion; this was the payment of a debt. This was a father giving up his only daughter to save himself.

Declan strode up to us, breaking the silence. "Hey, Sophia.

I'm Declan," he said, smiling kindly. Declan could do that when he needed to, he was as good an actor as I was. "I'm your new brother-in-law. Welcome to the family."

Sophia stared up at him, not sure what to make of him. My brother had that effect on people, it was why he was so effective at what he did. He disarmed people with his charm and his smile, leaving them wondering what the fuck just happened while they lay on the floor bleeding out.

I placed my hand on her lower back, steering her from the room. I wasn't going to hang around here in case Brennan suddenly found his balls. I wanted her out of this house. Brennan's wife, Celeste, motioned to Sophia's bags by the door like a game-show host.

Con and several of my men carried them out to my car, and Brennan finally pulled himself together and strode over to us. He pulled his daughter in for a hug, and Sophia stiffened in his arms, refusing to look at him.

"I'll see you soon...sweetheart," he said and glanced at me in question.

The endearment came out awkward, stilted. That was probably the first time he'd ever called her that. I dipped my chin, glad to see him already deferring to me—and showing again why he wasn't fit for the position he held. Good thing he wouldn't be holding it for long.

I shook his hand. "I'll be in touch." Then I led Sophia from the house and out to my waiting car. Con opened the door, and just as she was about to get in, the kid called her name and ran out of the house. She caught him in her arms and held him to her tight.

"I don't want you to go," he said, looking up at me like I was the devil.

He had good instincts. The boy obviously didn't take after his weak father.

She put him down and crouched in front of him. "I'll be back to visit soon, okay, buddy?"

"Promise?" he said, lips quivering.

"Promise." She planted a kiss to the top of his head, and he ran back inside.

She scowled up at me before she got in the car. I climbed in after her, and Con drove us away from the house.

To anyone looking, the Brennans and the O'Rourkes were once again a united front, but I was in charge of both families now, even if Brennan didn't know it yet. It was only a matter of time before his men were answering to me.

I'd done what I'd assured Alto I would do. I'd become the new head of the O'Rourke family. We'd returned Paolo to him somewhat unharmed, and once we finalized the terms of our deal, our mutually beneficial relationship could begin and our business interests could finally expand in ways I'd wanted them to for years. The Italians no longer had a reason to wage war, Brennan would keep breathing for now, and Sophia was mine.

"Where are we going?" Sophia said beside me.

I glanced her way. "Home."

Chapter Eight

Sophia

Cillian's house was right on the beach. It was dark, but I could hear the crashing waves, see the way light glinted off the water.

I hadn't thought too hard about what his home would be like, but if I had, this wouldn't be it.

He led me inside, and I took in the open-concept lower level. It was a big home, the furniture in this room understated—the artwork, though, was the complete opposite. There was no way Cillian had decorated this place; someone as cold as him definitely couldn't have chosen such beautiful, bright and vibrant paintings for the walls. These had been selected by someone else, someone with a soul.

There was a smell of newness to it, new paint definitely.

Conor, I'd learned his name on the way over here, strode past with my bags and carried them up the stairs.

"Are you hungry?" Cillian asked me.

I shook my head. I wasn't sure I'd ever be hungry again, not with this knot in the pit of my stomach. Conor walked back out.

"Bring in the rest of her bags, and leave them in here, make sure you lock up when you're done," Cillian said to him.

Conor jerked his chin up and headed back out to get the rest of my things.

I turned to my new husband, the murdering psycho standing across from me, and crossed my arms so he didn't see my hands shaking. "Now what?" If I was going to survive this, making him angry, fighting against this, running, would only make things worse, but I needed to know what he had planned for me.

Yes, I was so terrified that I was surprised I was still standing, but for now, at least, this was where I had to be. I would survive this, and when the time was right, when I got an opening, I'd run. I'd take Tommy, and I'd get the fuck away from this city and never come back. Which meant I had to be smart and not let my emotions get the better of me. I would survive this —*survive him.*

Cillian took me in, unmoved, his gaze piercing me like shards of ice. "Now I make you mine the way a husband does his new wife."

A tremor moved through me, and I hated that it wasn't all from fear. My body remembered the way he'd touched me back in my apartment, and despite how much I hated and feared the man standing in front of me, my traitorous body wasn't totally against being touched that way again.

I would not, could not, let the fear get the better of me. This wasn't a man to be trifled with. I could pretend to be someone I wasn't like he had. My father had taught me well after all. I knew how to be meek and obedient, but I was sure Cillian would see right through my deception. He was a liar, and he'd know exactly what deception looked like in other people.

So I straightened my spine and forced myself to hold his gaze. "Just so you know, I won't be your wife for long."

His green, fathomless gaze didn't leave mine. "No?"

I shook my head. "I don't care how long it takes, but I will find a way to get away from you."

He closed the space between us. "And I promise you, wife, wherever you go, I'll find you, and I will bring you back." He curled his tattooed, rough-skinned hand around my neck, the pad of his thumb at the base of my throat. "You are mine. I own every part of you, Sophia, and I don't give up what's mine, ever."

My heart thundered in my chest, fear spiking through me, and at the same time, a twisted darkness burned low in my belly. There had to be something seriously wrong with me—how could I stomach this monster's hands on me, how could my body react to his touch, while everything else inside me was screaming to run as fast and as far as I could?

The hand around my neck slid to the base of my spine, and he applied the slightest pressure to get me moving, directing me up the stairs.

When I got to the top, there were five doors, two on the right, two on the left, and one at the end. Cillian carried on past them to the last one at the very end, and directed me through the door.

A bedroom.

His bedroom.

I shivered, running my hands over my bare arms, hugging myself.

The room was clean and tidy, a large bed in the center, black lacquered bedside tables, soft light coming from the lamps on each one. There was a fireplace on the opposite wall, two chairs in front of it, with a matching black, glossy table between them. The door near the bed was open, the bags Conor brought up just inside what I assumed was a large closet, and I guessed the bathroom was beyond that.

"This is your room?"

"Yes."

I was finding it hard to breathe again. "You want me to sleep in here, with you?" I don't know what I expected. Separate rooms maybe? That he'd have his way with me, then leave my bed and go to his own, that he'd only come to me when he wanted to scratch that itch. Sharing a room, a bed? No, I definitely hadn't expected that. I couldn't do that, and not just for the obvious reasons. This man was a killer. How would he react when I lashed out at him in my sleep?

"Where else would you be?" he said, his accent thick.

His hand slipped away from my back, and a second later, the click of the door closing us in together had me jumping like he'd fired his gun.

Did he really think I could just move in here with him and we'd play husband and wife? "Why would you want me in here with you? This is insane. We don't even know each other," I said, staring out the window into darkness, finding it hard to meet his gaze, finding it hard to breathe.

"I know you better than you think," he said.

———

Cillian

I hadn't let down my guard, not once, not until this moment. Now Sophia was in my home, safe, with me.

She finally turned to me, and I barely stopped myself from dragging in a harsh breath.

My new wife looked like a wee fairy princess. My sleeping beauty.

Her long blond hair hung in loose waves almost to her waist. Her dress was modest but hugged her body. She had ample curves, but she still looked fragile. Breakable. I'd have to try really hard to be careful with her.

She was still young, eight years younger than me. Innocent. Pliable. My new bride was showing some backbone, but there were a lot of things she didn't know—about this life, about men —and whether she liked it or not, whether she'd admit it or not, eventually she'd be looking to me for guidance. Then I'd mold her into the ideal wife, and the kind of mother I wanted for my future children. The kind of mother I'd never had.

I'd never wanted any of this, but looking at her now? I was filled with possessiveness. Something about her brought out the monster in me, but instead of craving blood and death, Sophia made me want things I'd never had before, and it roared *mine*.

She was the first thing I'd ever truly wanted for myself, that I'd allowed myself to have, since I was a boy. Wishing for things as a child, wanting things, had been pointless.

She blinked up at me now, her rosebud lips coated in pink. Her mouth full and pouty. I wanted to taste her again. The desire to kiss wasn't something I'd experienced before meeting her. But now, god, I couldn't get enough of those lips. I wanted to fist all that perfect blond hair while I watched that pretty mouth stretched around my cock, watch her struggle to take all of me. I wanted to see that pink lipstick smeared on my dick when I held her legs wide and thrust inside her.

I didn't know if she was a virgin or not, not for sure, and I didn't care. What she did before I found her was of no consequence, but what I did know for sure was she'd never been with a man like me.

I wanted to shatter the innocence and fear I saw in her blue eyes and turn it into raw hunger. I didn't believe in love, I was incapable of the emotion, but the savage feeling growing inside me right then was all-consuming, and I wouldn't be happy until she craved me, and only me, for the rest of her life.

I closed the space between us, and the fear I saw on her face heightened. I got it. Despite making her come so hard, she squirted all over my hand, we'd only met a couple of times before today, at least while she was awake. She didn't know me, and thankfully, being sheltered as she'd been by her father, she might have heard of me, but nothing specific. How would she feel if she found out about the things I'd done for Seamus, that her husband was O'Rourke's monster, his twisted bastard son and as fucked up as his sadistic father?

I hated her looking at me like that. Most people feared me; I didn't want that from her. When I'd allowed myself over the last twelve months to imagine her here with me, there was never fear in her eyes when she looked at me, not in this room.

"I won't hurt you, Sophia," I said, forcing myself to gentle my voice as I tucked her hair behind her ear. She shivered as my hand traveled over the lace of her wedding gown, over her shoulder, then around to her back. I slid my hand under the thick curtain of her hair, finding the zipper and slowly tugging it down.

She froze. "I—I thought we might...take it slow. Get to know each other before we..." She glanced at the bed and back at me. "Before we, uh..."

"Fuck?"

She swallowed. "Y-yes."

I took her delicate jaw in my hand. "You are my wife, Sophia. From this night on, you're in my bed. I don't want to scare you, pet, but I'm no gentleman. I'll treat you with respect, but I'm not a good man or a patient one. You are mine now, and I won't wait to claim every inch of you."

She tried to take a step back, and I tightened my hold on her, grinding my fucking teeth. What I wanted to do was order her to strip and bend over the bed. I wanted to work out all the need that had been riding me since I first saw her a year ago. A driving hunger for her that had only increased when she'd walked toward me, trembling and wide-eyed, and stood opposite me in front of that priest.

This alliance was the only thing keeping Brennan alive and that old fuck knew it, but instead of fighting and dying with honor, he'd offered up his precious only daughter to the O'Rourke monster. He deserved to suffer.

But Sophia did not, and I'd do my best to avoid that.

I studied her again. I was going to have to find some patience because fucking her while she was this terrified wouldn't be good for either of us.

I was going to have to work for it, something I'd never had to do before.

Tilting her chin up, I brushed my thumb over her full lower lip, back and forth, letting a little of Dean slip back in, into my eyes, my voice, into someone I wasn't. "In your apartment, did you like the way I made you come, Soph?"

Her eyes widened, and I could see she wanted to say no. She wanted to deny it, but she couldn't. There was no hiding how hard I'd gotten her off. Rather than saying yes, she didn't answer, but her breath quickened. She was scared, but she was also turned on.

"It's okay to want me and hate me at the same time, pet." I brushed my thumb over her lip again. "Maybe you'll grow to like me a little?" I made my lips twitch, giving her what I knew others interpreted as a self-depreciating smile. "Maybe you won't, but out there"—I pointed to the door—"I'll protect you with my life. And in here, when we're alone, I'll worship every inch of your body. I'll make you feel good, Soph, because I'm your husband, and that's my job."

"I do...I hate you," she said, fiercely.

I swept my thumb over her jaw, her chin, tilting her head back. "Yet you still want me to kiss you."

Her face flushed pink.

I loved the way she blushed so easily.

I took her silence as an invitation and closed the space between us. And as much as I wanted to own that hot fucking mouth, to take it hard and deep, like the rest of her, I forced myself to dip my head slowly and gently press my mouth to hers. I'd never kissed anyone this way. I didn't do soft or gentle. I plundered. I fucked hard, then I walked.

But Sophia wasn't some random piece of ass. She'd be here in the morning, and the next, and the next after that. She'd keep on being here, and I needed to remember that. So I thought about all those movies I watched as a boy—learning what I could so I didn't scare people, so they'd believe I was like everyone else—and kissed her like the men in those movies kissed their wives or girlfriends. Imitating others was easy, I'd been doing it my whole life. I knew exactly how to be a good husband, a good father—I knew how to fool people into believing I was warm inside and not cold as ice. If that's what Sophia needed, then I'd give it to her.

Her lips were full and warm—

And completely still under mine. Frozen, like the rest of her. Her breath puffed from her nose like a frightened rabbit, her tits the only part of her moving, shaking against my chest from those panted breaths.

My terrified new wife was about to fucking hyperventilate from a kiss. How the fuck was she going to handle the full force of my hunger?

I touched my tongue to her upper lip, tasting her, trying to ignite the same fire I'd gotten from her the last time I'd kissed her...the first time *Dean,* kissed her. She made a strangled noise that was pure fear.

Fuck.

I had no plans of fucking around on her, I would never be

like Seamus, but there were things I needed. I had thought... hoped, what I saw in her, the stillness, the overt submissiveness, would come out in other ways if I showed her, taught her what I liked, if I coax it out of her—

Her lips moved—ever so slightly.

"That's it," I said against her mouth. "Now let me taste that sweet little tongue again."

She shivered as her tongue tentatively swiped over my lower lip.

"So good, Soph. Now open your mouth wider for me."

She did, and I threaded my fingers through her hair, sliding my tongue into her sweet, hot mouth, showing her that I owned it, that it was mine. It was probably too much, too soon, but there was only so much a man like me could take.

I held her tight to me, maybe too tight, but I had no control over that either. Only she made me this way. I let the iron grip I had on that part of me slip, and I took more. I couldn't get enough. I barely resisted tugging the delicate gown off her shoulders and dragging it off her body, stripping her bare.

She pushed against my chest, trying to pull away.

I wanted to fucking snarl. "It's okay," I said, then sucked on her lips, squeezing one of her tits.

She pushed at me again.

I took her chin and opened her mouth wider, kissing her deeper, demanding more.

She slammed her hands against my chest, jerking her head back. "Stop!"

Breathing hard, I lifted my head, but I didn't let her go.

"It's...t-too much," she stammered and tried to pull away. "You're too much. This whole day...all of it, is *too fucking much*. I don't know you. I sure as hell don't like you. I don't fucking want you kissing me, and I definitely don't want to sleep with you!"

This was all new to her, a shock. She'd change her mine, she had to. I wouldn't accept anything else.

I ran my fingers down the side of her face. "I know, pet, but you'll get used to it. You might even grow to like being here with me."

She stared up at me, eyes wide. "You're not just a psychotic monster...you're fucking delusional."

I'd heard variations of what she'd just said my whole life. As a boy I'd been confused, had wondered what was wrong with me, had tried to be something I wasn't to put others at ease. As I'd gotten older, I'd embraced it.

But those words coming from Sophia, no, I didn't like it, and without my say-so, the facade slipped, revealing the cold, twisted fuck I truly was, the *psychotic monster* she'd be sharing a bed with for the rest of her life.

"It's a good thing you're my wife, then," I said, taking her chin in my hand. "I may be a monster, but I take care of what's mine." I breathed in her sweet vanilla-and-cinnamon scent. "I don't break my toys, pet. As for being delusional?" I fisted the front of her dress and gathered it up slowly, shaking my head. "If I slid my hand inside your panties right now, are you telling me I wouldn't find your pussy fucking soaking wet?"

Chapter Nine

Sophia

My heart was racing so fast I trembled.

My mind screamed to shove him away, but I couldn't move, not when those cold green eyes had pulled me into his web and I couldn't figure out how to claw my way back out. Oh god, he was right. The throb between my thighs was so intense, I had to squeeze them together, and the slight relief that offered forced a whimper past my lips.

His scarred and tattooed hand worked its way under my dress, brushing my bare flesh, before a rough-skinned finger slid up the seam of my tightly pressed-together thighs, and I shivered.

"Spread your legs," he said.

I bit my lips, furious with myself. I should be fighting him, clawing and screaming, but what was the point? I was his now, my father had given me to this man, and if I ran, my brother would be in danger. Still, I tried to muster some kind of protest, but for some reason I couldn't make myself say the words. I couldn't make myself say no. My pride wouldn't let me give in to him either, though.

His hand brushed over my panties before he worked his

finger between my clenched thighs, grazing my clit through my underwear, and I whimpered again.

"Like I said, pet, fucking soaked."

My breath shook from me, and I bit my lip harder.

"Giving in to this won't change anything, Soph," he said, his voice gentler again, but it wasn't him, that was someone else's voice. Dean's voice. Even the Irish accent had vanished. He was giving me what he thought I wanted, and god help me, it was working. "You can still hate me while I fuck you so good you forget your own name. I won't judge you for taking something for yourself, something that feels good. You deserve a reward." He pressed his thumb to my lower lip, pulling it free from my teeth. "Now spread your legs for me."

My muscles jumped, and I trembled from head to toe. I had to be demented because I wanted it, wanted what he was offering. An escape from the fear and the hurt of betrayal. He pressed down on my lip with his thumb, opening my mouth a fraction, and slid his thumb in, just a little, touching my tongue. It was strange, but it also caused a deep pulse inside me.

He shook his head. "It'll be just between you and me." He pressed a kiss to the corner of my mouth. "Spread for me."

I couldn't resist, I was aching so badly I couldn't think straight. Soaking and swollen and desperate for him to take the fear and sadness away. I stepped out, just a little, and he instantly took full advantage, sliding his hand down the front of my underwear.

One of his thick fingers pressed in, right down the center, sliding over my slick clit, the tip of his finger notching at my entrance. "Such a good girl," he said.

My knees almost gave out. I was ashamed that just hearing him say that, in that deep mesmerizing voice, pretending he was someone he wasn't, nearly had the power to send me over the edge.

He pushed his thumb deeper into my mouth. "Suck it for me."

Like the obedient little pet he'd called me, I did what he said, I sucked his thumb into my mouth.

"Your lips are so pretty, Soph."

A coil of shameful pleasure tightened inside me at his praise. I felt as if I were losing my damn mind. His finger, still pressed to my opening, slowly, so slowly, pushed inside. I moaned around his thumb, and he started finger-fucking me.

"More?" he said, watching me closely.

I nodded, powerless to do anything else.

His finger slid from my pussy, and I whimpered my protest. He ignored me and quickly dragged down my zipper, helping me out of my dress, and again, I let him. I had nothing on underneath except my panties. My skin was feverish, every part of me on fire, desperate for release. He crowded me, walking me back until my legs hit his bed.

"Lie down."

Again, I obeyed, and my overheated skin felt so incredibly good against the cool, crisp cotton. He gripped my panties and dragged them down my legs, tossing them aside. I lay there bared to him, panting, uncaring as I watched him remove his jacket and drop it over the back of one of the chairs, unable to look away as he undid his shirt, revealing smooth, muscled, inked skin.

He kicked off his shoes and socks and climbed onto the bed in only his trousers, hovering above me as those unsettling eyes raked over my trembling, naked body. "So fucking beautiful," he said, then he leaned in and kissed me. "You've pleased me, Soph, so much."

My head was spinning. I should be saying no, I should be shoving him away, fighting this, but I was turned on beyond reason, confused, and desperate for him to keep talking. All the things he was saying were at odds with that look in his eyes, but I craved more. He was a freaking psycho and a murderer, but no one had ever spoken to me that way and I craved it. God, I felt as if I'd been starved my whole life and he was the only one who knew how to ease this all-encompassing hunger inside me.

The kiss was so deep, my toes curled and the throb between my thighs intensified. I let them fall wide, asking without words for him to give me more. I needed him to touch me right the hell now or I might actually cry. He kissed his way down my neck, my chest, his beard tickling my skin, sucking one of my nipples deep into his mouth. I jolted under him, making an unintelligible sound. His hips were hovering above mine, not giving me the contact I was silently, shamefully, begging for. He gripped my breast in his hand, the hold was rough, bruising, but his mouth was so gentle, his soft sucks and slow licks driving me wild. I lifted my hips, trying to reach him, but his other hand was at my hip holding me down.

"Please." The word burst from me without my say-so.

He lifted his head, looking down at me. "Please what?" he said as he slid his thumb back and forth over my now oversensitized nipple.

"T-touch me." I hated myself for begging for anything from this man, but if I didn't come soon, I didn't know what I'd do. I felt as though I might vanish completely, just cease to exist.

"I am touching you, Soph," he said, eyes dark now, glittering.

I felt tears well in my eyes, my mind and body were at odds, I was spinning out of control and didn't know how to stop it. Getting up and walking away maybe, but I couldn't do it. "Please," I said again, instead of giving him the words he wanted.

"I can't help you unless you tell me what you want, pet. Tell me what you want and I'll give it to you."

The enforcer stared down at me, but it was Dean's voice coming out of his mouth, and the fucked-up part of me that ached for this monster loved it. "Make me c-come. Please, I...need it."

"That's it. Now you get a reward." Watching me intently, he lifted to his knees and ran his hands down the insides of my thighs. He dipped his gaze, to my exposed pussy, and slid his thumb through the center, over my heated, slick flesh. "It pleases me when you tell me what you need, when you show me." He teased my entrance, and my inner muscles clenched all on their own, wringing a gasp from me.

Cillian bent over me, kissing my stomach, right below my belly button, then he carried on down. My face went up in flames. I tried to slam my legs closed. His beard scraped my thighs and I gasped for breath. His fingers dug into my flesh and he held me wide, closing his mouth over me.

My hips jerked and my back arched, a cry bursting from me as he swiped his tongue through my pussy and sucked my clit. Then he stayed right there, working the bundle of nerves in a way that told me he knew exactly what he was doing. I wanted his fingers inside me again, but he only teased my entrance, not sliding inside. Pushing me closer and closer to orgasm, but still withholding.

He reached up and squeezed one of my breasts as he flicked and sucked my clit, and my inner muscles spasmed, clamping down on nothing as I came so hard, light danced across my eyes. My hips had a life of their own as I cried out, rocking against his mouth, riding it until I'd taken every ounce of pleasure I could.

Panting, I opened my eyes when his weight left me.

Cillian stood over me, yanking the front of his pants open, then shoving them and his underwear down past his hips. I gasped, reality slapping me in the face. He took himself in hand

and crawled between my spread thighs, dragging the head over my sensitive clit.

"No." The word burst from me. Yes, I was naked, wet, and spread wide—god, I still ached for more—but I didn't want that, not with him.

He stilled. "I will fuck you, pet, you're just putting off the inevitable, you know that even if you don't want to admit it to yourself."

I shook my head. "I said no."

Cillian stayed where he was, his gaze on mine, then moving over my naked body. Then he grabbed my head, turning it to the side, and held his open palm below my mouth. "Spit."

"What? No—"

"Spit or I fuck you."

I quickly did what he said and spat into his hand. He wrapped it around his hard length and started stroking. His cock was long and thick and veiny. His fist tightened around the head with every upward stroke, giving it a little twist, and his abs tightened with every stroke. The ring I'd slid on his finger earlier glinted as his hand moved, and the weight of mine suddenly became unbearable.

His nostrils flared. "You came so good for me, Sophia, but I know your pussy's still aching. I know how badly it wants to be fucked."

He was jerking off, right there between my spread thighs. It was messed up, I should be pushing him away, running to the bathroom and locking myself in, but I couldn't look away as his strokes quickened, as his cheeks darkened and his chest pumped harder.

He dropped forward, to his elbows, hovering above me, slamming his hips down on mine, not pushing inside me but trapping his cock between us.

I pushed at his chest. "I said, no."

"And I'm not going to force you," he said as he rocked his hips back, then dragged his cock through my slit, working it between our tightly pressed-together bodies.

Every stroke teased my already sensitive clit, and god help me, I felt another orgasm building. I opened my mouth to protest, and he kissed me again, licking into my mouth, a deep kiss that wiped my mind of everything except what was happening between my thighs.

He moved faster, ground harder. "Wrap your legs around my waist," he said against my lips.

Like an obedient dog, I did it, too caught up in my impending orgasm to even think about refusing. He lifted to his hands. "Look between our bodies," he growled. "Look what you've done to me, Sophia."

I did. I looked down past his straining chest and flexing abs to his cock, fat and dark, glistening with my juices, spreading my pussy wide as he thrust against me. The sight undid me, pushing me over the edge. I jerked and cried out, coming a second time. That had never happened to me before.

Cillian's cock throbbed against me, and he came all over my stomach. He pressed his face to my throat, sucking hard on my neck, his teeth grazing my flesh, and groaned low, lifting goose bumps all over me.

"That's my good girl," he said against my ear. Dean was gone and Cillian was back, and my pussy spasmed at the sound of his rough voice praising me in that Irish accent.

I'd barely caught my breath and he lifted off me, climbing from the bed. Grabbing his shirt, he cleaned himself, then tossed it on the bed beside me. I lay there, shaken, unable to move as he tucked himself away and did up his pants. Then, grabbing a new shirt, he tugged it on and said, "I need to take care of some things." His voice was different now, harder. There was no sign of Dean anymore. Cillian had put him away again. "Shower's through there if you want one."

Then he turned and walked out, closing the door behind him.

I blinked up at the ceiling. What the hell had I done?

What the hell was wrong with me that I let him do those things without any real resistance? Cillian O'Rourke was the worst kind of monster, capable of killing his own brother, and possibly his father as well, who had admitted he would have killed mine if he'd been told to without a second thought, all to gain more power. The kind of man who became someone else completely to manipulate others and to get what he wanted.

I didn't know who I was going to get when he walked back through that door, but I had to be ready.

Shoving off the bed, I rushed to the bathroom, desperate to wash him off, to wash away what I'd just done. I turned on the shower and stepped in, letting the hot water pour over me. I reached for the body wash and paused. *Vanilla Breeze.* This was the one I used. What the heck was it doing in Cillian's shower? It was only available online, all-natural ingredients and made by a small business I discovered when Fiona and I stayed at an Airbnb for a girls' trip.

The bottle sat beside another one, more generic, the one Cillian obviously used because unlike this one, it had been used. There was shampoo and conditioner as well, the salon brand I always bought. He'd literally been in my apartment once, and there sure as hell hadn't been time for him to check out what was in my shower.

Unease filled me as I quickly washed and got out.

I was being silly. When he had someone pack up my stuff, they obviously saw what I used. But why did he care? This seemed at odds with the man who'd just walked out of the bedroom. What the hell was he playing at?

Grabbing my toiletry bag from the suitcase in the walk-in-closet, I brushed my teeth and washed off the makeup Celeste had put on me. I reached for a towel and froze...they were identical to mine, same brand, same dove-gray color. What was this? Another one of his mind games?

The unease crawled back, and I wrapped my arms around myself.

Cillian was a master manipulator, even worse than my father, this wasn't some olive branch or a kindness to make me feel more at home. How could it be when he didn't know the meaning of the word?

I couldn't drop my guard like I just had around him ever again.

He was far too dangerous.

Chapter Ten

Sophia

I'd spent most of the morning unpacking.

Did I want to unpack? Hell no. I spent all day yesterday avoiding any activity that would be seen as settling in.

But Cillian had ordered me to do just that before he'd walked out of the bedroom this morning.

He'd come back to the room sometime during the night, showered, then stood beside the bed. I'd kept my eyes firmly shut, pretending I was asleep. The very idea of looking into those cold-blooded eyes sent a shiver through my entire body. I'd lain there utterly still, holding my breath, pretending to sleep. I was still emotionally battered from what we'd done and wasn't ready to face him again so soon, not after the humiliating way my body had betrayed me. He'd stood there, watching me, for far too long before he'd finally gotten into bed beside me, and as soon as his breathing evened out, I'd dragged a blanket to the chair by the unlit fire. I'd tried to stay awake, scared what would happen if I had an attack, but I'd been exhausted. I'd woken still in the chair and injury-free, so that was something, I guess, but I'd been startled to find him looming over me, watching me again. He ordered me to unpack when I blinked up at him and walked out.

I'd found my way to the kitchen a couple of hours ago and made breakfast and a cup of coffee. I didn't know if Cillian was still in the house, but I found myself tiptoeing around, afraid I'd rouse the monster from wherever he was right now and give him cause to come looking for me.

Goose bumps lifted all over me when a sensory memory rushed out of nowhere, feeling way too real, like his hands, hot and rough, were grabbing my flesh, gliding over my skin, wrapped around my throat. I shook it off and searched the drawer by the front door. My car keys weren't among my things that Celeste had packed, but I needed my computer, my tablet— I had work to do, clients waiting, deadlines to meet.

I didn't even have my phone. Fiona had to be wondering where I was. Then something occurred to me that should have already. Steve, he was friends with Brian...Paolo. They met through me and Fi, but was that what really happened? Steve could be in on this whole thing. I needed to warn Fiona. I reached into the back of the drawer. Bingo. Keys. Snatching them up, I peeked through the peephole.

I didn't see anyone.

But I couldn't just walk out. Cillian might think I'd run away, and I wouldn't risk Tommy like that. I quickly scribbled a note, telling Cillian I'd be back in a couple of hours.

That should at least stop him from doing anything rash, and he hadn't actually said I couldn't leave the house. I wasn't going to give him the chance to tell me no, though, either.

Grabbing my wallet, I slipped down the stairs that I hoped led to a garage below and opened the door. Score. There were five cars lined up. Was this a stupid thing to do? Yes, without doubt. But I had to warn my friend and let her know I was okay.

I hit the button on the fob and a sporty little black car on the other side of the garage lit up. I rushed over and jumped in. The engine roared to life a moment later. No one came running, and I wasn't going to wait around until someone did. The garage doors opened automatically as I approached, and I sped out.

The engine revved as I drove down the expressway heading toward the city. Cillian lived a little ways out, but time seemed to rush by while I battled the nerves in my stomach. If Fiona got hurt because of me, because of my messed-up family—fear sliced through me and I glanced in the rearview mirror again to check if I was being followed. I didn't think so.

I drove straight to her work, and the perfume of a multitude of different flowers hit me as I walked into the shop. She wasn't at the counter where she usually created her stunning bouquets. She had to be out the back. "Fi! You back there?"

She rushed out. "Soph! Are you okay? You haven't been at your place, and you haven't answered any of my calls for two days." She searched me from head to toe.

Maybe that wouldn't sound like a long time without contact to some, but Fi and I talked several times a day, every day. "I'm okay, but we need to talk."

Concern filled her eyes. "What's going on?"

I did a quick scan of the shop to make sure it was empty. "Have you seen Steve the last couple days?"

Her expression shifted, hurt filling her eyes. "I tried to call him, but his number was disconnected. I couldn't get hold of Brian either." She shook her head. "Do you know what's going on? Have you seen them?"

That answered my questions about Steve. There was no way he would have ignored Fi before. He was in on it. "No. And if you do see either of them, you need to stay away. I can't explain, but...they're not who they tried to make us believe they were. They're not...good, Fi. They're dangerous."

"You're not making any sense." Color stained her cheeks. "You know something, don't you? Is he seeing someone else?"

"No, not that I know of, but that's not it and I wish I could tell you more…just, please, I need you to trust me, okay? If either of them contact you, or come by your apartment, don't let them in and don't talk to them."

I could see her frustration growing. She hated secrets and she wasn't a fan of people giving her only half the story, and I was doing both. Her gaze slid over my shoulder and her spine stiffened, her eyes kind of widening.

Panic welled, knotting in my throat because I knew exactly who had set off my best friend's flight instincts without even looking.

I made myself turn, standing in front of Fiona, like I had any hope of protecting her. Cillian was in a dark suit, the jacket undone and the white shirt beneath it fitting snugly against his chest and tight stomach. That impenetrable gaze was locked on me.

"You found my note?" I said as he reached me.

"I found it," he said, accent thick, then looked at Fi. "Whatever she shared with you, I'd advise you keep it to yourself. I'll be taking my wife home now."

Her mouth fell open. "Wife? What the hell's he talking about, Soph?"

Goddammit. "It was…sudden."

"Time to go," Cillian said to me.

"You're that guy." Fi frowned. "The one from the bar."

"Yeah, it was a bit of a whirlwind," I said and looked up at Cillian when his hand clamped on mine. "I seemed to have lost my phone. If I knew where it was, I wouldn't have had to leave the house at all, I could have just called," I bit out, my rising temper stifling my fear.

The muscle in his jaw jumped, and he slid my phone from

his pocket, handing it to me. "All you had to do was ask, Soph," he said.

I blinked up at him, at the sudden change in his voice. He curled his arm around my shoulders and tucked me in close. "Sorry I acted like a dick," he said to Fi. "I didn't know where she was and I overreacted." A self-deprecating half smile actually curled his lips.

Fi studied him, then me. "You're really married? You hardly know each other."

He chuckled like he was freaking possessed. "I'm actually a friend of the family. I've had a thing for Sophia for a while now. I guess, she finally saw me."

Fiona frowned at me. "But at the bar, you never said...so you knew him?"

"I didn't recognize him at first, with the beard, then I was trying to work through my feelings. Like I said, it's been kind of crazy."

"I saw my opening and I took it," Cillian said and grinned, like an actual human being.

I watched as the suspicion slipped from Fiona's eyes, as the charm he could switch on with the click of his fingers started working on my best friend. She looked between us.

"I was telling Fi to stay away from Brian and Steven," I said to Cillian.

He didn't even blink. "Brian was using Soph to get to her father. A business thing. He's not a good guy, Fi, and neither is his buddy. If you see them, if they ask after Sophia, or you're worried, please call. It's important."

She was already nodding, her lip trembling because she'd fallen for Steve pretty hard and this had to hurt. "I will. I promise."

Cillian looked down at me. "We need to get going."

"Will you be okay?" I said to Fiona. "I know you really liked Steve—"

Her lip quivered, but she shook her head. "I'll be okay. I just...I thought he was different, you know?"

"I know. I'm sorry, Fi. I thought he was a good guy as well."

She bit her lip, forcing a smile. "At least now I know the truth."

Truth? I had the sudden inappropriate urge to laugh. I swallowed it down.

Cillian's hand slid across my shoulder and curled around the back of my neck, not tight, but his grip was hot, firm.

"It was nice meeting you, Fiona," Cillian said. "But I'm going to steal my wife away now so we can get back to our honeymoon."

Fi held my eyes, still unsure. "Text me okay?"

"I will, promise." Then Cillian was guiding me away. Conor, the guy who had driven us to Cillian's house after the wedding, sat in a car beside the one I'd commandeered. He nodded when he saw us and drove away.

Cillian held out his hand. "Keys."

Tugging them from my pocket, I handed them over. He unlocked the car, and I quickly got in.

Cillian did as well, the engine roaring to life a moment later and he peeled out onto the street. He darted glances in the rearview mirror, his fingers tight around the steering wheel. "That wasn't very smart for you," he said in a deceptively calm voice.

Every instinct in me screamed that I should sit quietly and not poke the bear, but I couldn't stay silent. "Would you have let me go if I'd asked?"

"No," he said.

"They pretended that they met through me and Fiona, but

Paolo was obviously lying about that as well. I was worried about my friend—"

He glanced my way. "You have good instincts. Steve's real name is Walter Mazza, and Paolo brought him in to occupy your friend so he could get in your pants, get intel on you, make you fall for him, then use you as a way to seal an alliance between your family and his."

My stomach sank and humiliation at my mistake burned my cheeks. "What if Walter—"

"Walter won't get anywhere near you."

"And Fiona?"

He shifted gears and sped past the car in front of us. "She's no longer of use to him. His focus has shifted."

"How do you know?"

Cillian glanced at me again. "Because he tried to follow you from my place earlier, and we intercepted." His jaw hardened. "He got away, but he had zip ties and duct tape in his trunk."

I spun to him. "What?"

"I've made a deal with Alto, but his nephew has gone rogue. Paolo's pissed off. I worked him over pretty good the night he came to your apartment. His ego's bruised. He wanted to be one of the big boys, but his uncle cut him out of our talks. I should have killed him when I had the chance, but if I'd done that, we'd already be at war."

My stomach turned over.

"Your father's weak, Sophia, greedy," he said as if he were reading my mind. "If we'd left you with him, your family would be dead, Paolo would have you, and the decades-long alliance between us and the Brennans would be broken."

This was too much. My mind was in a spin. "God, you all treat me like I'm some kind of chess piece."

"Because in this instance, you were. And I won."

"Is that why you killed Adam? So you could win?"

"I killed Adam because I was Seamus's heir, not him. The men didn't trust him. They were never going to follow him."

I looked at his hard profile. "And they trust you?"

"I'll do anything for the good of the family, they know that. Adam was only concerned with himself."

"So you killed your own brother in cold blood?"

His expression didn't change, not even the slightest flinch. "Yes." He shifted gears, passing another car. "And I never considered Adam my brother."

I gripped the door handle as he pulled into the driveway and down into the parking garage under the house. The garage door closed behind us, and a cold knot coiled in my stomach. "And if one day I'm no longer fit for your purpose, will you kill me as well?"

He turned off the engine, and the car plummeted into silence. He turned to me, and I wanted to shrink in on myself. "What did I say to you last night, Sophia?"

I blinked over at him. I couldn't remember anything he said last night, it was all one insane, out-of-control blur. I shook my head.

He took a piece of my hair between his scarred fingers and rubbed it. "I take care of what's mine."

I was finding it hard to breathe.

His gaze moved over my face, and something disturbing flickered in the depths of his eyes. "My possessions are important to me. Once something belongs to me, I don't give it up. If you fuck with me, Sophia, I will punish you, but I'll never discard you, because I'll never give you up."

I stared back, my strength was a fragile shell around me and, in the wake of that dark promise, close to shattering.

"You are mine," he said, voice incredibly low.

I sat frozen as he shifted in his seat, the leather creaking, and angled toward me.

He cupped the side of my face. "And that will never change." His other hand wrapped around mine, his thumb running over the ring he'd put on my finger the day before, then sliding lower and gripping my thigh. Fear twisted with something dark and alluring had shameful heat flooding my veins as his hand slid higher. My pussy wanted me to spread wider for him and give this monster access, to let him make me feel good like he had last night, but when he tightened his hold on my hair and leaned forward, self-preservation and what was left of my pride kicked in and I turned away, denying him.

His mouth brushed my jaw instead, his whiskers tickling my skin, making me shiver. He stilled, breathing heavily for several seconds, then lifted his head, gave my hair a light tug, released me, and got out of the car.

I didn't move as he walked around and opened my door.

Then I scrambled out of the car and raced into the house and upstairs.

Chapter Eleven

Cillian

"It's done," Declan said, sitting in the chair across from me.

I glanced at Conor leaning against the doorframe. "And you've put more men on the house?" Walter hadn't come here alone yesterday, he'd brought another of Paola's men. I'd shot the other guy in the chest, but Walter got away. Dec and Con had taken care of the body, taking it out to the ocean and dumping it for the sharks to finish off.

"One of Brennan's men was sniffing around this afternoon as well," Conor said. "Said he was sent to check on Sophia, to make sure she was settling in okay, but I think it was something else."

"Considering Callum doesn't give a fuck about his daughter, I'd say that's a fair assessment." I sat back. "What did you tell him?"

Con smirked. "That it was her honeymoon and she was a little tied up."

Callum was already angry, unsure after I took control of the family and then his daughter. He'd be worried what that meant for him. Sending his man here, using Sophia as an excuse, told me just how worried he was. Con being a smart-ass would have only pissed him off more, and the angrier we made him, the more likely he was to make a mistake. "Has he been to see Alto?"

"Not yet."

I didn't know for sure if he would; he'd have to locate his balls first. Brennan had no idea I'd already made a deal. He'd want me out of the way so he could run both families himself, and the only hope he had to get me out of the way was to make a deal with the Italians. He'd be in for a surprise if he went that route.

Dec shook his head. "The guy's fucking delusional if he does. None of our men would follow him, even if by some miracle he did manage to take you out."

They wouldn't, but Brennan was arrogant enough to think otherwise.

There was a tap at the door and Janet poked her head in. "I'm heading off, Mr. O'Rourke. Sally's here for the night shift."

"Thank you, Janet."

The older woman smiled and ducked back out.

"How is he?" Dec asked.

"Alive." Seamus had collapsed when I killed Adam. He was already frail, but seeing his son's brains all over the floor had almost taken him out. "You want to see him?" Now he was here with around-the-clock nurses caring for him.

Declan's face hardened. "No. You should've just put a bullet in that fucker's skull as well."

It would've been easy enough. I'd thought about it many times. But some human part of me, buried deep but still gasping for life, had hesitated. It was a surprise, but that weak part of me wanted him to see what I was capable of, that I was more than just the killer he'd turned me into. It wanted to show him I could lead this family into bigger and better things.

It was late, and my mind kept wandering to Sophia, because

she was always there. I stood. "Make sure you keep eyes on Gaia. Brennan's desperate, and he could be capable of almost anything."

Declan stood as well, a grim expression on his face. "My new fiancée isn't making it easy."

Alto's daughter was a handful, but if anyone could handle her, it was Declan. "The sooner you're married the better."

Dec didn't look as convinced, but he'd get used to the idea. When she was under his roof, he'd have more control over her and things would settle down.

I thought about my new wife's escape yesterday, then again, what the fuck did I know? I had no control over my own wife. I'd been here in my office when she'd bolted. I'd watched her on a security camera as she'd taken off in one of my cars. Then I'd seen Walter. Con had tailed her to make sure she was safe, and I'd gone after our trespasser. I'd wanted to question him, but the fucker had taken off on foot, jumping over fences and running through backyards to get away.

Sophia had proven more than once that she wasn't the meek wee mouse I'd first believed her to be, and I found I liked it.

Declan and Conor left, and I made my way around the house, making sure the place was secured. I'd be working from home for a few more days until I was sure there were no immediate threats to Sophia and that she'd stay put while I was gone.

It was late when I walked into my bedroom and found her asleep on the chair in front of the fireplace again. She had a blanket tucked around her and a pillow propped under her head.

No, pet, that's not how this works.

In the car yesterday, when we got back to the house, I'd wanted to taste her so badly. We'd sat there in silence, and the way she'd looked at me, the fear in her eyes, the reluctant hunger, I'd suddenly been desperate to taste it, taste what was mine. I hadn't been able to stop myself, as if I was fucking possessed, but she'd turned away, shutting me down.

I got it, but I wasn't letting her walk all over me either.

My gaze traveled over her. I'd watched her sleep so many times, confused by how much I wanted her. Wanting her, but only allowing myself to hold her when she had an attack in her sleep. I rubbed at my chest, feeling restless. Fuck, she'd tasted so damn good.

My stubborn beauty. She had to know the risk of sleeping in a chair like this. But disorder aside, my wife did not sleep on a chair, she slept with me, and if I let her stay here again, not only would I be awake all night worried she'd hurt herself, she'd think I was okay with it—and I wasn't for some reason, not at all.

I could pick her up and put her in my bed, but I wanted her to come to bed on her own. I adjusted the thermostat for the room—I liked it cool, anyway—then walked to the bathroom and stripped.

The room smelled like her body lotion, vanilla and cinnamon, she'd been in here not long ago, and she'd used it.

The first time I'd smelled it, she'd been asleep in her bed at her apartment, her skin rosy after her shower, her cheeks pink. I'd looked down at her and found it hard to breathe. That scent on her skin, fuck, it made me hard. Everything about her had made me hard. I'd gone home and found the place that sold it online and ordered it. Seamus would say I was a sick fuck, and he'd be right.

That hadn't stopped being true just because Sophia was mine. I was still just as sick, just as fucked in the head. I opened the cupboard under the sink where I kept it and pumped some into my hand. Turing on the shower, I stepped in, my back to the spray, and smoothed it along my dick. Closing my eyes like I'd done so any times before—before she was mine, before I could touch her—and thought of how she looked in my bed, taking my fingers, squirting on my hand. The scent filled the shower while I fucked my fist, imagining she was in here with me, that I was pounding her tight pussy, that it was her squeezing my cock.

I shuddered as I stroked faster, the scent filling my head, the memory of her taste, of the way her pussy felt against my tongue, the way she begged for more, desperate for the slightest bit of praise, her needy cries, wanting her husband to take control and getting off so fucking hard when I did.

She was in the other room.

Sleeping beauty was mine.

I owned her.

The thought made me harder, made my balls tighten and my breath punch from my lungs. I squeezed my cock, stroked faster, and came with a grunt, panting hard. Relief flooded me. I'd needed that. All day I'd wanted to seek her out and make her come, but had resisted.

By the time I walked out of the bathroom, the temperature had dropped significantly. Sophia was still on the chair, but she'd pulled the blanket higher around her neck while she slept.

I got into bed.

My new wife was definitely stubborn. She lasted another hour, and by the time she darted across the room and got in beside me, I could hear her teeth chattering. I lay still, breathing evenly, letting her believe I was asleep, and my lips actually twitched when I felt her ease closer, just a little, seeking out some warmth. The bed trembled with her shivers. I didn't like knowing she was cold. My plan had worked, but it wasn't a tactic I'd use with her again.

I reached out and grabbed her. She squeaked. I ignored her weak protest and dragged her across the bed and against my side. Her skin was like ice. I'd feel guilty if I was capable of it. Instead, I kept her plastered to me so she'd warm up.

Sophia was mine, my wife, and I allowed myself to wrap my arms around her and hold her in place the way I had in her apartment while she thrashed as she slept, the way husbands did their wives in all those movies I'd watched. She was stiff in my arms, but she didn't try to pull away. I didn't care that it was only because she was cold, I liked her against me.

"Let me warm you, pet," I said against her ear. I knew what she liked, how she liked to be talked to. My wife was into praise, it made her wet. Good thing dishing it out made me hard as fuck, it always had. If I talked to a shrink, or referred to one of my psychology books, it'd probably say it had something to do with my mother's disdain for me and the ways she'd withheld affection. Then again, they might attribute it to my father murdering my mother in front of me, hiding his connection to my brother and me, or forcing me to make my first kill when I was fifteen years old.

Or it could just be that I got off on giving praise for the same reason as Sophia liked to receive it, because I'd never experienced it growing up.

Sophia whimpered and gave in, pressing her icy feet to my shins.

"You sleep in my bed from now on," I said. "You try and sleep anywhere but here, I'll pick you up and put you in this bed."

She nodded, but her body had stiffened. "There's...something you should know," she said in a hushed voice. "When I sleep, sometimes I—"

"I know about your sleep disorders, pet." She froze against me.

"You have nothing to worry about."

She was silent for several moments. "But what if I lash out, what if I—"

"Then I'll hold you to me until you settle back down. I

would never punish you for something that's out of your control."

Her body softened a little. "It can be...really bad."

"It's nothing that I can't handle. I promise you that." I slid my hand up and down her arm. "I know your world's been tipped upside down, Soph, but you're doing so good," I rasped, letting Dean come through, and she shivered. "You shared this with me, and you stayed here like I asked you to today. You've pleased me, pet." I felt goose bumps lift across her arms, but not from the cold this time. Maybe giving her what she needed, what we'd both been starved of all our lives, made some perverse part of me feel human.

It was dark in the room, snug under the covers. She was softening against me, and her breathing had quickened. "You've handled all of this so well, you deserve a reward." She quivered, and I knew I had her. "Lift your leg for me, rest it on mine." I gave her thigh a squeeze, and when she didn't move straightaway, I guided it where I wanted it, sliding my knee forward and resting her leg over mine. She hadn't moved herself, but she gave no resistance either.

I cupped her pussy over her panties, and yeah, they were already damp. I sucked the smooth skin under her ear as I slid my hand down the front. Her hips jerked and she gasped, but still she didn't try to pull away. I knew what she needed. She'd been so tense in the car yesterday, afraid for her friend—afraid of me. She'd avoided me all day today. I didn't like that, I didn't want her afraid of me, I wanted her to crave me.

She'd soon learn that I wouldn't hurt her. She was the first thing I'd truly owned that was all mine. I wouldn't let anyone take her. Nothing would hurt her, not even me. She needed out of her head, to clear her mind of everything except what she was feeling. That, I could give her, and right now, it was the only thing my new wife would let me give her.

My fingers were covered in her juices as I tested her willingness. She was growing wetter by the second. She had to be aching.

I nipped her ear as I thrust two fingers inside her tight pussy. A soft cry burst from her as she clutched around me tight. I wanted to feel that around my cock, badly, but I could wait a little longer.

I wrapped my fingers around her throat with my other hand and she gasped, grabbing at my wrist. My hold was firm but not tight, not interfering with her breathing, but enough that she'd try not to move in case it did. I wanted her to give in to me, give in to the pleasure I was giving her, and that could only happen if she felt a sense of powerlessness.

I started slow, fucking her with my fingers, working her up. Her gasps and whimpers, the wet sounds of her juicy pussy, filled the room.

"Your tight little cunt's taking my fingers so good, pet."

She groaned, her fingernails digging into my wrist, but she didn't ask me to stop, no, she lifted her leg higher over mine, spreading wider, silently asking for more.

"Fuck, my wife's got a greedy pussy." I increased the pace, thrusting into her faster and deeper.

Her mouth fell open and her hips moved restlessly against my hand.

"That's it, take it deeper," I grated against her ear. "I'm gonna need to stretch you out if you're ever gonna take my cock, pet. Can you take another finger?"

She moaned and shook her head.

"You can and you will, because that's what I want."

Her throat worked against my hand.

"Answer me."

"Y-yes."

I forced in a third finger and she cried out, her inner muscles spasming. I fucked her with all three digits, harder, faster. "You're taking it so fucking good. So good." Her pussy dripped more with every dirty thing I said, sliding down my fingers. Her thighs trembled, and her cries shifted, almost sounding panicked. The monster made her feel good, and it scared the fuck out of her. I felt her jaw tighten, gritting her teeth, holding back. "Let it go."

She gasped. "I c-can't."

"Yes, you can," I said, my voice harder.

"N-no. This is wrong. I shouldn't..."

I pulled my fingers from her and slapped her pussy twice in quick succession, then shoved them back in deep. Sophia screamed, instantly coming hard. Her pussy gushed, and her hips rocked and twisted against my hand.

Fuck yes.

"That's it," I said against her ear as she trembled and twitched in my arms. "That's my good girl."

When the last shudder moved through her, I carefully slipped my fingers from her and rolled her to her back. Straddling her hips, I shoved my underwear down, hooking them under my balls, rested a hand on the headboard, and fisted my cock. She was wearing a soft T-shirt and shorts, and I shoved the shirt up so I could look at her tits. What I wanted to do was tear those shorts off completely and fuck her senseless, but we weren't there yet.

I didn't think I'd ever been this hard before, and I stroked my cock brutally. Sophia stared up at me wide-eyed, her gaze moving over my face, my chest, down over my stomach, and as soon as her eyes locked on my cock, she licked her lips. It was involuntary, I was sure, and probably didn't mean what I wanted it to, but right then I told myself it was because she wanted me to fuck her face.

Just the thought was enough to push me over the edge. I

groaned, coming all over her tits. She watched, not looking away, and I held her wide blue eyes.

When I was finished, I slid my hand over her skin, smearing my come across her tits before carefully tugging her shirt down again. "Don't wash it off."

I don't know what possessed me, but I pressed a soft kiss to her lips before I rolled to the mattress beside her.

She started to roll away. Again, I didn't know what the fuck possessed me, why I...felt I needed this closeness with her, but my arm shot out. I hooked her around the waist and I dragged her back against my side.

Oh no, sweet little Sophia, you aren't going anywhere.

————

I woke an hour later to my sleeping beauty's screams. She kicked and fought, hitting out with all her strength. I quickly grabbed her wrists, crossing her arms over her chest, pinning them down by wrapping mine around her tight, then hooked my legs around hers, immobilizing her completely, so she didn't hurt herself. "Easy, pet." She continued to fight, not waking, her fear so real, she trembled against me, sweating and jerking against my hold. "It's okay, pet, you're safe," I said against her ear.

Slowly, she stilled.

Then my new wife pressed closer to me with a soft moan and relaxed in my arms.

————

Sophia

Cillian was still asleep beside me, his arm over my waist.

I couldn't believe I'd let him touch me again last night, god, that I'd begged him for it. He'd come on me, rubbed it in, commanded me not to wash it off, and I'd obeyed like the good little pet I was. What the hell was wrong with me? His alarm would go off soon, and I didn't want to be here when it did. I carefully slid his arm off me, eased out of bed, snatched up some clothes from the closet, and shut myself in the bathroom.

Turning the shower to hot, I stepped in and let the hot spray sink into my bones as I lathered up and defiantly washed him off my skin, moving quickly. Even with the door locked, I was afraid he'd come in. My brain tried to fire images at me of what we'd done last night, and my skin heated, my nipples tightening without my say-so. How could I want him? He was everything I despised, he was a monster, *the* monster. I hated him for what he'd done, for the way he'd helped my father destroy my life.

His deep voice filled my head.

Then I'll hold you to me until you settle back down.

I fought a shiver.

That was the last thing I'd expected him to say when I'd tried to tell him about my sleep disorders, when I'd asked what he'd do if I lashed out.

I shoved down the images, the sound of his voice, and got out, drying off quickly, then reaching for the bottle of body lotion sitting on the bathroom counter. I frowned at how light it was, and my gaze slid to my toiletry bag. Another bottle of the same vanilla-and-cinnamon body lotion sat inside, my new almost-full one.

My gaze slid between the two bottles. The one in my hand was over half empty. For that to be the case, it had to have been here a while, longer than a few days, definitely before Cillian, pretending to be Dean, walked into my apartment for the first time and fucked my life up completely.

What the fuck was this?

Quickly dressing, I grabbed the bottle and strode into the bedroom.

Cillian was up. He stood in the middle of the room, shirtless and in the process of doing up his pants. I hated that he was so beautiful, that I couldn't stop myself from eating up the sight of his lean, muscled body. He looked up, his gaze slicing from my face to the lotion in my hand, and a darkness moved through his eyes.

My belly wobbled, but I ignored it and held up the bottle. "What is this?"

He said nothing.

"You've obviously had it a while, it's half empty. How did you know I used it? You have the same towels as me and you had the same shampoo and conditioner as well." I glanced at the bed. "Hang on, are those the same sheets as mine?" The unease grew to something else, bigger and awful. "How did you know what I used, the things I like?"

Cillian still said nothing, just watched me, and there was this...god, odd look on his face that lifted the hair on the back of my neck.

"You came into my apartment, didn't you? Before you pretended to be Dean?"

I forced myself to hold my ground when he continued to stare for several more seconds, then finally nodded.

My stomach dropped, prickles of fear crawling all over me. "When I was there?" He didn't move, stayed completely still. "How many times?" Again, nothing. "Did you come in while I was asleep? Did you watch me?"

His emotionless gaze moved over me, then locked on mine again. "Aye."

Oh god. "Why? Why would you do that?"

The muscle in his jaw pulsed.

I drew in a deep breath, refusing to tremble. "Did Seamus want you to hurt me?"

He shook his head. "He wanted info on you."

"And that included coming into my place while I slept."

"No, that part was all me."

Oh god. "Did you want to hurt me?"

"No."

"How many times? How long were you doing that... watching me?"

"A while."

"Months? Longer?"

He nodded again.

I knew he was capable of a lot of terrible things, but this? I couldn't believe what I was hearing. "That's how you know about my sleep issues?" He'd seen me, watched me while I'd fought the invisible monsters in my dreams, seen me at my most vulnerable. Seen my secret shame.

The look on his face changed. He was looking at me the same way he did when he touched me. My heart thundered in my chest. "Did you touch me?"

"I held you down when you needed it."

I wrapped my arms around myself. "You held me down? Is that all, is that the only way you touched me?"

Another nod, and his eyes darkened.

"Did you get off on it, is that it?" I fired at him.

His nostrils flared. "Aye, I did."

My fingers tightened around the bottle in my hand, and I glanced down at it, realization hitting me. "And what? You came home and used this to...to..."

"To stroke my cock," he said, his accent thicker. "Thinking of you while I did it."

Everything he'd just said was wrong, terrifying, violating,

but again, my body responded in a way that it shouldn't. I had to be as twisted as he was.

"Why?" I whispered.

He grabbed the shirt he'd draped over the chair beside him and slid it on, unhurriedly doing it up. He tucked it in, then looked over at me. "Because you were mine, pet, you just didn't know it yet."

Then he walked out.

Chapter Twelve

Sophia

I looked out the living room window. The ocean was wild today.

I'd been living with Cillian for a week. I didn't see him that much during the day, he was either out or working in his office here at the house. When he was out, he didn't often come home until late at night, and every time he got into bed beside me, he'd pull me against him, waking me slowly from my sleep with his hands or his mouth.

Because you were mine, pet, you just didn't know it yet.

He'd said that after he admitted he'd stalked me, watched me, that he'd broken into my apartment, and, on occasion, got into bed with me while I slept and he held me down. That when he came home after doing that, he'd used the same lotion I did to touch himself while thinking about me.

And still I let him do what he wanted to me. Despite everything I knew, I still let him do it.

Because in the darkness, he became someone else, he played a role that he knew I craved. He was Dean. And I was so needy for affection, for attention, I let the monster, my stalker, my jailer, give it to me. I became his pet, his toy to play with. He told me how wonderful I was, and I caved completely. He called me his good girl, and I spread wider, desperate for him to touch me. He took command of my body until I was wet and squirming, then he'd make me come so hard I didn't know what to do with myself.

After, he'd stroke his cock until he came as well, usually on me, and he'd hold me to him again, tight, to stop me fighting in my sleep.

I didn't remember having the attacks, but I knew I was, the familiar aching muscles gave it away, because I'd been struggling with everything I had, my throat raw as if I'd been screaming. There were never any injuries, though, Cillian made sure of that, like he had been for months without me knowing, holding me down until the attack passed, like he said he would. He'd never once mentioned it in the morning.

I didn't know what it said about me, that knowing he took care of me while I was so vulnerable actually made me feel safe, or that I'd started anticipating the sound of his footfalls on the stairs, the dip of the bed when he got in beside me, his strong hands wrapping around my waist and tugging me across to him so I was plastered against his body.

My feelings for him hadn't changed. I despised him, yet I let him do those things to me.

Every morning, I told myself that I'd pull away next time, that I'd tell him no, but then in the darkness, his room became a safe haven where no one knew my shame or the dirty things I let him do to me—or how much I wanted him to do them.

I rubbed at the goose bumps that had broken out across my arms and tried to shove him from my mind. God, I felt restless. I'd already cleaned the kitchen, living room, and bedroom, even though Cillian had a regular cleaner and it was already spotless, then I'd texted with Fi for a while, and she filled me in on everything that was going on, and that she hadn't seen or heard from "Steve," which was a massive relief.

I paced the room some more. What I really wanted was my computer, my tablet, my things, the rest of my clothes. The jewelry my mom gave me before she died. I wanted to work. I'd emailed my clients and told them there'd be a delay, but I couldn't expect them to wait much longer.

Three nights ago, before I'd fallen asleep, I'd asked Cillian if I could go to my apartment and get my things. He'd said no. That's it, nothing else. I glanced at my phone on the coffee table. He'd said if I needed anything, to call or text him. Until now, I hadn't even contemplated it. Straightening my spine, I strode over and scooped it up.

Nerves rioted in my belly. Yes, I let him touch me every night, but it wasn't like we were having deep and meaningful conversations in the dark. We spent no time together during the day. I slept in his bed beside him, but I didn't know him. Did anyone know the real Cillian O'Rourke? Or did everyone in his life get the version he wanted them to see? The idea sent shards of ice through my veins.

Wrestling down my nerves, I hit his number and braced for some weird reason. Probably because I didn't know who I was going to get. He'd shown me two different people. Was there any of Cillian in Dean? Did some of the real Cillian come out when he made that transformation? Or was he just that much of a sociopath?

He stalked you, broke into your place, and watched you sleep. He murdered his own brother and forced you to marry him.

"Sophia?" His voice was low but utterly unreadable.

"Uh, hey. Can you talk or are you busy?"

There was a beat of silence. "Is something wrong?"

"No...well, nothing life-threatening."

More silence, and this time it dragged on. "Why are you calling, Sophia?"

I jumped, his roughened voice startling me. "You said to call if I needed something."

"I know."

Shit, I sounded like the biggest idiot.

"Sophia," he said, and there was a bit of growl to his voice.

"Right, yes, sorry. I have clients waiting for me to finish their projects and I need my computer and tablet from the apartment."

"Fine."

I was expecting him to tell me no again. "So I can go get them?"

"No, I will. Anything else?"

Yes, but this felt weird. I was about to ask the O'Rourke monster to go pick me up a few things, like he was just your average domesticated guy, not the head of a family of mobsters. "The rest of my clothes in the big dresser, my jewelry on top of it, and there's makeup in the bathroom cabinet that I want... I mean, if that's okay?"

"I'll get it." There was another pause. "I'll see you later."

Why the hell did my heart just skip a beat? I opened my mouth, not sure what I was going to say, but he'd already disconnected.

After that awkward interaction, I took a nap. I hadn't been sleeping as much as I needed, for obvious reasons, and when that happened, my body forced me to rest. So I surrounded myself with pillows and gave in to it.

I woke a couple hours later and, not sure what to do with myself, went wandering. The house was broken into two wings. There was a single-story section that jutted out the side, that I'd seen when we drove in yesterday. You had to go through the kitchen to get to it. The first door I opened was a massive gym, with all the equipment you could ask for. Another bathroom, a kitchenette. A fully self-contained addition by the looks. Down from that was a small living room and a bedroom. It looked like someone was staying here. There was a bag by the bed and a half-empty glass of water. Is this where his men slept when they were guarding the house?

I ducked back out. There was one more door beside it. Gripping the handle, I pushed it open—and froze.

Seamus O'Rourke lay in a bed across the room. He was alive, yes, but he looked frail and was hooked up to a bunch of tubes. Cillian had spared him for some reason, but I doubted it was from the goodness of his heart. He'd have to have one for that. A nurse sat beside him, and she was reading aloud. She looked up, catching me before I could get the hell out of there.

"I'm sorry," I said. "I didn't mean to disturb...I..."

"Come here, girl," Seamus said, his green eyes, so like Cillian's, locked on me.

I hesitated.

"It's not like I'm a threat," he said, voice reedy and thin.

The last time I saw him was with Adam at our house. He'd given me the creeps then, and he did now too. It didn't matter that he was bedridden and frail. Those eyes, they made it hard to disobey, and I found myself stepping into the room.

"Give us a minute, would you, Sally?" he said to the nurse.

"If you promise not to get worked up," she said.

He chuckled. "Woman, the only thing that gets me worked up is that round ass and those massive tits of yours bouncing around in front of me all damn day."

She shook her head at him but didn't seem fazed or grossed out. I had to fight not to cringe. She walked out, closing the door behind her.

"Take a seat, girl, I don't bite. Or at least, I can't, not

anymore." Those dead eyes moved over me from head to toe. "Though, I wouldn't mind taking a bite out of you, sweetheart."

I fought my shudder and took a seat like he asked, not sure why I'd stayed, it wasn't like he could force me to. I'd been told to respect my elders my whole life, my father had demanded it, but this creep had done nothing to earn it. I had no doubt Seamus was the biggest monster of them all.

"So he married you, then? I wondered," he said. "Did he tell you he killed my son?"

I nodded.

"I guess I only have myself to blame. His mother always said he wasn't right in the head. I brought him and his younger brother here when they were young, thought some time with me would straighten Cillian out. He was like a stray dog, angry, untrusting. Trust is dangerous in our world, so I beat him to make sure he never forgot it, then I beat him until he could take it and not even flinch. I made him the stone-cold killer he is. Only problem with that is, he doesn't understand loyalty. I created a monster, then he turned on me."

Horror filled me. I didn't think I could ever feel sorry for Cillian, but at that moment I did. My heart broke for the boy he'd been, unwanted, angry, untrusting. How could a father beat their own child? No, I hadn't spent much time around him or his men, but Seamus was wrong, Cillian was sure of their loyalty, and there was no missing that he trusted Declan and Conor.

"Why are you here, then?" If Cillian had turned on him, why was he still alive?

His gaze darkened. "He wants to watch me suffer. I'd rather he put a bullet in me and be done with it." His hand shot out, grabbing my wrist, and despite his frailty, his hold was bruising. "You could help me."

I shook my head, trying to pull from his hold. I didn't want any part of this, whatever it was.

"You get me out of here, and I'll do the same for you." I winced when he squeezed my wrist tighter. "He'll kill you, girl. One day you'll let down your guard, you'll think everything's fine, then he'll blow your brains out where you sleep. You're not safe here."

I tried to yank my hand free again, but he wouldn't let me go. "He said he'd never hurt me—"

"And you believe him? Cillian's broken, he's cold to his core, an emotionless monster. He doesn't have a personality of his own, so he pretends to be other people. He used to watch movies for hours, read a bunch of books on psychology and shit, learning how to act like a fucking human being. He pretends to be what people want to get what he wants." He yanked me closer, fear in his eyes. "He's a fucking psychopath."

The door flung open and Cillian stood there, eyes blazing, not cold, not emotionless. They locked on Seamus. "Let go of my wife or I'll remove your fingers one at a time and make you eat them."

The fear on Seamus's face slipped away like it'd never been there. He didn't blink, didn't flinch as he slowly released me, and in that moment, I wasn't sure which of them truly was the psychopath.

Sally rushed into the room. "Is everything all right?"

"My father's worked himself into a state, best you give him something to help him sleep." Cillian stared him down, and the look in his eyes lifted goose bumps all over me.

Seamus went red, his gaze slicing between Cillian and Sally. "Don't you fucking dare sedate me, and I'm not your father. I'm not your fucking father," he yelled, actually working himself up now, doing exactly what Cillian wanted. "I never wanted you. I told your mother to get rid of you and your brother, but she thought having babies would keep me tied to her."

"Calm down," Sally said, taking a small vial and filling a syringe.

Seamus started flailing, not letting her near him. Cillian strode over and held him down, a look on his face I couldn't read. Was he enjoying this? Holding all the power now over the evil bastard who raised him, abused him? I couldn't tell.

Sally emptied the syringe into the IV in Seamus's hand and a moment later, his struggles eased and he slumped back. Cillian thanked her, then grabbed my hand and dragged me from the room.

"What were you doing down here?" he said as he pulled me along the hall and back into the kitchen of the main house.

"I was bored and lonely... I was just exploring the house. I didn't know you had Seamus here." He towed me into the living room. "I kind of thought...I thought..."

"That I'd killed him?"

"Yes." There was no point pretending otherwise.

"As you just saw, he's very much alive. I don't want you going back to that part of the house, understand?"

I nodded and he started walking again, taking me with him, leading me up the stairs and into the bedroom. There were bags and boxes, my stuff piled just inside the door.

"You can set up the room down the hall as your office. Con's put your desk and chair in there already. If there's anything else you need, let me know and I'll make sure he gets it."

I stared at the pile. It wasn't just a few things. "That's everything? All my stuff."

"That apartment isn't your home anymore, Sophia, this is." He pulled off his jacket and hung it up. "I'm ordering dinner. Anything in particular you want?"

I shook my head.

He nodded, his gaze moving over me. "I got you a dress."

That stopped me in my tracks. "Why?"

"Your father's telling anyone who'll listen that you're my prisoner, that I'm abusing you. I wouldn't usually give a fuck what people thought of me, but Alto's big on family. If he thinks I'm hurting you, it could jeopardize our deal."

"You made a deal with Alto Leone?"

"Aye, but it's tentative."

"So my family's safe?"

"It's complicated. Things are still volatile. There are other families, allies, business partners, enemies watching us right now. The change of hands, with me taking over, has some people uneasy. We need to show everyone the alliance between our families is strong, that we're a united front, and an attack on one is an attack on both. Alto's invited us to one of his clubs tonight. He wants to see us together for himself."

"Will Paolo be there?"

"After what he did? No fucking way. Alto knows better. It'll be low-key. We'll go, you'll show them you're happy, we'll leave."

I stared back at him. He couldn't be serious. "But I'm not happy."

"Then you'll pretend," he said without missing a beat and walked out.

Chapter Thirteen

Cillian

I stared out at the ocean and sipped my drink.

We'd eaten not long ago. I'd ordered from the Thai place in the city because I knew Sophia liked their khao soi. She used to get it a lot when she was living on her own. I'd seen the receipts in her apartment on the table by her door.

When Sophia was enjoying food, she made these appreciative noises, similar to the ones she made when I ate her out. My dick got hard every night just watching her.

Tonight, though, the churning in my stomach overpowered anything else. I didn't know what was wrong with me, but it was like something had reached up behind my ribs and squeezed. I pressed my hand to my chest. My heart was beating faster, the same way it did after a good workout.

We'll go, you'll show them that you're happy, we'll leave.

But I'm not happy.

Her words, that look on her face when she said it, were on repeat in my head. How the fuck would I know what happy looked like? I'd assumed she was because she was still here, right? She hadn't tried to run again.

Because you threatened her family.

I rubbed my temples, confused. I'd mastered my self-control, if I hadn't, I would've fucked Sophia already. But this spinning feeling in the pit of my gut, like I wasn't on solid ground, was unsettling, and I didn't know how to make it stop. Sophia was safe, protected. She had all her things. An office to do her work. A big house, a comfortable bed. I made her come hard every night. I assumed those things would make her happy. But when I'd said it out loud and she'd contradicted me, I'd been —surprised.

When I used to go to her apartment and watch her sleep, I'd hoped we'd end up here. That I'd somehow make her mine. I'd bought this house with her in mind, wanting to give her the kind of home she was used to growing up. I'd had the walls painted the same color as she'd painted her place, same sheets, same towels. I'd done what I thought she'd want. But I was doing something wrong, obviously.

Why do you care?

Did I? Did it matter to me if she was content? Well, considering I was standing here still laboring over four fucking words that she'd said three hours ago, it looked like I did. It was a realization I hadn't been prepared for. What did that mean? What the fuck was I supposed to do now? A woman's emotions, fucking anyone's emotions were beyond my understanding. I didn't know how to fix this.

A noise came from behind me, and I turned as Sophia walked down the stairs. She was in the dress I'd bought her. I hadn't selected it, Dec had organized it. He knew the right people, and I didn't have a fucking clue where to start. He'd sent me pictures of two different dresses, and I'd chosen this one.

It was peach, the color almost the same as her skin, making her look naked at first glance. The hem stopped mid-thigh, and there was a slight glitter to the dress when she moved. The fabric skimmed over her curves, hugging her perfect tits, and was held in place by straps so thin it looked as if they would snap if she moved the wrong way. Her shoes matched the dress, the heel spiked, and I wanted to wrap her legs around my waist and fuck her in it.

"Do you like it?" I said before I knew the words were coming out of my mouth.

She ran her hands over her hips, her mouth twisting to the side. "It's a bit more revealing than I'm used to." Her long, blond hair was down in soft waves, and her pale blue eyes locked on me. "I feel kind of naked."

My stomach clenched, and my palms grew fucking sweaty. My mouth actually watered. I wanted her to like it. Usually, I'd have to search my mind for the right thing to say, what was appropriate, something I'd seen in a movie. I didn't need to this time. "You look beautiful." My voice was deep and gritty as fuck.

The heavy lashes that shadowed her cheeks flew up, and she eyed me almost suspiciously. I wasn't surprised. I'd never said those words to anyone in my life.

"You don't think it's...too revealing?" she asked, her cheeks growing pink.

I shook my head, on the verge of telling her I'd changed my mind and dragging her upstairs. I couldn't seem to get enough of touching her.

I'd been waking her every night with my hands, my mouth. Making my wife come was an addiction. I didn't need to be still and silent and gentle anymore, not like I had when I'd held her in her apartment. Instead of making sure she stayed asleep, I teased and toyed with her, growling dirty shit in her ear, touching her, playing with her until she woke from her deep sleep, wet and writhing and desperate for more.

Someone tapped on the door. It opened and Conor walked in. "You ready?" His gaze slid to Sophia and his chin jerked up, just a little, but I didn't miss it, before his gaze sliced down her body from head to toe.

I wanted to growl like a fucking wild animal. Instead, I forced it down, and when Con looked over at me again and realized I'd seen him ogling my wife, he grinned.

Sophia walked out the door.

"If you were anyone else," I said to him.

"You'd slit my throat?" he said, not in the least bit worried.

He and Dec were the only two people in this world I completely trusted. Sophia was fucking gorgeous, and Conor had eyes. Still. "No, but I will fuck you up."

He chuckled. "Fair enough. Best you sharpen your knife, big man, you're about to take a tasty little snack into a room full of hungry lions."

Sophia

I sipped my drink and glanced around the room again. I felt like a minnow in a shark tank.

I didn't know anyone here, but several people had been over to congratulate Cillian and me, shaking his hand and kissing my cheek like we were old friends instead of enemies.

Alto Leone stood in front of us now, and he smiled kindly down at me. "It's nice to finally meet you, Sophia. I must say, you are breathtakingly lovely. I see why Paolo was so enamored of you."

Cillian stiffened beside me.

Alto chuckled. "I've spoken with him. He's no threat to either of you," he said to Cillian.

"Walter Mazzo stopped by my house a week ago. I still have his car—and the zip ties and duct tape he had in the trunk," Cillian said to him. "If he wants it back, tell him I'll be waiting."

Alto stiffened. "That's the first I'm hearing of this."

"He got away, and he hasn't been back." Cillian held the other man's gaze. "Please pass on that if he comes anywhere near my wife again, he'll be coming back to you in pieces."

Banked rage blazed in Alto's gaze. "Our families have a truce, he broke it. I'll take care of it."

Cillian nodded. "Or better yet, you send him to me when you find him."

He gave a stiff nod. "I can arrange that."

My stomach twisted. Cillian was going to kill Walter.

"Right, enough of these unpleasantries," Alto said, and the warm smile was back on his face. "Tell me, Sophia, how are you enjoying married life? Does your new husband treat you well?"

I forced myself not to think about the murder that had just been so easily discussed and arranged in front of me and plastered a smile on my face. I had to keep Tommy safe, and that meant lying through my teeth. I could feel Cillian's stare burning into me. "Yes, very well."

"Glad to hear it. I know these alliances can be difficult at the beginning. My own wife, Luciana, took some time to adjust when we first married." He pointed to a scar on the side of his throat. "She wasn't happy about her father marrying her off. One night I woke with her knife at my throat." He chuckled, eyes dancing like he was remembering something heartwarming. "She didn't cut the artery, thankfully. Now look at us, married thirty-seven years, with five children."

"She tried to kill you?" I choked.

He shrugged. "She was afraid. I eased her worries, we made babies, life was beautiful." His gaze slid to a dark-haired girl across the room, then back to Cillian. "Best you tell Declan to sleep with one eye open when he marries my Gaia. She's a lot like her mother."

Declan and Gaia Leone were engaged? And by the sounds of it, she had no say in who she married either.

Cillian grunted. "My brother is the charming one. I think he'll be okay."

Alto laughed again and shook his head. "If you say so, but don't say I didn't warn you." He smiled broadly. "It was lovely to meet you, Sophia. Please, stay, enjoy the wine and the music." Then he strode off toward a woman I assumed was his wife.

Cillian looked down at me, and instead of ice, there was something else in his eyes. "Don't get any ideas, pet."

Was he teasing? I couldn't actually tell. My heart raced. "You'd already be dead if that was my grand plan," I said and smirked.

His nostrils flared and his chest expanded sharply, but the look on his face didn't change. He curled his fingers around the side of my throat, his thumb pressing lightly against my skin. "How would you do it? Wrestle me into submission in the middle of the night?"

"Maybe," I said, sounding breathless.

"I'm down for naked wrestling anytime you want," he said, his gaze sliding over me, as if he were seeing me naked now.

Heat burned my cheeks. He'd stripped me out of my pj's last night, and I'd let him. I'd let him lick me, and fuck me with his fingers. I'd begged him to do it, and like every night, he hadn't asked or pushed for more. The hand around the side of my throat slid higher to the side of my face before he brushed his thumb over my no doubt glowing cheeks.

His lips twitched.

Not a smile, but close. This Cillian was different. I didn't know who I was looking at right then, who this was teasing me. Seamus said Cillian had watched movies, read books to learn how to interact with others—well, he'd actually said to learn to be fucking human. Was that where Dean had come from? Was that what was happening now? Cillian definitely couldn't let his guard down in this room full of sharks, though, so who was he giving me now? I didn't think this was some iteration of Dean.

I was pretty sure I'd almost made the O'Rourke monster smile.

I'd somehow broken through his mask, just a little. All I needed was for him to drop his guard, to give me some freedom, and when my opening came, I'd plan my and Tommy's escape.

"I may be smaller than you, but I'm no lightweight," I said, and I was surprised to realize I was actually enjoying myself. It excited me to ruffle that hard exterior. "I saw this woman in a movie once, and she choked a guy to death with her thighs."

His green eyes sparkled. "So in your scenario, my head's between your legs?"

I bit my lips. I hadn't actually thought about what I was saying. "Uh...well, yes."

"If you'd like to practice your technique later, I'm available."

My breathing was growing ragged. I may not want to be married to a murderer, but that didn't stop my traitorous body from getting hot around him. "I mean, if you're up for getting your ass kicked."

His eyes lit up, dancing.

What the hell was happening here?

"Cillian," a rough voice said.

He immediately straightened, and the glint in his eyes vanished. His body stilled and his hands dropped, now loose at his sides, like an old movie gunfighter getting ready to quick draw.

A large sweaty man with a big gut closed the space between us. His fleshy mouth looked greasy, like he'd just been chowing down on spareribs and hadn't bothered to clean up. His eyes were black and utterly devoid of anything. When they came to rest on me, I actually shivered. Those were the eyes of someone who could do all kinds of awful, disgusting things and not only never lose sleep over it but enjoy every moment of making someone scream for mercy.

"This must be your wife." He held out a beefy hand.

I had no choice but to take it. His hand was hard, but his skin was soft and sweaty.

"Pretty little thing, isn't she?" he said to Cillian. "Fat ass, big tits. Bet she's a good ride."

I yanked my hand free and automatically stepped closer to Cillian. What I wanted to do was tell him to fuck off, but I knew men like him. Saying shit like that earned you a split lip. My father had never hit me, but I'd seen others do it without batting an eye. It'd be better for me and for Cillian if I kept my mouth shut, but it was hard. Cillian's arm came around me, as if he sensed my unease, and pulled me tight against him. His body was hard, unyielding.

"You speak about my wife like that again, Vince, and I'll cut your tongue out." The ice in Cillian's terrifyingly calm voice left no doubt it was not a threat, but a promise.

The older man's gaze slid back to Cillian and he flushed red. "Careful, boy."

"Not your boy, old man. Best you remember who the fuck you're speaking to," Cillian said, his hard gaze locked on the other man.

Vince took a step back. "I meant no offense." His glanced at me again. "Your wife's very beautiful. I was paying her a compliment—"

"Don't look at her," Cillian said. "Don't talk to her, don't think about her. I don't give a fuck that you're Alto's family. I will slit your throat without a single thought, understand?"

I pushed deeper into Cillian, wanting to be anywhere but

there. I knew with every part of me that he'd never let this man hurt me, but I felt the controlled violence coming off him. He was showing none of it outwardly, but his body was rock solid against mine, like he'd fly apart at any moment. He was braced, ready to do exactly what he just said. No, he wanted to do it. I didn't doubt that he'd kill Vince right here and now in front of all these people.

That would be a big mistake, here in Alto's club, with all these witnesses. There would be no avoiding a war then. I pressed my hand to Cillian's chest. "Cillian?"

He dragged in a breath, like he'd been holding it.

Vince inclined his head, then took another step back, careful not to look at me as he turned and quickly strode away.

Cillian took my hand, still on his chest, and wrapped it in his, heading for the door. Declan spotted us, and he and Con, who were on the other side of the room, followed.

"What's going on?" Declan asked as we stepped outside.

"Vince was running his mouth," Cillian said. "I'm taking Sophia home. It's probably best you and Con stay."

Declan nodded.

Conor strode out with us, searching the streets as we walked to a waiting car. Cillian opened the car door and ushered me in, then followed.

Another of Cillian's men, Danny, was in the driver seat, and he pulled out onto the street.

Cillian sat there like stone, those scarred and tattooed hands fisted so tight on his knees that his knuckles were white.

I looked over at him but remained silent. I wasn't afraid, even with the wild energy radiating from him now. I don't know what had changed, and I'm sure it was dangerous to let my guard down around him, to trust him, but since forcing me to marry him, he'd done nothing to hurt me.

I thought of the things Seamus had said, the horrific way

he'd treated Cillian when he was just a child. No wonder he was the way he was. I really wanted to keep hating him, after all the things he'd done, but he'd gone out of his way to make me comfortable. He'd gotten my things, made room for me in his house. He'd been patient with me when I knew a lot of other men in his position wouldn't have been. There was more to him than he let most people see, and I realized I wanted to understand this man. He'd been shaped by a monster, but the real Cillian was under there, and tonight he'd given me a glimpse of him, I was sure of it, and I wanted him to show me more. I wanted to know who he truly was.

Yes, I should hate him, but maybe if I could get to know him, get through to him, he'd let me go, he'd release me from this insane arranged marriage.

I studied him as, jaw still tight, he uncurled his fingers and started twisting the wide wedding band I'd put on his finger. He seemed to do that often. I covered his hand with mine. "Are you okay?"

He didn't move for several seconds, then he turned to me, staring down at me for what felt like forever, a look on his face I'd never seen on him before and had no hope of reading. I wanted to squirm under that look.

He moved suddenly, hitting a button on the door, and a blackout screen slid up between us and Danny.

"Cillian?"

"No one's ever asked me that before," he said in an odd voice.

I blinked up at him, confused. "No one's ever asked you if you're okay?"

He shook his head, then he grabbed my legs, sliding me around on the leather seats. I shrieked, but he was already down on the floor, kneeling there. He shoved up my dress and gripped my underwear in his fists, the sound of them tearing came next, a moment before he threw my legs over his shoulders, grabbed my butt, and covered my pussy with his mouth.

I cried out, arching against the seat. He gripped my ass tighter in his strong hands and feasted on me like a man starved. His eyelids fluttered as he slid his tongue over me, teasing my clit, sucking on it gently, making me tremble. I thrust my fingers in his hair, my mind in a whirl, trying to catch up as my hips lifted on their own, seeking more. We may not know how to communicate, like at all, but what we did at night, in the dark of his room, came easy.

Now when I went to bed, I'd lie awake, waiting for him. I anticipated the way his arms would come around me and pull me up against him, the way he'd manhandle me where he wanted me, the dirty praise he'd rasp into my ear while he made me feel so incredibly good.

He lifted his head, spread me wider, and then spit on my pussy before plunging his fingers deep inside me, giving it to me in a way he knew I loved, the way that had me losing all control. His eyes locked on mine as he plundered me, fast and hard. The coil in my lower belly swirled in a way I knew well.

"Cillian, no, slow down...I'm going to..." My stomach trembled and my thighs shook. The muscles inside me contracted hard. I groaned.

His gaze sharpened and he didn't let up, knowing exactly what he was doing to me. "Let go, pet. Give me what I want."

The orgasm slammed through me and I cried out, whimpering and jerking, gushing all over his hand. I rocked against his fingers, my body completely under his control.

"That's it," he said low. "That's what I want."

He didn't let up until the last tremor moved through me and I'd slumped back, breathing hard, limbs like jelly. I watched as he used my torn underwear to wipe down my thighs before sliding them in his pocket, then he tugged my dress down and lifted me onto his lap, doing what he did when we were in bed, in the dark. He held me close.

I was too spent to move, to do anything but lie against his strong chest. "You pleased me so much tonight, Soph," he said finally, gently.

Warmth filled my belly and darkened my cheeks, not from embarrassment but from pleasure. I didn't know what it was, but when he said things like that, I melted. God, I was starting to think that I might do anything to please him, to hear him call me pet—to hear him tell me I was his good girl in that sexy, rough voice.

The car slowed, then stopped.

Danny's voice echoed around us. "Garage door's jammed."

Cillian cursed, put me down beside him, and shoved the door open. He scanned the area, then held out his hand for me. I took it and slid out.

We started toward the house—

Something hit the wall with a thud, then dinged off the steel railing beside me. Cillian grabbed me, throwing me to the ground, his body crashing down on top of me. Thunder exploded around me a moment later.

Someone was shooting at us, and Cillian was returning fire.

Chapter Fourteen

Cillian

Someone dressed in dark clothes spun and ran. I fired, aiming for the back of their head, but they were too far away. Danny took off after them, and I scooped a frozen Sophia into my arms and sprinted for the house. I wasn't sure that was the only gunman, and I wasn't going to stay out here like a fucking sitting duck.

I punched the security code into the door and rushed in. Sally was standing in the middle of the living room, eyes wide, in obvious shock.

"Everything's under control, Sally. Go back to Seamus."

She nodded, spun around, and took off back down through the kitchen. I carried on through the living room and up the stairs to the bedroom, carrying Sophia to my bed.

She was shaking hard against me. She'd trembled at the restaurant tonight as well when Vince got close to her at the party. Something inside me had snapped, knowing she was afraid, that she was seeking comfort from me, a man who had never given comfort to anyone in his entire life. Now someone had fucking shot at us, had barely missed her out there, and she was clinging to *me* with every bit of strength she had—and I didn't know what the fuck to do.

"It's okay, pet," I said. "You're safe in here. This house is a fortress. No one is getting in here, Soph." Was that the right thing to say? Fuck if I knew. I heard the door slam downstairs. "I need to go talk to Danny," I said to her even though she hadn't said one word in return. I took her chin and tilted her head back so I could make sure she was with me. "Soph?"

She nodded woodenly but didn't let me go.

I carefully pried her fingers loose, and there was a kick in the center of my chest as I climbed off the bed. I didn't want to leave her like this. "I'll be right back."

She nodded again, and I strode out and back down to the living room. Danny stood there, teeth gritted. He'd taken a shot to the shoulder and was bleeding all over the floor.

"He got away. Had someone covering him. They winged me when I went after them."

"Paolo?" I said.

Danny nodded. "That'd be my guess."

"We need to find him." I jerked my chin toward the kitchen and the door to Seamus's wing of the house. "But first, go see Sally, she'll patch you up. I need to talk to Alto."

Danny strode off, and I headed back upstairs to my office, hitting Alto's number as I went.

"Cillian," he said, his voice smooth.

"I'm calling you first as a courtesy, nothing more. Sophia and I were shot at tonight, at my home. When I find Paolo, and I will, he's a dead man."

Silence. "And you know it was him for sure? You saw his face?"

"I didn't need to. It was him, and he wasn't alone. Anything you want to tell me, Alto?"

"I'm a man of honor, Irish, and I don't like that put into question. We need to meet."

The truce and upcoming alliance between our families was under threat, and I fought to gather my control. For the first time, I struggled to put the good of the family first and not say something that could jeopardize everything I'd done to get to this point. But I was struggling to think about anything but Sophia trembling in my arms. "Where?"

I called Danny and got him to double security on the house, then strode down the hall to check on Sophia.

She was curled in a tight ball, somehow, she'd fallen asleep, and as I looked down at her, I realized I didn't want to leave, even knowing she was safe in my home, but I had to go. This needed to be dealt with, now.

Her hair had fallen over her face, and I brushed it back. Jesus, she was so incredibly still. I held the backs of my fingers to her slightly parted lips to feel the warmth of her breath. How many times had I stood in her room at night, staring down at her while she'd slept, fighting the urge to touch her, confused over my obsession with her? Trying to figure out why I was in her apartment again, why I couldn't stay away?

Now I could touch her whenever I wanted to. She was in *my bed*. She was mine. And I was still confused. I didn't know why this tiny woman was able to reach deep inside me and drag that gasping, drowning part of me from the darkest, murkiest depths. A part of me I didn't think I possessed anymore, but she had, without even knowing it, and the more time I spent with her, the more I couldn't bear to be parted from her.

I ran the backs of my fingers over her soft, warm cheek. No, nothing and no one was going to be taking her from me. No matter the cost.

I tucked pillows around her to minimize any damage if she had an attack while I was gone. It was all I could do for now.

Then I forced myself to walk away.

———

I met Declan and Conor back at the club. The party was over and most of the guests had already cleared out.

"Take a seat," Alto said when I walked in, all good humor from earlier gone.

I didn't want to sit. I wanted to blow a hole in Paolo's head, then watch him bleed out all over the floor. "This needs to be dealt with," I said to the older man, not letting him see my fury. I was known as a cold monster who would slit your throat without batting an eyelash, and when Sophia wasn't involved, that description was more than accurate, but I didn't feel cold right then. Anger burned the back of my neck, in my gut, brighter, hotter with every passing moment that I didn't get to hurt the fuckers who'd fired shots at us and almost hit Sophia.

"I can't allow the O'Rourke monster to kill my nephew, you must understand this. I can't align with the family who killed my sister's only son."

"And I can't align with a family who shot at my wife. Your nephew doesn't care about an alliance, Alto, he wants war."

Alto's jaw tightened, then he snapped his fingers. Two of his men appeared, dragging Walter and another guy with them. They were bruised and bloody. "Paolo is just misguided."

"Misguided? He opened fire on my *wife*," I said, barely keeping my anger in check, something that had never been an issue before.

"I can't give you Paolo, but after your call, I sent my men to find those responsible. These are your gunmen, and they swear they were acting alone."

"And you believe them?"

"I do."

He was lying, trying to prevent a war between us, to save his piece-of-shit nephew's ass, and a whole lot of money that our alliance would bring him, and us. "I'm not stupid, Alto. Paolo wants Sophia, and he won't stop until he gets what he wants." I wasn't sure what that was. I assumed he wanted her for himself. I thought I was his target, but then his mindset could have shifted more toward *if I can't have her, then no one can.*

Alto's gaze locked on mine. "Paolo is on a plane as we speak. I've sent him home to his mother in Sicily."

I refused to show weakness, but it was hard to stay in my seat and not blow the old fucker's head to pieces. "You insult me and my family. I'm owed retribution for what happened tonight."

Alto didn't move, didn't look away from me, but several of his men had closed in. Declan and Conor moved to stand beside me, my own men now on full alert.

"Paolo will be watched," Alto said and sat back. "I hope we can put this unpleasantness behind us now."

I wanted my pound of Paolo's flesh, but that wasn't going to happen. At least not right now. What I so desperately wanted to do was tell him the alliance was off, the wedding between Declan and Gaia was off, then shoot every last motherfucker in this room, but I wasn't just the O'Rourke monster anymore, I was the head of the Irish mafia in this city. Brennan was nothing, and everyone knew it. My moves needed to be strategic. This anger was new for me, and I had to get a handle on it. I couldn't let it rule me. A war right now would be bad for all of us—including Sophia.

So instead of pulling out my gun, I waved my men forward. My only option was to take Alto's conciliation prize.

They strode forward and grabbed Walter and his sniveling friend and dragged them from the club. Then I walked out, Dec and Conor right behind me. "Take them to the warehouse," I said and got into my car.

———

Three hours later, I was walking back into the house.

Danny stood from his chair in the living room. His arm was wrapped and in a sling. He looked pale. "Go home. I've got things covered here."

He nodded. "Everything sorted?" He eyed the blood spatter on my white shirt.

I quickly filled him in, all the while wanting to check on Sophia. There'd been this knot in my gut since I walked out of here, this sense of urgency to come home. I couldn't see her like this, though. I needed to shower first. I hadn't gone easy on Walter or his friend, another of Paolo's followers, to get the information I needed, and things had gotten messy.

Walter had confirmed Paolo's obsession with my wife, that he wanted Alto's seat, then he'd begged for his life before I'd finally shot him.

Danny left, and I took the stairs two at a time. The bedroom was dark when I walked in, Sophia nothing but a small lump in the bed. The bedside lamp switched on before I could get to the bathroom, and she sat up. The pillows I'd put around her were scattered, and I quickly scanned her body for injuries.

"You left," she said, accusation in her voice.

"I had to sort some things out. Danny was here."

Her gaze slid over me, taking me in from head to toe. "You look different. What happened?"

"Nothing you need to concern yourself with. Just know you're safe now."

She shoved back the covers and got out of bed, her gaze searching mine with more courage than she'd ever had as she closed the space between us. She took in the rest of me, the blood splattered on my neck, on my shirt, and she paled. "What did you do?"

"Sophia—"

"You killed someone."

She immediately tried to retreat, to get away from me, and something inside me snapped. I grabbed her wrist and wrenched her back against me, so close our bodies were pressed tight. "Yes, I killed someone. Walter and another of Paolo's men. They were the ones who shot at us tonight. I took them to my warehouse, I beat them, tortured them, then I shot them both between the eyes, and I felt nothing, pet, not one fucking thing. They deserved to die. They almost killed you. If those first two shots had been just an inch closer, you'd be dead now." Her eyes were huge. She was afraid, afraid of me, and I wanted to fucking snarl when she tried to pull away from me again.

Her eyes glistened with tears. "Seamus really did turn you into a monster, didn't he?"

I was breathing hard as her words arrowed through me, slicing and cutting as they went. "Aye," I said, not bothering to pretend to be something else, not this time. All she had to do was look into my eyes to see the truth. "Are you afraid?"

"Yes," she said, her chest rising and falling fast with her panted breaths.

She blinked and a tear streaked down her cheek, her body trembling, but she hadn't tried to pull away again, no, she leaned into me, getting closer. My cock was hard as steel, my need for her yawning wider. I swiped her tear away and sucked it from my thumb, needing to taste every part of her. "Are you wet, pet?"

Her lips trembled and another tear slid down her face. "Yes."

I leaned in and lapped it up this time.

"Is your heart made of stone, Cillian? Do you truly feel nothing at all?"

I lifted her off her feet, and her legs came around me. "I honestly don't know anymore. Since I met you, something changed." I thrust my fingers into her hair and covered her mouth with mine. I kissed her so hard and deep, she whimpered against my mouth, her nails digging into my shoulders. But there was no stopping this time. I wasn't letting her pull away from me, not in any way. I was going to own every part of her, and I was going to do it as myself. No act, no pretending to be what I thought she wanted, I was going to give her the truth.

I strode to the bed and laid her on it, then yanked my bloody shirt off and tossed it aside. I jerked her pj top over her head and tore her sleep shorts and underwear down her legs. She lay there pale and small in the moonlight, and looking so fucking vulnerable I had to suck in a desperate breath to hold myself back. Seeing her like that caused an ache behind my ribs.

"Did you get this hard when you watched me sleep all those times in my apartment?" she whispered.

My chest expanded sharply. "Aye."

"And when you got into bed with me...did you want to fuck me?" Her cheeks darkened as she said it.

"Aye," I rasped. She was breathing harder, her perfect round tits shaking with each panted breath. "Some nights, when you thrashed and cried out in your sleep, and I climbed onto your bed and I held you, I almost lost control."

Her eyes widened. "But you didn't." She fisted the covers, but she didn't try to get away.

"Every time I was close to you, I barely resisted taking what was mine."

I stripped off the rest of my clothes and climbed on top of her. She trembled beneath me as I slid the backs of my fingers over her hot cheeks. "You know what I'm about to do, don't you, Sophia?"

She nodded, and I took her mouth again, fucking owning it, giving in to the driving need I had for her that was so fucking raw and wild there was no stopping it. A need that had become a monster of its own over the last twelve months. I wanted to take. I wanted to hear her scream my name. I wanted to fuck her so hard the fucking house shook.

Sucking her throat, I dragged my teeth along the tendon there, nipping at her delicate skin and making her cry out. Gripping one of her tits, I sucked the little puckered nipple into my mouth and kneaded the other, teasing and pinching and sucking until her nipple was darker, swollen, then went to the other and did the same thing. Sophia arched and writhed beneath me, fisting my hair, trying to yank me away, then holding me to her instead.

Her thighs rubbed together, and I forced them apart, shoving mine between them as I worked my way down her soft belly. "You fucking soaked for me, pet?"

"Y-yes," she sobbed.

"My good girl's wet for her twisted fucking husband. You want me to fuck you hard, don't you, Soph?"

She nodded as another sob burst from her. "Y-yes."

Sophia didn't know what to do with that. She wanted me, her pussy ached for me. But she was scared of what I was, what I'd done, and turned on by it all at the same time. That was okay. In time, she'd realize I'd never hurt her. I could work with lust. Lust made people do all sorts of fucked-up shit, like letting the O'Rourke monster, still stained with another man's blood, fuck you. Right now, it was all I needed. If she wanted me, she might not try to leave me.

I shoved her thighs wider and covered her dripping cunt with my mouth. My fingers dug into her thighs as I swiped my tongue through her pussy and fucking feasted. She planted her feet in the mattress and lifted her ass, rubbing her hot little pussy against my face, begging for more. She wanted my fingers, was desperate for me to fill her up while I sucked her clit. Not this time. Her pussy would be aching to be filled before I slid my cock inside her.

I dragged my tongue up to her clit, flicking it, then sucked it between my lips. She groaned and tensed, and I lifted my head.

She cried out. "No, don't stop."

I climbed over her, fisting my cock, and pressed the head to her opening, pushing the tip in a little, then pulled it back out. It took all my self-control, but I held there, just the tip, again and again. Sophia's cheeks were flushed, her lips apart, her thighs trembling under my hands. "Every time I watched you sleep, I wanted to climb under the covers with you, pet, all warm and soft. I wanted to taste your skin, breathe in the scent of vanilla and cinnamon, that scent that made my dick hard as fucking iron, then peel off your panties while you still slept and slide deep inside your sweet little cunt."

"Oh god, yes. Please," she moaned. She shook harder, her belly trembling, her hips rising on their own trying to take me deeper while I tormented us both.

I'd been dreaming of this for so long, of sinking inside her. "Legs around me," I said, my voice so deep and rough it didn't sound like my own. "You still on the pill?" I'd seen them in her apartment.

"Y-yes, but what about—"

"Never fucked anyone raw, pet. Only my wife gets that."

A breath shuddered from her, then she was locking her thighs around me, her body flushed and hungry.

No more teasing, I couldn't wait another moment, even if I'd wanted to. I filled her in one hard stroke.

———

Sophia

I cried out, arching against Cillian as he filled me, stretching me to my limits. "Oh god." I clawed at his shoulders as he pinned me to the bed with his hips and slid out, then slammed back in. Pleasure and pain, all mixed together, had me trembling hard beneath him. On the next thrust, I cried out, the orgasm he'd brought me to the brink of crashing through me. My pussy contracted around him hard, repeatedly.

"That's it, come all over my cock, pet," Cillian growled as he pounded harder into me. He shoved my legs back and swatted my ass, and another wave of pleasure washed through me. I gripped his shoulders, and he grabbed my hands and dragged them over my head, pinning them to the mattress.

I looked down and watched as his thick cock, wet with my juices, slid out of me and slammed back in. He didn't hold back. Cillian took me hard, filling me over and over, his vibrant green eyes locked on me.

"Look what you do to me," he growled. "You make me lose control. You make me lose my fucking mind."

He wasn't the only one. I could feel another orgasm building, and I strained against him, gasping for breath, for grounding, while his cock plunged into me without mercy.

I called his name, not sure if I wanted him to stop or fuck me harder—then the next orgasm crashed over me so hard, white light covered my vision.

"Fuck," Cillian snarled as his thick cock pulsed heavily inside me, his come filling me as he ground his hips into mine. "Take it, take all of it," he said as he shuddered.

Then his big body collapsed on top of me, his cock still inside me. He nipped my ear and kissed my jaw, my chin, then gently kissed my lips. "You are mine, Sophia. You know that now, don't you?" he said roughly against my ear.

My heart fluttered wildly. "Y-yes."

This was wrong. The whole situation was messed up and insane, but whether we were together or not, here with him or somewhere else, there was no denying that Cillian O'Rourke had taken ownership of me.

And god help me, no matter what the future held, I got the feeling he always would.

Chapter Fifteen

Sophia

"Look at me!" Tommy called and jumped into the pool.

I laughed and held up both hands. "Ten!" He beamed at me and swam to the side of the pool to do it again. When we'd arrived, Cillian and Dad had immediately closed themselves in my father's office. He said he needed to speak with Dad after what happened last night. Paolo was back in Italy, but Cillian was still concerned.

I shifted on my seat, still sore from what we'd done, then shivered. Despite the ache, I'd been wet all morning just thinking about it. I felt guilty, and obscene, like there was something very wrong with me. Cillian had still had blood on his clothes, and I'd wanted him so badly, I'd leaned into him, telling him without the shame of asking for what I wanted out loud. Cillian hadn't missed it.

Dean had been nowhere in sight when he'd taken me to bed. He'd been all Cillian, and he'd wanted me to know it.

Celeste walked out and plonked into the chair beside me. "So how's married life treating you?" She sipped her wine, watching me over the rim, eyes glittering.

Usually, I'd make polite conversation, do what I could to try to keep the peace, even when she said shitty things. She'd treated me like crap since the first day she walked into this house, had made my life hell. Celeste had relished the thought of me being married to a man who kills without conscience. She'd also known the kind of man Adam was, that he hurt women, and she hadn't cared about that either. No, she'd taken pleasure in scaring me right before my wedding.

Cillian hadn't hurt me, though, and somehow I knew he never would, but for some reason Celeste hated me and was hoping for the opposite. I turned in my seat and did something I rarely did. I held her sharp gaze, not looking away, not backing down or excusing myself to avoid her venom. "What do you want me to say?" I said to her. "What would make your black heart happy, Celeste? I'd hate to disappoint you."

She gripped her glass tighter and forced a shrill, ugly laugh. "Not going that well, then, Soph?"

I smiled. "On the contrary. My husband likes me very much." I sat forward in my seat and lowered my voice so only she would hear me. "He came home last night covered in someone else's blood, then fucked me while it was still on his skin."

She jerked back, and I grabbed her hand, stopping her retreat. "He's obsessed with me, you know. I think he'd do anything I asked." I held her gaze another beat, then released her and sat back, not taking my eyes off hers.

Celeste's glass trembled in her hand, and she quickly set it down on the table, but her eyes were still filled with hatred. "Are you threatening me?"

Tommy called for me to watch him, and I stood, but turned back to her before I walked away. "Yes, that's exactly what I'm doing."

Then I walked over to Tommy and sat on the edge of the pool and hung out with my baby brother.

Fifteen minutes later, the door to my father's office opened and Cillian strode out. My father followed, red-faced and obviously furious, but he was keeping his mouth shut. He'd barely greeted me when we arrived and didn't really look at me now. Cillian came straight to me and took my hand before he took hold of my chin and kissed me. My heart instantly burst into flutters, and I felt Celeste's eyes burning into me, watching the whole thing.

Cillian's eyes scorched into me, and when he lifted his head, he didn't tamp it down. This was a show for my father, for some reason, and I wasn't sure how I felt about it. I didn't like being lied to about who he was, or manipulated, but then the truth of who he was, was also terrifying.

He turned to Dad, giving him a hard look. "I'll be in touch."

Dad nodded, and then we left.

"What was that about?" I asked, feeling uneasy.

Cillian opened the car door for me. "Our families are tied together more so now than ever before. We're also in business together, and I needed to remind your father of that."

I frowned, but he ushered me into the car and strode around to the driver's side. He wasn't going to elaborate, I knew that, but he still shared more with me than my father ever had. "Where's Danny this morning?"

He glanced my way as he started the car. "He got shot last night. I gave him the day off."

"What?" I spun to face him. "Is he okay?"

"He's fine." We drove out onto the street.

"But he was *shot*, Cillian. Oh my god. He could have been seriously injured." I stared at Cillian's unconcerned profile. "He could have died."

Cillian was quiet several seconds. "You seem awfully concerned about Danny's well-being."

"Of course I am. He's one of your men. I like him, and he's nice to me."

"You didn't seem to want nice last night, pet. Nice was the last thing you wanted." His gaze slid to me.

I stilled at what I saw. What the hell was going on here?

"Tell me, Sophia, exactly how much do you like Danny?"

I stared at him in shock, until it hit me what was going on here, and with how crazy everything had already been the last couple weeks, and what happened last night, a manic feeling filled me out of nowhere. I couldn't hold it in. I laughed. No, I snorted loudly, *then* I laughed.

He glanced at me, an expression I couldn't read on his face. "What the fuck's so funny?"

"You are," I said and shook my head. "Are you actually jealous right now? Really?"

The muscle in his jaw jumped. "No."

"You are. You're jealous." I laughed again at how insane my life was.

His hands clenched tighter around the steering wheel. "Do you want to fuck him, Sophia? Is that it?"

I couldn't believe what I was hearing, I'm not sure why I was so surprised by his reaction, but I was. "No, I don't want to sleep with Danny. For fuck's sake, Cillian, I know we don't know each other that well yet, but up until last night, I was a virgin. And in case you're not paying attention, which you obviously are not, the only man I seem to want to sleep with is my stalker, a man who can kill without remorse, then come to me covered in another man's blood, and still I'll let him fuck me into the middle of next week."

His chest expanded with his sharp indrawn breath. "You were a virgin?"

That's the part he focused on? "Yes, but I'm certainly not anymore." I turned to him. "There are things you should worry about, *husband*, like if your wife is slowly losing her damned mind with all the ways her world has been thrown on its head, or if I'll do to you what Alto's wife did to him, or whether I'll run away in the middle of the night—because sometimes I have to seriously talk myself out of both of those things—but me wanting to fuck some other guy isn't one of them, okay?"

His gaze dipped to my mouth and back up, before it returned to the road. "Okay."

———

I'd spent all morning setting up my office and had finally got to work after lunch. I'd added a few more little touches: a rug I found in one of the other bedrooms, a lamp I'd swiped from the living room, and a vase full of flowers sitting on my desk that I'd picked outside, a bandaged Danny in tow.

I was working on some ad images for a client when Cillian walked in.

"You've been up here all day," he said.

I checked the time on my phone. I hadn't realized how late it was. "I have a lot to catch up on." I watched as he took in the room. "What do you think?"

He turned back to me. "Do you like it?"

"I do. I even like the color it's painted. Good thing, too, since I'm assuming you just had the whole place done not long ago? The only additions I can think of is maybe a few pictures for the walls and a whiteboard over there, oh...and I wouldn't mind a couch under the window. But other than that, I like it very much."

"I had the whole place painted so it'd be fresh when I brought you home."

I realized it was the same dove gray as my apartment. Yes, he was a stalker, my stalker, but he'd painted his entire house for me, to make me...feel at home? And happy? "You wouldn't have had much time."

"No."

"But you did it anyway. Why?"

He pulled out his wallet. "I thought you'd like it better." He slid out a card and held it toward me. "You want to buy something, I'll get it. Or just order it online. Whatever you want."

I stared at the black card he'd put in front of me. "You're giving me your credit card?"

"I'll get you your own, but use that one for now."

Did he think he could buy my acquiescence? That having *things* would make up for tearing me from my life and forcing me into his? Maybe the towels and sheets and wall color would be romantic if he hadn't broken into my apartment multiple times to watch me sleep. "I don't need it. I have my own money."

He shrugged. "Your money's your own. I want you to use this."

I didn't want to take it, and I sure as hell wasn't going to use it, but the look in his eyes said this wasn't up for discussion, so I took it from him. I expected him to leave, he never usually sought me out during the day, but he hovered.

I waited for him to say whatever it was he wanted. Finally, he motioned to my computer. "What are you working on?"

That was the last thing I'd expected him to say. "Some marketing graphics for a local pottery artist. I love her stuff. It's not hard making her images look enticing." He came around my desk and took a look at what I was doing. Why was my heart racing all of a sudden, my palms sweaty? If I was at home with my father, this would be the part where he'd tell me I was wasting my time, that what I was doing was pointless.

Cillian studied my computer screen, taking it all in, then his gaze slid to mine. "You're talented. This is really good."

My hands started to shake, and for some stupid fucking reason my eyes stung. I was not going to cry, no way. My face grew hot, humiliated over my reaction to Cillian saying something positive, because he was the only person besides my tutors and Fiona to ever say something encouraging about my work.

He studied me, and I quickly looked away. "I should probably get this done."

He didn't move for several long seconds. "We're invited to a party tonight," he finally said. "If you want to go, I'll take you."

"If it's a repeat of the one at Alto's club, I'll pass," I said, not looking his way because my belly was all flippy-floppy, and he smelled really good, and my eyes were still stinging because I was an idiot, and if I looked at him right now, I might cry and beg him to ease the ache rapidly building between my thighs.

"Nothing like that. It's at Declan's. It'll just be our men and their women. It'll be safe, relaxed. I think you might like it. It'll be good for you to meet everyone. Maybe you'll make some friends."

I was starting to go stir-crazy in this house. Maybe it wouldn't be so bad? "Okay, sure, that sounds all right."

Still, he didn't leave. Clearly there was something on his mind. Something he was hesitant to say.

I stared over at him, biting my lip as the tension in the quiet room grew.

He moved suddenly, gripping the back of my neck, and I jumped, an involuntary gasp bursting from me. His thumb swiped across my jaw, and his gaze dropped to my lips.

He dipped closer, and I held my breath.

But instead, his mouth went to my ear. "I'm proud of you, pet," he said roughly, setting off shivers all over me.

Then he released me and headed for the door, while I tried to get my breathing back under control.

"We'll leave at nine," he said, then walked out.

Chapter Sixteen

Cillian

Declan had parties all the time. I never went, but I thought Sophia might like it. She'd said she wasn't happy.

I didn't like that she felt that way. It was new, thinking about someone else's feelings so frequently when I had little understanding of my own.

But I was, and I didn't like leaving her every morning, knowing she felt that way. She seemed to like her new office and being able to do her work, but that wasn't enough. Sophia needed more than that. I just had to figure out what that was and how to give it to her. A party might be a step in the right direction.

As we took the elevator up to Declan's apartment, I could feel her eyes on me. The door opened, and I took her hand. She let me, and that pleased me more than was rational.

We reached Dec's apartment and walked in. The place was full, and I scanned the room.

She was safe here. Every man in this room knew she was mine. No one would fuck with her or try to touch her.

My brother spotted us and his brows lifted, then he grinned, striding over. "You came. Is the fucking sky about to fall?" He turned to Sophia. "Hey there, Soph, welcome to my humble abode." He flashed a grin, the one that did an excellent job of convincing everyone my brother wasn't a lethal killer, that he was the less monstrous one out of both of us, when that was a complete lie. Declan had been molded by Seamus just like I had, and he was as fucked up as me, only instead of shutting his shit down like I had, he covered all the dark, barbed parts of himself under his natural charisma. Kind of like Charles Manson. He was good with people, it came easily, and they were drawn to him, but he had no conscience to speak of.

"Hey, Declan," Sophia said and smiled up at him. "I like your place."

"Thanks." He tilted his head to the drinks table. "Follow me, and I'll get you a drink and introduce you to the family."

The family. The men we knew would follow me when I took out Adam, the ones who no longer trusted Seamus to lead and were open to the change had been brought into the fold, the rest, well, they were no longer of consequence. Thankfully, there hadn't been many. Sophia looked up at me, and I nodded for her to go with Dec and watched as she walked off. She was wearing a dress that made her look even more fucking innocent than she was. The light, floaty-looking fabric was the same color as her eyes and had thin straps. The top part hugged her tits, while the bottom flared out a little, draping over her round hips and ass and ending just above mid-thigh. If we were going anywhere else, I would have made her change.

Conor strode over, and I tore my eyes from my wife.

"Never seen you at one of these parties before," he said, grinning. "At least not voluntarily."

I grunted.

"You know, I thought you'd run right over that girl," he said. "But I think I got it the wrong way around. I think Sophia might actually be good for you."

"You think too much," I muttered.

He barked out a laugh, then the smile slipped off his face. "Fuck me."

I followed his gaze. Gaia Leone had just walked in. She strode straight to Declan, who was still talking to Sophia and another woman, one of a few he casually hooked up with. I quickly weaved my way over to them. Gaia had proven herself to be unpredictable.

"That's my fucking fiancé you're groping," she was saying to the girl.

"Gaia," Declan bit out.

"You're engaged?" the other woman asked, yanking her hand out of Declan's back pocket.

He winced. "It's...complicated."

The girl turned red. "I'm out of here," she said and took off.

Gaia looked up at Declan, her eyes were wide and filling with tears. "You're cheating on me? But I...I thought..." A tear streaked down her face.

Declan jerked back, horrified. "Whoa. Hang on a minute. I thought you understood, I assumed you knew—"

Gaia threw her head back and laughed loud, wiping away her crocodile tears as she did. "That was way too easy. Jesus, you should see your face." She imitated it. "I—I assumed you knew," she said in a deep voice.

Declan scowled. "What the fuck, Gaia?"

She ignored him and turned to Sophia, who was watching the whole thing with wide eyes. "I hear your father's a selfish pig like mine. The kind who'll use his daughter as a bargaining chip and sell her off like a cheap whore to make more money?"

Sophia opened her mouth, her eyes darting to me, then closed it. "Um..."

"Seems we're going to be sisters-in-law." She turned back to Declan and grinned. "Isn't that right, honey bunny? I'll be your wife, right there at your side twenty-four seven. Everywhere you go, I'll be *right there*. When you eat, shit, sleep, I'll be there. When you close your eyes at night." She winked. "I'll be there." Her gaze hardened. "Are you a deep sleeper, sweet cheeks?"

Conor had joined us, and he bit back a laugh beside me.

Declan flashed a grin, taking a piece of her dark wavy hair between his fingers. "Baby, who said there'll be any time for sleep?"

Her eyes narrowed, and she jerked her head back, pulling her hair free. "You're a pig."

"Yet you'll be the one doing all the squealing," Dec said, his eyes glittering, a smirk on his face.

Gaia hissed. "I'm going to enjoy making you bleed," she said, then grabbed Sophia's hand. "Let's dance." She led a stunned Sophia out into the middle of Dec's large living room where a couple others were dancing.

"You're fucked," Conor said. "And not in the good way."

Declan sipped his Jameson, his gaze on Gaia as she danced. "Oh, I don't know. I'm kind of looking forward to it."

Several hours later, I was sitting with a few of my men having a drink, and Sophia was tipsy and laughing with Gaia like they were old friends. Sophia twirled, and her pretty dress lifted a little, flashing her yellow panties, and my heart skipped a fucking beat in my chest. Gaia grabbed Neville's hand and spun around, then pressed herself against him. Neville's gaze sliced to Dec for help, but my brother was already stalking over. One minute Gaia was dancing and flirting, the next, Declan had picked her up, tossed her over his shoulder, and walked out of the room.

Fucking around and flirting with our men in front of Dec wasn't a good idea, and my brother was about to explain why to her now.

Sophia looked around, confused, then shrugged and kept

dancing with some of the other women. Conor's girlfriend, Becca, was there, and she'd been with them most of the night.

Jesus, I couldn't take my eyes off my little wife. I twisted my wedding band around my finger. Seeing her like this, I liked it. I liked seeing her laughing, enjoying herself. Happy.

She turned and her gaze fell on me. I didn't look away, eating up the sight of her all flushed and bright-eyed. Instead of blushing deeper, like she often did when I looked at her, she said something to Becca and headed straight for me, then she kept coming, moving in so close I sat back to make room for her. Sophia climbed right onto my lap in front of everyone in the room, wrapping her arms around my neck.

A grin curled her lips. "Have you been watching me?"

"Aye." A thrill raced through me. I liked her claiming me as hers in front of everyone.

"Why?" she said, running her fingers over my jaw, over the beard I still wore even though my assignment pretending to be Dean was over.

I'm not sure why I'd kept it, other than I'd wanted Sophia to see me differently than I'd always seen myself. "Because you are so beautiful, pet, that I can't keep my eyes off you."

She blinked down at me, an exhale shaking out of her. "You really think I'm beautiful?"

"Aye, pet." How could she not know? "You're my sleeping beauty."

Her gaze searched my face for several seconds, then her arms tightened around my neck, and she kissed me, the first kiss Sophia had ever initiated between us. Her tongue was hot and slick, and I could taste the wine she'd been drinking. She squirmed on my lap, pressing against me. I slid my hand up her thigh, her hot, smooth skin against my rough palm, and squeezed. I didn't take over the kiss, though, I let her lead. I wanted her to show me how much she wanted me, to feel it, without eclipsing her need with my own. To know that she wanted me as much as I did her. Her hand slid over my jaw, her fingers into my hair, holding me to her as her mouth moved over mine, as her tongue dueled with mine.

I slid my hand higher, and she whimpered against my mouth, pressing closer, wriggling on my lap, and my hard cock strained against my pants.

"You need something, pet?" I said against her lips.

"Yes."

"Say it."

"I want you, Cillian. Please, I want you."

I lifted her off my lap, stood, took her hand, and led her from the room and down the hall. I opened the door to Dec's office and led her inside, then turned the lock. "How badly do you want it, Soph?"

"So bad."

I kissed her again, so fucking hungry for her. She whimpered against my lips, her hands dropping to my belt, clumsily trying to undo it. I backed her up to the desk, grabbed her hands, and spun her around, bending her over it, then shoved up her dress.

I kicked her legs out so they were spread. "You want it hard, pet?"

"Y-yes. Fuck me like you wanted to the first time you watched me sleep," she said, arching her back.

Jesus fucking Christ. She'd asked for the monster more than once now. I could see how wet she was without even touching her, her panties clung to her pussy. Gripping them, I dragged them off and shoved them in my pocket, then I freed my cock and pressed the head to her slick pussy. "Are you lying in your bed, Sophia?"

She nodded, whimpering. "Y-yes."

"Sweet little Sophia, all alone, pussy so empty and aching,

dreaming about the monster who sneaks into your room to take what he wants?"

"Yes, oh god. Take it," she moaned, pushing her round ass back, trying to impale herself on my cock.

Grabbing her hips, I slammed inside her. She cried out, her core instantly clutching me tight. I slapped her round ass. She wanted to feel helpless, the monster's object. She got off on what I'd done, watching her, wanting her. "Quiet, no one will help you now, dirty girl." I leaned in and pressed my mouth to her ear. "No one else gets to hear the sounds you make when you get fucked. Only me."

I gripped her hips and gave her what she wanted. I fucked her hard, pounding her tight pussy like it was my full-time job.

When she groaned, I swatted her ass again. "Quiet."

She gasped. "I...I can't."

I came down on top of her, covering her mouth with my hand, muffling her cries. "Has my sleeping beauty woken up with the monster's fat cock inside her?"

Her pussy spasmed around me, and she nodded, eyes glazed with pleasure.

"Fucking dripping." I gripped her ass with my other hand and spread her wider. "Gonna fuck this ass one day soon. Gonna claim every fucking part of you, pet."

Her pussy spasmed around me, and she shrieked against my fingers, already coming for me. I pressed her harder into the desk, covered her mouth more firmly, and slammed into her, hard and fast, fucking her like the fucked-up monster I was, just the way she wanted. "That's my good fucking girl," I said against her ear, her muffled cries growing louder. "Take it. Fucking take it, Sophia."

As soon as I said it, the convulsions of her pussy, that had started to slow, contracted hard, and her eyes rolled back. Her tight cunt gripped my cock repeatedly as she came a second time.

"Fucking made for me, Sophia. Every fucking inch of you is mine." I slammed into her again and again, but I was struggling to hold back, especially after the way she'd just come for me. I loosened my grip on her mouth, and she instantly grabbed my hand and sucked one of my fingers into her hot mouth, shattering my control completely. I bit her shoulder and pulsed hard inside her, filling her up, over and over, shuddering and groaning.

Panting, I kissed her shoulder where I'd fucking *bitten her* and rocked into her until I was completely spent. I didn't move right away. I stayed buried inside her, kissing along her shoulder and up the side of her throat. "Can't get enough of you. So beautiful, my perfect wee wife. My precious beauty." The words tumbled from me as if they were coming from someone else, and there was no stopping them. I breathed in her vanilla-and-cinnamon scent, like a fucking addict getting a fix.

Her lashes fluttered. "You don't...you don't need to pretend to be someone else anymore, Cillian. I don't need you to be someone else."

I stilled, realizing in that moment that I wasn't pretending. The thought hadn't even occurred to me. With her, it was coming naturally, a part of me I thought was long dead, a part of me Seamus hadn't managed to beat out of me. "I know," I rasped.

A part that only Sophia could access.

I lifted her carefully, sliding out of her, and turned her to face me. I held her gorgeous blue eyes. "I know."

Chapter Seventeen

Sophia

Fiona sipped her drink. "I can't believe you live here. I mean, this is...wow. This view is insane."

Things had calmed down the last week. No one had tried to shoot at us, and Paolo was still in Italy and staying there, according to his uncle, which meant Cillian had eased up a little.

Well, he'd let Fiona come and visit. I still wasn't allowed to go off on my own, and Conor or Danny were always here, but still. "It's definitely taken some getting used to."

Fi tilted her head toward Conor, who walked by below us, in the middle of a perimeter check. "Who's the hottie?"

"Conor, the head of Cillian's security."

"First, Cillian needs security? And second, and more importantly, does Conor have a girlfriend?" Fiona walked to the railing and waved down at him when he glanced up.

He gave her a flirty grin and swaggered off.

"He does actually." But now I was questioning the seriousness of it.

"Not sure he knows that," Fiona said with a smirk. "Right, let's move cocktail hour poolside."

Several hours later, we were sitting on the steps in the shallow end, past tipsy and laughing our asses off. Cillian had walked out thirty minutes ago with his laptop and a glass of Jameson, and he'd been working there since.

Fiona cackled and held out another shot. I took it and we both downed them.

"This was an excellent idea of mine," she said.

"It really was." My life had been insane the last few weeks. I'd been betrayed by my own father, married off to the O'Rourke monster, my stalker, who had murdered his brother on our wedding day but had also protected me. He'd thrown himself over me when I was shot at. I glanced his way. He was also obsessed with me and turned me on like no one ever had. That was a lot to process, and my feelings had become confusing as hell. My emotions were all over the place, heightened, and seriously conflicted. I wasn't sure I knew myself anymore, my moral compass was seriously on the fritz, and that was really scary.

I tried to stand and plonked back down. "I think we might have had one shot too many." Yep, I was totally slurring my words.

"You know," Fiona slurred back, "I think you're right—"

She kind of slumped to the side, tipping over, her head going under the water. "Shit!" I grabbed for her, unbalancing myself.

Conor was suddenly there, scooping a sputtering, laughing Fiona from the pool, at the same time strong hands lifted me out as well. Cillian hoisted me up. "You're done, pet."

"No...hang on. I'm..." My head spun. "I don't feel so great," I said, staring up at him.

"Not surprised," he said in that sexy-as-hell accent.

I twisted in his arms. "Fiona, I feel like shit."

"I think I'm gonna hurl," she called back as Conor carried her in the opposite direction. "It's okay, though. Mr. Hottie security guy's gonna take care of me."

Conor shook his head, a grin teasing his lips, and carried on walking.

"Where's Conor taking my friend?"

"Home," Cillian said.

I grinned up at him. "Well, aren't you a sweetie."

His brow lifted.

I wrapped my arms around his neck, feeling...kind of soft toward him. "You may have killed a bunch of people, but you're really a big old softy under there, aren't you?" I patted his chest.

He carried me into the house and up the stairs. "My sweet, sexy, murdery husband," I said and booped him on the nose. "You're cute, you know that? Not like fluffy-bunny cute but like the emo boy in school who's all silent and broody and you want to ask him what he's thinking all the time."

"Yeah?" he said.

I nodded. "And you just want him to grab your hand, take you to the music room when no one else is there, and play you some of his emo music while you make out like crazy."

He muttered something.

I ran my fingers over his lips. "So are you going to make out with me like crazy or what? 'Cause I really want to."

He looked down at me, then his lips twitched, then holy hell, they curled up and there was a flash of straight white teeth. Not the Dean smile that I now knew was fake but the Cillian smile.

"You're smiling," I said breathlessly.

"I don't smile." He was still smiling.

"Swoon."

He chuckled.

"*Oh my god.* You laughed. I think I'm going to spontaneously orgasm."

"Fucking hell," he said, shaking his head. "You wanna use the bathroom or straight to bed?"

I grinned. "Bed, naked, with you." I touched his lips. "You know, you've made me have all kinds of dirty thoughts."

"Have I now?"

I nodded. "Do you want to know my deepest, darkest fantasy?"

"Tell me," he said and nipped my fingers, making me giggle.

"Well, ever since you told me that you watched me sleep, and we did that um, you know, role-play thing at Dec's party... I've been thinking I'd like it, for real."

"What do you want for real, pet?"

"Sometimes, I have these...um dreams, dirty ones, and I wake up and I'm wet and know I've been moving, acting out the things happening in my sleep because my muscles ache...you know like I've been—"

"Fucking in your dreams?"

I nodded. "Did I ever do that when you watched me?"

His nostrils flared. "Yeah."

"Did you like it?"

"The way you moved, the sounds you made, pet, made me fucking jealous. Made me want to kill whoever you were dreaming about."

I liked that more than I should. "The guys, they used to be faceless, no one I knew, but now, the only man I dream about...is you."

"You dream about me, beauty?"

"Yes...and the next time you see me have one of, um...*those dreams*...I want...I want you to strip me, carefully, so I stay asleep, then ease between my thighs, slide deep inside me... and...fuck me awake."

His chest expanded sharply, and he gripped my hair. "That right?"

"Yes." He laid me down and the room did a full three-sixty. "Uh-oh."

"Uh-oh, what?"

"I'm gonna throw up." I scrambled out of bed, tripping and stumbling into the bathroom, then dropped to my knees in front of the toilet and emptied my stomach. "I'm never drinking again," I wailed and heaved.

A few moments later Cillian was there. "Okay, baby," he said behind me. I felt his hands in my hair, tying it back. "Here." He tilted my head back gently and wiped my face with a cool cloth. "Better?"

"I think so," I muttered, then another wave of nausea hit. "Nope." I spun around and heaved again, nothing much coming up, since Fi and I kind of forgot to have dinner, but that didn't stop my body from trying anyway.

"You're all right, pet," Cillian murmured, rubbing my back.

"Keep rubbing my back," I said between retches. "It makes me feel better."

"Not gonna stop, Soph."

His voice was soothing as well. Man, I was tired. "Never drinking again," I said again and groaned.

"I know, beauty."

"You think there's something wrong with me—"

"No."

"All the things you did..." I swallowed convulsively. "You kill people...and I...I want you anyway. I want you and I shouldn't, should I?"

He rubbed my back again. "Nothing wrong with you, Soph, not one fucking thing."

My eyes grew impossibly heavy. I rested my head on my arms and closed my eyes.

I woke hours later in bed. As soon as I stirred, Cillian was handing me painkillers and a glass of water. I drank them down and fell back to sleep.

———

It was after ten in the morning when I finally woke and stayed awake, and Cillian was gone. I remembered him murmuring to me softly, holding my hair out of the way while I was sick, wiping my face with a cool cloth, rubbing my back. He'd held me all night, I knew that as well because every time I woke, he was there, making sure I was okay, making me drink water, taking care of me in a way no one had for a very long time.

The last person to look after me when I was sick was my mom. Fiona was awesome, too. She'd drop off soup if I had a cold, make sure I was stocked up with flu medicine. But what Cillian had done was something else, he'd wiped my face after I puked and promised everything would be okay, and I'd believed him.

The rest came flooding back, and my face heated.

My sweet, sexy, murdery husband.

You're cute, you know that?

I'd booped him on the nose, then I'd asked him to make out with me.

He'd smiled.

God, he'd laughed.

Warmth flooded me, but not from embarrassment this time —well, not only embarrassment.

That is, until I remembered the rest. I'd asked him to "fuck me awake." I mean, I'd thought about it, more than once, but I'd actually said it out loud.

Cringing, I shoved down the memory, tossed back the covers, and eased out of bed, more than a little relieved that, besides a dull headache, I didn't feel too bad. No doubt thanks to the painkillers Cillian had given me earlier.

I checked his office, then headed downstairs, but he wasn't there either. Conor was sitting out on the deck. He turned to me and grinned. "Headache?"

"Not as bad as it should be."

He huffed a laugh.

"Fiona get home okay last night?"

Conor gave me a bewildered look. "Your girl's a handful. It took some fucking doing, but yes, I got her home. Stayed with her until I was sure she wouldn't choke on her own vomit, then left."

"Thanks, I owe you one."

"Nah, haven't been that entertained in a while," he said with a smirk.

"Oh god, what did she do? I love Fi, I really do, but when she's drunk she can get a little—"

"Handsy?"

I winced.

"Yeah, think I have a bruise in the shape of her hand on my ass," he said.

I wanted to call her, but there was no point. She'd be asleep. Her hangovers were bad, and she usually had to sleep them off most of the next day. "Sorry about that," I said, though he didn't look that upset about it.

"No problem."

"Did Cillian say when he'd be back?" Despite all the humiliating things I'd said, I had this really strong urge to see him.

Conor shook his head. "He and Dec have some business. It'll probably take a few hours."

Disappointment surged through me. "Okay, well, I'll just grab a shower, then."

"You want some pancakes? I can whip you up a stack while

you wash the puke out of your hair," he said, that grin back on his face.

"What?" I touched my hair, the strands around my face were stiff. "Oh god. That's disgusting." I spun and rushed for the stairs.

"I'll start on the pancakes... And, Soph?"

I stopped and turned back.

"Next time, you might wanna put pants on. Not sure Cillian would be too happy with me seeing you like that."

I froze and looked down at myself and my face exploded with heat. I was in only my shirt and panties. "I thought... Oh god, I'm not wearing my bathing suit anymore."

"Nope," he said, winked, and strode into the kitchen.

Face on fire, I sprinted upstairs and into the bathroom. My bathing suit was in the laundry basket, also covered in puke. I was wearing one of my T-shirts, a short one. Cillian must have grabbed it and a pair of panties, they were dark pink with a lace cutout. My face heated again. No, he wouldn't like anyone else seeing me like this. Not at all.

I felt much better after I'd washed my hair, cleansed my face, and scrubbed my teeth. I pulled on shorts, my most comfy bra, and a soft T-shirt. Then tied my hair back in a ponytail and headed back downstairs, feeling decidedly more human this time. I was really hoping Cillian would be back, but he still wasn't, and my disappointment was kind of extreme. I pulled my phone from my pocket and tapped out a quick text.

Thanks for looking after me last night.

For some reason my heart sped up when I hit send.

Conor fed me a stack of pancakes, and I ate them all. Then I headed out to the pool to nap and wait for Cillian to get home. I woke several hours later in the midst of a nightmare, when I flipped the lounger and hit the ground. Thankfully, no one saw and I only grazed my elbow.

Cillian still wasn't home and he hadn't replied to my text. I paced around inside the house again, then tried to get some work done, but I felt fidgety and restless. It was nuts, but I thought I might actually miss him. How was that possible?

Ever since the party at Declan's, things had changed between us. He was trying, I could see it. He talked more, always asking if I had what I needed, making sure I was okay. He brought me things—a beautiful lamp for my office that I knew had to have cost a lot, he made me pick a couch the day after I mentioned I wanted one. The list went on.

Then last night—

I stood and paced to the window, looking for his car in the driveway, but he still wasn't home. A knot of worry curled in my gut. What if this business he and Declan had was dangerous? What if he was hurt somewhere?

I paced the house some more, asked Conor for the tenth time if he'd heard from Cillian, then forced myself to watch some TV. I couldn't focus. Somehow, I drifted off again on the couch. But then, no matter what was happening, I could always sleep whether I wanted to or not, my disorder meant it was out of my control. Conor eventually gave me a nudge and said I should go up to bed.

I changed into one of Cillian's shirts, closed the door, and got into bed.

My mind raced, but I still fell back to sleep, and when I jolted awake again, it was mid-flail with a cry about to burst from my throat. The room was dark and my hand shot out to the other side of the bed.

Empty.

I hadn't woken like that in a long time, because of Cillian, because he'd held me down until it passed. Pushing back the covers, I jumped out, my legs shaky since I'd barely given myself time to wake up. I was about to run downstairs and ask Conor if he'd heard from Cillian, when I saw light coming from under his office door. Relief rocketed through me, and I ran down the hall and pushed the door open.

Cillian looked up, surprised, as I rushed into his office. His suit jacket was off, his shirt undone at the throat, no tie, sleeves rolled up. Not a single mark on him.

"You're okay," I said, my legs shaky now for a different reason. I rounded his desk.

"Soph—"

Without thinking, I climbed onto his lap and wrapped my arms around his neck, holding him tight. "I thought...when I didn't hear from you. I thought..."

"Hey," he said rubbing my back. "I'm fine."

"Why didn't you answer my text? You always answer my texts." I was trembling, and I hated that my reaction was so strong. Someone on the outside looking in might say my growing attachment to Cillian was unhealthy, that I was projecting, that I had fucked-up daddy issues and a need to be wanted that was extreme, therefore being here with him was dangerous to my mental health, and they'd probably be right—but I couldn't lock this feeling away.

"Somehow my phone ended up on silent. I didn't see your messages until I was almost home," he said and tilted my head back. "I didn't want to wake you." He studied my face. "You're upset."

Now I felt like an idiot, but I refused to blush or pretend I wasn't feeling what I was feeling. "I was worried."

"I should have thought, but I've never had anyone—"

"If you tell me no one's ever worried about you getting home late, I'll cry. Do you want me to cry?" I wasn't lying. Somehow, I'd grown to care for this man. I hadn't planned it, I'd tried to fight it, I'd tried to keep hating him, but I just didn't anymore.

He searched my face, and shook his head, then his gaze went to the Band-Aid on my elbow. "You're hurt."

"I fell asleep by the pool, I'm fine."

He made a rough sound and grabbed my arm to get a better look.

I stopped him. "It's just a graze. You're trying to look after me again, like you did last night."

He didn't reply, just tucked my hair behind my ear and looked into my eyes in a way that made my breath hitch. How we came together was insane, but the head of the O'Rourke family, Seamus's brutal monster, had been nothing but kind to me. Maybe not everyone's definition of the word, but slowly getting to know Cillian, I knew I was right. For me, he'd ignored the cold cruelty instilled in him by his father, the neglect, and he'd treated me with care and kindness.

No one had ever asked him if he was okay, and no one had ever taken care of him like he had me last night.

He gave to the people he surrounded himself with and all he asked for in return was their loyalty.

He'd asked nothing of me.

Not one thing.

I slid off his knee and his fingers dug into my hips for a moment as if he were going to stop me from climbing off him but then changed his mind. He expected me to walk away. Instead, I lowered to my knees in front of him. Confusion filled his eyes, until I reached for his belt. He said nothing, just watched me as I slid the leather through the buckle, undoing it. I looked up at him as I undid the button of his pants. "You've had a long day," I said and slowly slid down the zipper.

"I have a lot of long days," he rumbled.

"I've noticed."

He didn't reply, just waited for what I'd do next.

He wasn't getting it, not yet. He thought I was playing some game, that maybe I wanted him to make me feel good, that I was teasing. He'd made me feel good so many times since I came here. But I'd never just given to him, just to give him pleasure.

"You take care of everyone, Cillian, and never ask for anything in return," I said.

His muscled body tensed, stilling completely.

I gripped the top of his pants and yanked. He lifted his hips automatically, and I slid them down a little so I had better access. "You know, I've never done this before, not with anyone."

His eyes flared. "Sophia," he said roughly, but that was it, that was all. Just my name, but there was confusion, conflict in his eyes.

"I know this isn't a first for you, not the physical act, but you need to know that I don't want or expect anything in return. You don't need to make me come afterward, I don't want gifts or credit cards or furniture." He sat like stone in front of me, gaze going blank, a look of retreat filling his eyes. I got the feeling he was so out of his element right now, he didn't know what to do or say. So I ignored that look in his eyes and curled my fingers around his brutally hard length through the fabric of his briefs. He hissed. "You took care of me last night, Cillian. You've been taking care of me since you hijacked my wedding, and now I want to take care of you."

He gripped the arms of his chair tight, a wariness in his eyes that I felt in the center of my chest, like he was waiting for the other shoe to drop. "And how are you going to do that, pet?"

"Watch and see," I whispered.

Chapter Eighteen

Cillian

Sophia ran her hand up and down the length of my cock, her wide blue eyes on me. I couldn't fucking look away. Somehow, this perfect, innocent, sweet girl saw me in a way no one else ever had. I wasn't sure that version of me existed anywhere else but in her eyes, but seeing it reflected back at me was...mesmerizing. I wanted to be that man, the one she saw—and I'd do anything to make sure she believed it was true.

You kill people...and I...I want you anyway. I want you and I shouldn't, should I?

Then again, maybe she saw more of the real me than I realized, and that fear, that doubt worried me.

Her hand shook a little as she tugged down the front of my boxer briefs. I helped her, tucking the fabric under my balls, out of the way, curious to see what she'd do next. As she stared at my cock, she licked her lips, and I swear I felt it against the already swollen head.

"You're beautiful, Cillian, everywhere," she said in that soft fucking voice that sent tingles across my shoulders and down my arms, while she blushed for me prettily. "I never thought a...a cock could be beautiful, but yours is. It's so long and thick, and the skin's so...god, so soft."

I'd had women try to flatter me when they got on their knees, telling me how big I was. I'd ignored it. It was just noise before I got off. But this was different, it felt different. Soph wasn't trying to flatter me, not really, she was trying to be sincere, honest, and my cock jerked in her hand. I was desperate for what came next.

My sleeping beauty, my wife, had me in her fucking thrall. Someone could fire a bazooka through the living room windows and I'd stay right the hell here in this spot. She literally held me in the palm of her hand, in every sense of the word. I sucked in a sharp breath when she leaned over my lap and finally sucked the head of my cock into her hot mouth.

I gripped the arms of the chair tighter, barely stopping myself from lifting my hips and thrusting deeper. "Fuck." Her mouth on me was torture. She wasn't trying to tease or toy with me, but every tentative and unschooled lick and suck had me fighting back my need to fist her hair and fuck her face.

She looked up from what she was doing and swirled her tongue around the ridge, lapping at the slit like a lollipop, and my eyes almost rolled back into my head. Her gaze went to my mouth, watching as my breath hissed through my gritted teeth.

"Does that feel good?" she asked.

And fuck me, the tentative, unsure way she asked was like a fucking haymaker to the sternum. "Aye, pet, it feels really fucking good." Her eyes brightened, and shit, there went another one of those right hooks to the chest.

"Tell me what you like, Cillian?" she asked, her voice a little stronger, her confidence growing.

I caught up her hair and twisted it in my fist, holding it back so I had a better view of my bride sucking cock for the first time. "Wrap your hands around the base and stroke while you suck," I instructed, and there was no disguising the edge to my voice.

She nodded, smiling up at me, then did what I said. She gripped my length in both hands and started stroking in time with her mouth, sucking down as much of my cock as she could. She bumped the back of her throat and gagged, and my balls drew up tight.

I cupped her jaw. "That's it. Take it. Take my cock. Show me what a good girl you are." I fisted her hair tighter, and she moaned around me. I was already fighting not to come. Nothing had ever felt as good as my perfect wife sucking my cock for the first time. She sucked harder, and my ass left the seat, thrusting deeper into her mouth before I knew what I was doing. She gagged again, but she didn't stop. No, she did it again, sucking me harder still, hungrily.

I tilted her head back, watching as she gave me everything she could, until tears ran down her face, her mouth stretched wide around me, her chin glistening with spit. She was sitting on her heels and squirming as she worked me faster.

"You love it, don't you, Sophia? You love sucking your husband's cock? Pussy's dripping now, isn't it, pet?" She hummed around me, nodding, her fingers digging into my thighs. "I wish you could see how perfect you look. So messy, so fucking beautiful."

She said this was all about me, taking care of me, and looking at her now, I knew she meant it. She was fucking choking herself on my dick, working it like nothing else mattered. Like making me feel good was her entire world.

No one had ever given this to me, not like this. My balls throbbed and my cock fucking swelled. "Gonna come, pet," I rasped, brushing her cheek with my thumb. I didn't expect her to swallow, not this time, I expected her to pull back and work me with her hands until I was done, but she didn't, no, she gripped me tighter and groaned around me, lapping and sucking the precome that was a constant stream now—then she sucked me so fucking deep, I knew she wasn't going to pull back.

Fisting her hair so tight she couldn't move, even if she wanted to now, I held her in place and thrust into her mouth, coming down her throat. She had me fucking spellbound as she swallowed urgently, not even trying to pull away as I flooded her mouth with come.

When she'd swallowed every last drop, she released me, panting. Her lips were swollen and red, her cheeks and chin glistening. Without a word, I tucked myself back in, then hooked her under the arms, lifting her off the floor, and stood, carrying her to the couch against the wall. She said she didn't expect anything in return, but not making her come, not making her scream my name after that was fucking sacrilege. Making her feel good made me feel good.

I sat on the couch, standing her in front of me, and tore her panties down her legs.

"Cillian, you don't—"

"Quiet," I said, and there was, fuck, real emotion in my voice. I wasn't ready for her to hear how deep it ran. I was still trying to come to terms with this feeling inside me. Somehow, in such a short time, Sophia had brought back to life what I was positive Seamus had destroyed forever. I snatched up her panties and used them to wipe her chin, then kissed her swollen, red lips before I lay back, gripped her hip, and tugged her forward. "Sit on my face."

Her tits shook with her panted breaths, her thighs slick with her juices, so fucking turned on from sucking my cock that I knew she was aching.

"Now," I said.

She moved then, jumping into action, unable to hold out or tell me no, needing what she knew only I could give her. She climbed on, and I dragged her up my body. She looked down at me, trembling with need.

"I want you to fist my hair and work your pussy on my mouth until you come, understand, pet?"

She nodded, licking her puffy lips as she straddled my face and lowered her slick pussy.

I lapped at her and groaned when her taste filled my mouth, but she was still letting me lead, and this time, I wanted her to take from me. So I grabbed her hand and put it on my head, then I gripped her hips and tugged her down harder. She cried out, her fingers instantly fisting my hair as her hips rolled, seeking more contact.

I kept my hold on her hips, not giving her any room, and that was all the encouragement she needed. A minute later, Sophia was grinding against my mouth, fisting my hair tight as fuck, totally lost in her need to come. It was perfect. She was all over my face, so wet, she had to be close to coming.

"Sh-shove your tongue inside me," she said, pussy directly over my mouth.

Fuck me. I was rock hard again and her demand was so hot, my hips rocked up. I shoved my tongue inside her with a groan, and she stayed right there, rocking and grinding against me, crying out as she came against my mouth, shuddering and shaking.

Before she was done, I lifted her again, stood, and strode to the desk, laying her over it. Quickly freeing my cock, I slammed inside her, and she cried out, coming again.

"Hungry fucking pussy," I snarled, thrusting into her. "Can't get enough of your husband's cock, can you, wife?"

She shook her head and moaned. "Harder."

"Even want it when you sleep. You still want me to fuck you awake, pet? Next time you have one of your dirty dreams?" I hadn't been able to stop thinking about it.

*"Oh, fuck...*yes, yes, I want that."

Christ. She'd be the death of me. I fucked her so hard the desk shook, impaling her on my cock over and over again. I gripped her throat and pinned her to the desk. Her head was to the side, her face a mask of utter bliss. I couldn't look away. I could spend every day, all day fucking this woman. I shoved my thumb into her mouth. "Suck. Make it wet." She did, then I slid it between her spread ass cheeks, pressing it to her tight hole. She tensed. "Relax," I growled, and unbelievably she did, trusting me with her body, even with me sounding like a feral animal.

I slipped my thumb inside her ass as I fucked her pussy, and she wailed, tightening her legs around me, trying to lift her ass to take more. I held her down, fucking her deep and hard, keeping my thumb inside her the whole time. "Told you I'm gonna fuck this tight little ass, pet, and you're gonna love it, you're gonna beg me for it."

Then she was coming again, writhing and bucking underneath me as I fucked her, lost in the sight of her. I came down on top of her, groaning against her ear as I filled her again and again, as I came, pulsing deep inside her.

When I finally slid out, she lay there, panting, exhausted, and I carefully lifted her and carried her from my office.

Kissing her forehead, I laid her on our bed, and got in beside her, holding her warm and sated against me. When I first saw her, I knew I would have her, now I knew there was nothing I wouldn't do to keep her—to keep this feeling inside me.

I'd never felt more human—or more out of control in my entire life.

Chapter Nineteen

Sophia

My belly went all weird and my palms itched to touch him when Cillian walked into the bedroom. He was shirtless, his trousers still undone, his hair wet from the shower, slicked back, and droplets of water had landed on his tattooed shoulders and chest. His muscles danced as he shoved his hair back.

I shivered thinking about what happened in his office last night.

I had no idea what the hell I was doing anymore. I was a jumbled mess of raw emotions. How was it that someone who barely had any himself could make me feel this way?

He ran a hand over his freshly trimmed beard, then grabbed a shirt and slid it on, his abdominal muscles flexing as he did. My mouth went dry. He glanced up and caught me watching. His expression didn't change, those intense green eyes never leaving me, and god, my heart galloped faster in my chest.

He was unreadable, dangerous, but he'd never hurt me. I believed that unequivocally. He wanted me, maybe even held affection for me, whatever that meant for him. I knew he cared about his brother, his men, but love? I wasn't sure Cillian was capable of the emotion in any of its forms.

"I thought I might look for a painting for my office today and wondered if you'd tell me who chose your paintings?"

"I did."

I blinked up at him, I definitely hadn't expected that. "You have a great eye."

"I know nothing about art," he said.

"But the paintings in this house, they're all so beautiful."

He stilled, just a split second, but I noticed it. "I had a certain criteria."

"And what was that?"

"Does this make me think of my sleeping beauty," he said.

"What?" My voice came out barely more than a whisper.

"That's why they're all bright and colorful. Why when you look at them from a distance the brushstrokes look deliberate, but when you get closer, you see that they're not at all, they're more wild and haphazard, free."

Sleeping beauty.

I stared at him in shock. Is that truly how he saw me? "You think I'm wild and free?" I whispered.

"I know you are." He tucked his shirt in. "You just don't let many people see it."

But he'd seen it, hadn't he? He made me wild, and despite this life that had been forced on me, he'd made me feel free. I didn't know what to say.

"I have a couple meetings, but I shouldn't be late." He slid on his belt, doing it up, still aiming all that intensity my way—then he strode toward me. Like often happened when he took me off guard like that, I kind of froze. He was just that...overwhelming.

He stopped right in front of me. "When I get home, you can choose what we have for dinner, okay?"

"O-okay..." I cleared my throat. "Okay," I said again sounding less like a demented toad.

He frowned. "Everything all right?"

I nodded. "Yep, you're just...really, really intense and also really, really hot, and sometimes I forget to breathe and get a little dizzy," I said, because what the hell, it wasn't like I was hiding shit from the people around us, and since my new husband seemed to have trouble reading emotions, he was at a disadvantage. It was only fair I filled him in as well.

He blinked, those thick dark lashes coming down over moss-green eyes once, twice, then they were burning down at me—and he smiled. Not just a minor curling of lips, this was deeper, with a flash of white teeth and, god save me, a dimple. Declan had the same one, but on the opposite cheek.

"You have a dimple?" I said.

"Do I?"

"You don't know if you have a dimple?"

He shrugged.

"You haven't smiled in the mirror before?" I said, then scoffed. "Sorry, I forgot who I was talking to there for a moment." I shook my head. "You realize that's a large part of what makes your brother so endearing, that wicked grin of his. If you flashed that dimple around a bit more, maybe you'd be a little more approachable."

"I don't want to be more approachable."

I studied his lips. They were far too pretty for the O'Rourke monster, but add in that smile, those white teeth, and the dimple, and it all made sense. It all worked.

"You think my brother's endearing?" he asked, an odd look on his face.

"Well, yeah, he's kind of sweet. Your face isn't meant to be so stern all the time, refusing to smile the way you do. You've been hiding major components of your face."

He did the blinking thing again. "Apparently not, you just saw all my...components."

He had this befuddled look on his face. Dear god, I loved it. Was it mean that I enjoyed confusing him so much? Probably. But I enjoyed the hell out of it. "When was the last time you smiled?"

"Ten seconds ago."

I shoved his chest with a laugh. "Smart-ass. Before that?"

"Haven't had a lot to smile about, Soph. I don't feel things the way other people do. I never really have." He frowned. "Or at least I didn't think so."

"What changed?" I asked studying his handsome face.

He tucked my hair behind my ear. "I married this nerdy, cute, sexy-as-fuck little virgin, who says a whole lot of weird shit no one else has ever said to me, who talks nonstop through dinner so nearly every night she ends up eating it cold, who looks at me like she wants to lick me from head to toe while I dress after a shower, and fucks like she can't ever get my cock deep enough, then sleeps pressed into me all night as if I'm her favorite childhood stuffed bear... That's what changed. The urge to smile, it's come over me more since you've been here than it has my entire life."

Now it was my turn to blink up at him, stunned into silence.

He gripped my chin in a possessive hold, stopping whatever I was about to blurt, and kissed me. "Be back around eight," he said against my lips, then turned and walked out.

I stared after him, trying to catch my breath.

———

Danny walked in carrying the grocery bags. Conor was with Cillian a lot lately, and Danny seemed to be the poor bastard stuck with me more often than not.

"That's the last of it," he said and dumped the bags on the counter.

"Thanks." I still felt weird telling a guy like Danny what to do, forcing him to drive me about and trail me around the store. Thankfully, he didn't seem threatened or offended by it. My father would have lost his shit if Mom had told him what to do. Celeste never did. I didn't know if that was because she only sought out Dad when she wanted something, usually his credit card, or she'd learned the hard way like the rest of us.

He gave me a chin lift and left.

While I put everything away, all I could think about was what Cillian said to me earlier, that I'd somehow changed him, or brought something to life inside him that had been buried for a long time. The whole situation, this marriage, what he was, was messed up, but I couldn't help the way I felt about him. I was falling for the O'Rourke monster, all of him, and there was nothing I could do to stop it.

The realization hit that I didn't want to stop it.

I don't know what that said about me, but I wanted to keep on casting light on the shadows inside him. I wanted to keep reviving the parts of him that had been gasping for breath for so long.

I wanted to make him smile.

Cooking for others was one of my love languages. Cillian seemed to order in a lot. He'd never asked me to cook, but I wanted to. It was a small thing, but I wanted to do something nice for him, to show him that I appreciated what he'd done for me.

How good he'd been to me.

I searched the cupboards for the biggest pot I could find.

Cillian had spent his childhood in Northern Ireland, in Belfast. I was born and raised here, so I had no idea what he considered a taste of home. My dad liked stew, one his mother had made for him when he was a boy. My mom had made it for us over the years, and I'd helped her. It was delicious, so that was on the menu. I'd had to google what to have with it. Mom had always made mashed potatoes, but I was going with a side of colcannon, mashed potatoes with cabbage mixed through it, and Irish brown bread.

I started with the bread, making the dough and leaving it to rise, then cut up the lamb. The stew would need a few hours to cook slowly. I spent the rest of the afternoon in the kitchen.

The table was set and everything was ready by eight o'clock. But Cillian didn't show.

He hadn't texted to let me know he'd be late, and he hadn't replied to my messages, which after last night and him knowing how worried it made me, made me extremely nervous. Danny said he was just held up and he'd be home when he was done, but that didn't stop me from worrying. I looked at my table, the candles were almost burned all the way down now. So stupid. Cillian wasn't romantic. He struggled with emotion, for fuck's sake. What was I trying to do here? I blew out the candles and carried my glass of wine to the couch.

I watched TV, waiting. When I looked at the time again, it was eleven. I should just go up to bed. Instead, I closed my eyes, just to rest them for a few minutes.

I woke with a start to the sound of low voices. Cillian was talking to Danny, telling him he could head home. Sitting up, I immediately scanned his body for injuries. He spotted me then, sitting in the dark living room.

He looked surprised, then frowned. "I thought you'd already be in bed."

"I was worried. Did none of what I said last night register with you, like at all?"

His frown deepened, his mouth opened, then shut. "You waited up for me?"

I guess I had. "Looks that way."

He slipped his jacket off and strode over to me.

He was so tall and strong and beautiful.

So deadly and cold and ruthless—but not to me, not anymore.

He crouched in front of me. "I heard you last night, I just... didn't think..." He shoved his fingers through his hair. "I'm sorry. It won't happen again. I'm just not used to people worrying—"

I pressed my finger to his gorgeous lips. I couldn't hear how neglected he'd been his whole life, not right then. "You do now," I said, letting him in a fraction more, letting him know a small part of how I felt.

His expression didn't change, but his Adam's apple slid up and down his throat. "I'll be right back. Don't move."

He strode off, but I couldn't stop myself from following. It was pathetic. I was pathetic but I'd missed him. I'd been worried about him. I walked into the bedroom in time to see him putting his gun back in the safe.

"Did you use that tonight?" I asked. Women like me were raised not to ask questions. Depending on the man, questions like that could get you the back of a hand and a split lip, making sure you never got any stupid ideas and did it again. Cillian was cold and scary at times, but he'd never hurt me like that. Not physically at least, and not on purpose.

He slid a wicked-looking knife from his boot next and put it in the drawer in front of him, then turned to face me. "Do you really want to know the answer to that, pet?"

"Yes."

His eyes burned into me. "I did." He watched me, waiting for what I'd say, what I'd do.

What was there to say? He was who he was. He wasn't going to change. This was his life, the way he'd been raised, and it was my life as well. He studied me, and at my silence, a shift came over him. The sharpness of his eyes, the way he held his mouth, even the way he stood all changed, as he put Cillian away and let Dean slide forward. He thought he'd scared me. He thought being himself wasn't enough. God, it hurt to watch.

I walked over to him and pressed my hands to his chest.

"Soph," he said, all Dean.

I hated it.

He cupped my face, and I saw a drop of blood on his sleeve.

He saw it as well and tried to drop his hand, but I held on, turning it over and undoing his cuff link. I did the same with the other, then slid my hand down his chest, undoing the buttons. He was utterly still, watching me with an intensity that made me breathless. I moved behind him and pulled his shirt off, tossing it in the laundry hamper, then moved to stand in front of him again, and tilted my head back, staring right into those unreadable eyes.

Right then, they were full of smoldering intensity.

"I'm not afraid, Cillian," I said. "You don't need Dean. I don't need him."

His chest expanded on his sharp indrawn breath.

"Do you feel anything? After you hurt someone?" I asked, needing to know all of this man, even the dark and ugly parts.

He studied me for several seconds. "No."

That should terrify me, horrify me, but for some reason it didn't. I wasn't afraid. "Seamus said you used to watch movies, read psychology books, that you needed them to understand how to interact with others, is that true?"

He went very still. "Yes," he finally said. "I watched movies and read books to help me understand the people around me, and to understand why I am the way I am."

I nodded. I had no right to be horrified. I'd asked and he'd given me the truth, that was more than I'd ever gotten from my father. I wasn't going to push for more, though, not now. "Are you hungry?"

"I could eat," he said, his voice deepening, rolling with my change of subject as his gaze moved over me, trying to read me, my reaction to the things he'd said.

He meant me, but I ignored that as well, which wasn't easy and took his hand. "Come on. I made you dinner."

He stilled again, and I had to tug on his hand to get him moving. He followed me, an unreadable expression on his face. I sat him at the table and lit the candles again. He didn't look away from me as I heated his dinner, then brought it over and put it on the table in front of him.

He stared down at it.

"Stew, colcannon." I slid the bread board over. "And brown bread. I thought you might like a taste of home. I hope it's okay? I wasn't sure what to cook. I looked it up online," I said and chuckled, suddenly feeling self-conscious.

He looked up at me. "My ma didn't cook, and we lived on chips and curry sauce when we lived with Seamus's sister." He looked back down. "No one but my nan ever cooked for me like this."

His grandmother was the last person to cook for him? "Is she still in Ireland?"

"She died when I was ten," he said and picked up his fork.

I felt my lips tremble. "What did you eat when you were at your father's?"

He forked stew into his mouth and made a low sound. "I was fifteen, they put me and Dec in the basement. I cooked for us." He looked up at me. "This is amazing."

"The basement?"

He looked up again, the horror in my voice making him pause.

"It was fine. It had a kitchenette and a bathroom. I cooked

for me and Dec every night. That's probably why I don't like cooking now."

"What about on your birthday?"

He frowned. "What about it?"

I shook my head, trying to fight back my emotions. Seamus was a fucking monster. "Try the bread," I said to distract him from looking at me. I didn't want him to see how furious I was on his behalf, how close to angry tears I was.

He sat there, shirtless, beautiful, eating like he'd never eaten before. Seeing him like that, it satisfied something inside me. I wanted to take care of him, please him, give him the things he'd missed out on. When he finished, he sat back and stared at me across the table.

"That's just about the best thing I've ever eaten," he said, and those gorgeous, terrifying eyes weren't cold, they were bright, hot.

"Just about?" I said, and it came out breathlessly.

"Nothing beats the taste of my wife," he said.

I had to bite my lips as I walked around the table. "Come on, I'll clean this up in the morning."

"Where are we going?" he asked, and there was actual amusement in his voice.

"We're going to shower, then we're going to bed."

He said nothing else as I took his hand and headed upstairs. He let me lead him to the bathroom and watched as I stripped off and turned on the water. He kicked off his shoes and socks, then his pants. He was hard, so incredibly hard.

There was a slice in his arm that I hadn't seen before.

He followed my gaze. "It's nothing."

I got in the shower and he followed, crowding in behind me. I turned, and he stepped back into the spray when I pushed against his chest. For now, he was letting me lead, but the way his fingers flicked at his sides, the way his chest rose and fell faster, the hunger in his eyes deepening, told me he was close to the edge. Cillian liked control, and he was humoring me now, but not for much longer.

I scrubbed him clean, working my way across his muscled body, soaping him up, and rinsing him off. He watched me avidly, like the predator he was, waiting to see what I'd do next. My pussy was hot and aching. I was so wet, but I didn't drop to my knees like I wanted to, no, I turned off the shower and got out. Cillian released a shaky breath but did the same, still letting me lead, still choosing to follow. The cut on his arm was bleeding again, and I took a Band-Aid from my cosmetics bag, tore off the wrapper, then took his arm, dried it, and covered the cut.

He looked down at it, then up at me, and his lips curled, flashing his teeth. "Race cars?"

"I bought them for Tommy," I said.

He nodded. "You've fed me, cleaned me, tended my wounds." He took my jaw in his hand, his thumb pressing against my lower lip, and my tongue darted out on its own, touching the tip. He made the same rough, appreciative sound he made while he ate his dinner, then pressed his face into the crook of my neck and up to my ear. "You gonna let your husband take care of you now, my wee fairy princess?" Then he gripped my towel and tugged, and it dropped to the floor.

Cool air hit my nipples and they grew even tighter. "What if I haven't finished taking care of you?"

"I'm all yours," he rasped.

I pressed my hand to his chest, and he backed up into the bedroom. I kept advancing until we reached the bed, then gave him another shove. He got the hint and fell back, lying on the bed, watching me with hooded eyes.

"You gonna ride me, pet?"

We hadn't done that yet, and that's exactly what I planned

to do. "Yes." My thighs were slick. I was desperate to feel him inside me, but I took my time admiring him. His body was utter perfection. "You're beautiful," I said, unable to hold it in. "Every inch of you."

The cocky grin slipped from his face.

"You were honest with me yesterday. You don't hide things from me, and I want to give you that as well." I let my gaze move over him.

"Yeah? And what do you see, Sophia, when you look at me?" His words were a low rumble, and his stomach muscles tightened as if he were bracing for a hit.

Despite the things I'd done and said, he was still expecting me to say a monster, killer, to strike out at him in some way, but I saw more than that now, so much more. "Your hands are big and strong. I know what they're capable of, what they've done, but it doesn't matter, I don't care, because I crave the feel of them on me all the time." I crawled into the bed, straddling his thighs. His chest was heaving. "I should be scared of you, but I'm not, not anymore. You stalked me, you broke into my apartment and watched me sleep, you forced me to be your wife." His gaze darkened. "I should be plotting my escape, but instead I lie awake, listening for you to get home, achy and desperate for you to touch me again with those rough hands that can be brutal and violent, but I know they never will be toward me." I took his painfully hard cock in my hands and stroked. "I feel safer here with you than I ever have in my entire life."

"Sophia," he growled.

"I don't want a lie, Cillian. I don't want Dean. I want *you*."

His fingers dug into my flesh, every muscle going hard beneath me.

He was on the verge of snapping, and I wanted it, I wanted to push him over the edge. "I love this cock," I whispered. "It's so long and thick and fills me so good. I'm glad you're the first man I let fuck me—"

"The only man," he all but snarled. "I'm the only man who will ever know what it feels like to be inside your perfect, tight little cunt, Sophia. Say it."

"You're the only man," I said and stroked him again. Maybe this was wrong, I was wrong, for wanting this, for wanting him, but I did. He was all I wanted.

He was breathing so hard now, his chest and stomach, his thighs rock solid. I slid my body higher and rocked my hips, dragging my pussy up his hard length, then back, but not taking him inside, teasing him even more.

"Sophia," he growled again.

"What?" I chewed my lip and ground my wetness against the underside of his cock. "Don't you like it?"

There wasn't just thunder in his eyes now, he was on the verge of devouring me. "Fuck me, pet," he snarled.

"No," I said, playing with the monster.

Why are you testing him?

Because I was falling in love with him, despite all the reasons I shouldn't, and I needed to know that part of him up close and personal. I need him to show the monster to me.

He gripped my hips and tried to lift me so he could thrust inside. I shoved back and shook my head.

"Let me in, Sophia."

"Not yet."

His eyes went bright, gleeful menace transforming his features. Somehow, he'd worked out what I was doing. Now I was the one panting in anticipation, while nerves flew wildly around in my belly.

I slid my pussy along his cock, rolling my hips, then back one more time.

Cillian shot up, hooked me under the arms, and stood. I

shrieked in surprise. In two strides he had my back to the wall, manhandling me like a doll. He hooked his arms behind my knees, so I was almost folded in half, my legs spread wide, then he impaled me on his cock, slamming up inside me.

A scream burst from me.

He nipped my jaw. "You want me to lose control, you got it." He slammed his hips forward. "You wanted an introduction to the monster in this fucked-up fairy tale, sleeping beauty? Well, here he is."

He'd seen right through me.

He pinned me more firmly to the wall and fucked me with more force, his cock, hard steel, filling me over and over again. "I will never hurt you, Sophia, no matter how hard you push me. From the moment I laid eyes on you, you were mine." He took my face in his hand, not letting me look away, his eyes boring into mine. "You are the only thing in this world I will die to protect, do you understand?" He pulled almost all the way out and slammed back in, jarring my body.

I wailed, my legs shaking. It was too much, but there was no escape. I was at his mercy, and, god, I wanted it. I craved being controlled, manhandled, fucked, cherished by this wild thing, this man capable of anything, but knowing I was the exception. I clawed at his back, wanting more and terrified of the huge feeling inside me.

Cillian was a furious storm and I was barely hanging on, but I was terrified if I clung too tight, he'd throw me away like everyone else. "Don't let me go," I sobbed.

"Never," he snarled.

I wouldn't survive it, not losing him. I knew it now. This feeling inside me was too big. It was violent and unapologetic and wrong, but so incredibly right. We were right, together.

"Whatever happens, promise me, you'll never let me go," I said again because I was spinning out of control, my feelings, my fears all there, so raw and exposed and there was no hiding them.

He pulled me from the wall and took us to the bed, falling to his back and taking me with him. He was still inside me, and I clawed at his chest, grinding down on him, fucking him, claiming him like he had me.

His hands came up and he fisted my hair and pulled my face close to his. "I promise, pet, I will never, ever let you go."

I threw my head back, crying out, shaking and rocking against him as I came so incredibly hard.

Finally, I fell forward, and Cillian rolled me, still thrusting into me, growling and snarling like the monster he was, not letting up until he came with an unhinged roar, bucking inside me until he was spent.

He fell beside me, pulling me into his arms, and kissed me tenderly.

I shook against him and quietly sobbed, unable to hold it in.

Cillian rolled me to my back, studying my face as he swiped my tears away. "Why are you crying?" he asked, only curiosity, fascination, in his gorgeous eyes, no fear. He'd sworn never to hurt me and he knew he hadn't caused me pain.

"Because...because it was so good. Because I never knew that...that it could be like this," I said through my tears.

"Me either." He slid his thumb over my cheek. "Fuck, pet, you're so beautiful when you cry." He made a low sound, deep in his chest. "Mine," he said, then pulled me back against him.

His.

Chapter Twenty

Sophia

I walked into my father's house, Danny right behind me.

Celeste had called earlier that morning. Tommy was missing me. He was home from school with a cold, and she'd asked me to stop by to cheer him up. "Is he up in his room?" I asked her as she strode toward me. I wasn't interested in making small talk with her. If it wasn't about Tommy, we had nothing to say to each other.

"Go on up," she said and smiled at Danny. "There's lunch on the terrace, please help yourself."

Danny ignored her and followed me toward the stairs.

"Tommy doesn't know him, Sophia. He'll be scared with your guard dog hovering," Celeste said.

I smiled at Danny. As annoying as it was, she was right. "Have some lunch, I'll be fine." He shook his head, about to argue. "I'm fine. I'll call if I need you."

His jaw tightened, but he did what I said. Danny didn't go out to the terrace, though, he stood at the bottom of the stairs, and I knew he wouldn't budge until I came back down. He didn't trust my father in the slightest, that much was obvious.

None of them did. What they thought he could do, I had no idea. He'd already done his worst, right? Luckily for me, his worst was starting to look like the best thing to ever happen to me.

I walked down the hall, tapped on Tommy's door, then walked in. "Hey, buddy..." The bed was empty. I walked into the room, assuming he was in the bathroom. "Tomo?"

The bedroom door clicked shut behind me and I spun around.

My father stood there.

"Where's Tommy?"

"At school." He was nervous.

"Celeste said he was sick."

"I needed to talk with you, privately," he said, still blocking the door.

Unease settled behind my ribs. What the hell was going on here? "Then you should have called. Not lied to me about my brother."

"I'll do whatever the fuck I want. I'm the head of this family—"

"Yet you're hiding in your son's bedroom so one of Cillian's men doesn't hear you—"

He stepped forward, his hand flying back—

"You mark my face and Cillian will end you," I fired at him. Shock rocketing through me. He'd never even tried to hit me before. I felt sick.

He dragged in several breaths and dropped his hand. "God, I'm so sorry, Sophia. I don't know what came over me...I'm under a lot of stress."

"What the hell is going on?" I'd never seen him like this, and he'd never in my entire life apologized to me for anything.

"You need to listen to me, trust me."

"You're scaring me."

His gaze hardened. "Your time married to Cillian O'Rourke is over. I'll come for you tonight. Wait until he's asleep, then come outside. There'll be a car waiting down the street for you behind the house, be there by two."

I froze. "What?"

"He's going to kill me, Sophia. Can you live with that? With your father's death on your conscience? I'm organizing an annulment now. I know a judge, he owes me. You can walk away. You don't have to stay with a man who murdered his own brother. You're not safe."

An annulment? What was he doing? And he hadn't cared about my safety when he'd planned to marry me off to someone with Adam's reputation or Cillian's for that matter. "Why would he want to hurt you?" I was done staying quiet and doing what I was told.

His jaw tightened. "He's about to find out about some... deals I've been doing in his territory."

"You betrayed the O'Rourkes again? What were you thinking?"

"I'm looking out for our family, and I'm not giving that fucker a dime of my money."

Oh fuck. "Dad—"

"Things are about to change, and you won't be a goddamn O'Rourke when they do."

"What do you mean, change?"

"That's none of your concern. You'll do what you're told and that's the end of it."

My hands shook with anger, that he was doing this to me again. "I need to leave. Danny will come looking for me soon."

His dark eyes were locked on me. "The car will be waiting for you at two, and if you tell Cillian, if you don't come, what happens next will be on your head."

The dread swirled higher. "What will happen?"

His gaze darkened. "He will kill me when he finds out what I've been doing, Sophia. You know he will. He'll kill Celeste... and he'll kill Tommy."

"He wouldn't do that," I bit out.

"You have no idea what he's done, what he's capable of. I do. I've seen it, things that would give you nightmares, make you sick to your stomach." My father was a manipulator and a liar, but the fear in his eyes, it seemed real.

I shook my head, my stomach twisting, my mind flashing to the blood on Cillian's shirt, the gun, the knife. He'd never hurt a child. He'd never hurt Tommy. But my father, Celeste...

He grabbed my arm and shook me. "Even if he doesn't kill your brother, who's to say Tommy won't get caught in the crossfire? Or that he'll be forced to watch both his parents executed in front of him. Cillian isn't called the O'Rourke monster for nothing, you have to know that by now." He gave me another shake. "Be ready tonight." Then opened the door and walked away.

I stood frozen. I wasn't stupid, I knew what Cillian was. He wasn't like other people, he didn't have much of a conscience, if he had one at all. He'd told me that he'd been prepared to kill my father for his betrayal to Seamus, that first night in Dad's office. That was how his world worked. My father had been given a second chance because of me, because of our alliance, and he'd squandered it. He'd thrown it back in Cillian's face. Cillian couldn't let that go. He was the head of his family now, he couldn't show weakness.

Dad had fucked up, and when Cillian found out what he'd done, he'd have no choice but to make him pay.

I made myself move, stomach churning.

Danny watched me come down the stairs, and as soon as he saw me, he frowned. "Okay?"

Celeste stared at me, and the fear I saw on her face was as real as my father's.

I forced a smile. "Yeah, I just...I don't like seeing Tommy unwell. We should get back."

My mind raced the whole way home, my stomach in jagged knots. I headed to the bedroom as soon as we got there. Thankfully, Cillian was out. He'd know something was wrong if he saw me now. I needed time to think. What would he do if I told him? Would he tell me the truth?

My father wasn't a good man, but I didn't want him dead. I sure as hell didn't want Cillian to be the one to kill him, or Celeste. She was Tommy's mom, it didn't matter how much she hated me. If Cillian did that, if he murdered them, how could I stay here with him? I couldn't.

I paced until my feet ached and then sat on the bed. What the hell was I going to do?

What my father planned, going back on his deal with Cillian, taking me back, on top of what he'd done, would only make everything worse. It would start a war. If I told Cillian what my father did, what he had planned, then he'd definitely kill him. Cillian wouldn't be able to let that slide. He couldn't let that go, not in his position, and whether I told him or not, he would find out because my father had already set this thing in motion. He'd organized an annulment for fuck's sake. If I didn't do something now, if I didn't try and stop this, my father would die. He'd signed his own death warrant when he decided to betray Cillian.

But if I was there, if I was at my father's house, it might keep them safe?

What the hell was I going to do?

I curled up on the bed, the same scenarios running through my head over and over again, but no matter how hard I tried, there was no fighting the tiredness I felt.

I woke to Cillian helping me out of my clothes.

"You fell asleep still dressed," he said, searching my face.

My gaze sliced to the clock by the bed. 10:57. "I was tired."

He sat me up, lifted my shirt over my head, and tossed it aside, then unhooked my bra next and slid it down my arms. One of his hands cupped my bare breast, squeezing lightly before dropping to the button of my jeans. He undid them and slid them off. I watched him, trying to read the expression on his face, but couldn't. He was focused, every bit of it on me.

His gaze flicked up to mine. "How was your visit with Tommy today?"

Guilt slammed through me. "Yeah, okay."

"He feeling better?"

I nodded.

"You eaten?"

I nodded again, lying. I couldn't stomach even a mouthful of food, and if he knew I hadn't had dinner, he'd make me eat.

"Get in bed, pet. I'll grab a shower, then I want to show you something."

He strode off and I watched him go. I thought I might actually be sick. Cillian would never hurt my brother, I knew that without a doubt, but losing both his parents would hurt him.

My father was a manipulator, though, and as real as his fear looked today, I wasn't going to just believe him, I knew better. Dad said things were about to change, and the more I thought about it, the more concerned I became. He'd do or say anything to bend me to his will. I needed proof, of what he said, and until then, talking to Cillian was out of the question. There was too much at stake.

I set an alarm for 1:30, put it on vibrate, and slid it under my pillow. I had no idea what I was going to do, but I did know I needed to try and stop this. I needed to talk to him. I needed to try to defuse this situation before it went any further and it was too late. And if my father was telling the truth and he'd been making deals in Cillian's territory, I had to try and convince him to come to Cillian to pay him his dues; then he might actually walk away from this whole thing.

I flicked off the bedside lamp. If Cillian looked into my eyes now, he'd know I was hiding something.

The bathroom door opened. I got a flash of Cillian's naked body, all smooth inked skin, his hair damp and swept back, before he shut the door behind him, then strode to the bed. The mattress dipped as he got in and instantly pulled me into him.

"You had a big day?" he asked.

"Hmm," I said and prayed he didn't feel how fast my heart was racing.

He kissed the back of my neck. "Love you like this, Soph, all soft and sleepy." He cupped my breasts, squeezing in a leisurely way, toying with my nipples until they were hard points and I was squirming. This was like the first nights I was here, when he'd get into bed with me and make me come in the dark, like it was our little secret and no one else had to know. Something I could pretend hadn't happened in the cold light of day.

"You want me to make you feel good, my beauty?" he asked against my ear and slid his hand down the front of my panties.

I did. I wanted him. I always wanted him. "Yes."

He shifted so he was leaning against the headboard, taking me with him, and pulled me in between his legs so my back was to his front. The light from his phone broke through the darkness and he held it out in front of us. "Watch this," he said with more than a little growl in his voice.

An image came onto view. I stiffened when a room appeared on the screen. My first thought was he knew something, that he knew my father had ambushed me in Tommy's room and he knew what he'd done. But then I saw Conor.

"What is this?"

"Keep watching," he said.

A moment later I walked into the room, my hair was all over the place. Conor looked up and smiled. I walked farther into the room and the rest of my body came into view. I was in a T-shirt and panties, lace ones that didn't cover much of anything. The morning I was hungover. *Shit.*

"I can explain…"

"Best you do, pet, 'cause I have to tell you, I'm not fucking okay with my men seeing my wife in her underwear." His lips went to my ear. "I can see your pussy right through them, which means so could Conor."

"I was hungover, and I kind of blacked out some of the night before. I thought I was in my bathing suit. I hadn't realized that you'd changed my clothes."

"You're lucky I didn't take Conor's eyes out. The only reason I let him live was because I know I can trust him."

I was trembling, but not from fear, from the way his hands had moved up my inner thighs, kneading my flesh.

"Take off your panties," he said.

I shoved them down, spreading my legs for him instantly.

"My dirty girl, always so eager," he said and hooked my legs around his, trapping them and spreading them wide.

"I'm sorry. It won't ever happen again," I said, need making my voice tremble.

He put the phone aside, and the room was cast in darkness again. Then his hand was back, and he started circling my clit gently, grinding his hard cock into my ass. "How sorry?"

"Really, really sorry," I whispered.

His mouth went to my ear again. "You know I have to punish you, don't you, pet?"

Yes, I wanted him to punish me. Tonight, of all nights, I

wanted to be punished. "W-why?" I said, even as I silently begged him for whatever it was he wanted to do to me. My pussy was bare and spread and dripping for him, for whatever happened next. I was vulnerable and at his mercy, and that was exactly what I needed.

"So you never do it again," he said and spread me with the fingers of one hand right before the other came down on my bare flesh, the wet slap ringing out in the quiet room.

I cried out and arched against him. "*Oh fuck.*"

"No one sees this perfect pussy but me," he growled and spanked my clit again.

I jerked in his arms, my thighs trembling.

"Understand?" he growled, then did it three more times in fast succession.

I screamed, coming, my pussy clenching against nothing, around nothing. I tried to shove my hand between my legs, and he gripped it in one of his, stopping me, then slapped me again. My mouth fell open, and I tried to pull away even as I begged for more. It was too much and not enough.

One of his arms banded across my chest, one big hand gripping my breast while the other started circling and rubbing my clit, making me whimper and squirm. I was sensitive, and he still had my legs trapped and spread. I wanted to scream for him to stop, yet wanting to keep riding the high. My orgasm hadn't fully ended and the next was right there. "Punish me...please...I need you to punish me."

"Such a greedy, wee pet," he said and thrust two fingers inside me.

His hand left my breast and gripped my throat, then he was finger-fucking me so fast all I could do was sob and plead for him to make me come. He spread me wider and pushed in deeper, hitting me where I needed him the most. Then I was arching against him, coming again, writhing against his hand, my pussy clamping around his fingers hard. I knew I'd soaked the sheets, and I'd come twice, so fucking hard, but it wasn't enough, not tonight. I felt mad with lust. I wanted more. "Please, I want it. Fuck me. Please, Cillian."

He growled against my skin as his mouth moved over my throat, sucking hard before kissing the tender skin there. "Then put me inside you, pet."

He let my legs free and I shifted, putting my feet under me and I reached back, taking his cock in my hand and pressing the head to my opening. I sat down, taking him inside me, and he groaned. I started moving instantly, riding him hard and fast, reaching for it, desperate to come again, to feel Cillian come inside me.

"Fuck," he grated against my ear. "My wife loves being stuffed full of her husband's cock."

"Yes," I sobbed as he grabbed my hips and took over the pace, but it was too slow, too intense. With his arms now locking me against him, I couldn't move like I wanted to. He had me pinned, totally in his control, the way he liked it—the way he knew I loved it.

He held me still, then thrust up into me over and over. "Pussy's dripping all over me, pet. Such a hungry little cunt. You ever let another man see what's mine again, I'll fucking kill them, understand?"

I sobbed, so close to coming a third time.

"Answer me, Sophia," he growled.

"Y-yes."

He moved suddenly, pulling out and shoving me to my back. He pushed my legs wide and filled me again, making me cry out. He ground into me, staying deep, making my head spin. He stared down at me, eyes glittering in the dark, compelling me to look into them, holding me captive.

"Play with your clit," he said, hushed, urgent.

I reached down between us and rubbed. He watched, his gaze searing into me as he increased the pace of his thrusts, faster, deeper, harder.

"Beautiful," he said.

My orgasm hit me like a rolling wave, flowing over me, through me. I arched against him, calling his name. He grabbed my jaw and made me look at him, and I watched as his face contorted with pleasure. His deep groan and the heavy pulse of his cock setting off aftershocks through me.

He pressed his forehead to mine, our panted breaths mingling. "So fucking perfect," he said huskily.

I clung to him, looking into his beautiful face, into eyes that could be as cold as ice but burned hot for me, and the realization struck me. I wasn't falling for him—no, I'd already fallen in love with Cillian O'Rourke. Completely.

He kissed me, soft, tender, still inside me, the way he liked. He always stayed inside me as long as he could. The emotions inside me yawned wider, so wide I couldn't contain them any longer.

"I love you," I whispered into the darkness, so quiet, my voice so small. I should keep it to myself, but I said it anyway.

His expression didn't change, but every muscle in his body tightened above me. His jaw twitched, but he didn't say anything. Humiliation burned my face, but I knew this would happen, didn't I? I knew this man wasn't capable of loving me back.

"Pet," he said roughly. "I—"

"You don't need to say anything." I glanced at the clock. 11:48.

He studied me for long seconds, the muscle in his jaw working. "I'll protect you, look after you, give you everything you need. But love...it's not something I'm capable of, Sophia. I don't know if I ever was," he said roughly.

"You don't have to explain." This made it easier, didn't it? Whatever happened tonight when I left this room, this house, and walked to my father's car would be easier because Cillian didn't love me back. He could never love me back. My heart didn't agree, but that was why I said it. That was why I'd thrown myself on the sword, because the truth hurts and it was what I needed to hear. If he loved me, if he said the words and I had to leave tonight, it would hurt so much more.

Sure. The dagger currently buried in your chest barely hurts at all, right?

I shut down the voice in my head. I needed to remember the truth of my situation. I was a pawn. This marriage was a business deal. None of this was real, and it never had been. Yes, he cared for me in whatever way Cillian was capable of, but this wasn't love, it wasn't some fucked-up fairy tale. I wasn't his sleeping beauty and he sure as hell wasn't my prince.

His rough-skinned fingers drifted across my brow, down the side of my face, then gently over my lips. "But knowing you love me, pet, it pleases me more than I know how to adequately express."

I flinched when he called me that name. It didn't feel nice, not anymore. It made me feel like a thing, his thing. Pain sliced through me, and my throat ached from fighting back my sob. "Can you let me up, please? I need to pee."

He blinked down at me, but then moved, rolling to the side. I scrambled out of bed and rushed to the bathroom. It was hard, but I didn't let my emotions take over, I couldn't. I had to go back out there.

I cleaned up, walked back out, and got into bed. Cillian dragged me closer like he always did, so I was pressed against him, and kissed my jaw.

"Night, pet."

"Night," I whispered.

A few minutes later he was fast asleep. I blinked through my tears, staring at the clock, watching the minutes tick by. Tommy was all that mattered, and I'd do whatever necessary to protect him, to stop his life from being blown apart.

Chapter Twenty-One

Sophia

God, my heart was banging wildly in my chest as I keyed in the code to turn off the alarm. I'd seen Danny do it enough times that I'd memorized it without even knowing I needed to.

I slipped out the door, my sneakers silent on the path as I eased along the side of the house toward the pool area. Leaving out the front wasn't an option when at least one of Cillian's men would be patrolling. Moving as quickly and quietly as I could, I grabbed one of the chairs from under the pergola and sprinted across the grassy area behind the pool to the fence.

Any minute now, one of the guys on security detail would make their way back here, or Cillian would wake and wonder where I was. Shoving the back of the chair against fence, I took several steps back and ran at it, jumping into the seat and throwing myself at the fence to get higher. My fingertips curled around the top, the tips of my shoes trying to grip the planks, scrambling for purchase. I didn't know how I did it, probably fear and a huge amount of adrenaline, but I managed to get high enough to hook my arms over, so I was hanging by my armpits, then hooked a leg across the top and finally got over.

I dangled down the side, let go, and winced as I hit the ground. My shoes sunk into sand and then I jogged toward the street behind the house. There weren't many streetlights along this stretch of road, so it wasn't hard to spot the headlights shining several houses down the street. I straightened my spine. If my father thought I'd do what he said without question, he was wrong. I hadn't been his to give away in the first place, and I sure as fuck wasn't his to take back now. I didn't know what he was up to, but betraying Cillian and voiding the alliance between our families behind his back, by attempting to take his wife from him, was an insult that couldn't be ignored. Not in our world. I couldn't let that happen. Whatever this was truly about, doing dealings in Cillian's territory, or something else, I needed to try and talk my father down, so we could all walk away from this in one piece.

I reached the car and the back door was shoved open. My father sat there looking nervous.

"Get in."

"No." I hated the way my voice shook. I didn't defy my father. Ever.

"Get the fuck in the car," he said, fury in his voice.

I took a deep breath. I needed to keep him calm or there was no way he'd hear me out. "Dad, you can't just expect me to leave. Taking me away from Cillian will only make this whole situation worse. You said things are about to change, what did you mean by that? Were you telling me the truth, the things you said in Tommy's room or is this some ploy to force me to do what you want."

He leaned forward, his eyes black in the shadows of the car. "I don't explain myself to you, now get in."

I shook my head. "I'm not a child anymore. You can't—"

Fingers curled around the back of my neck, and I felt hot breath against my ear. "Hello, Soph."

Paolo.

He pressed his body against mine, then thrust his hips forward, ramming his hard-on against my ass, making me stumble forward. "In you go."

I tried to pull away, to yank out of his hold, but he jerked my arms behind me, forcing me to bend forward with a hand at the back of my neck, and shoved me in the car. I fell on the seat beside my father and quickly struggled into a sitting position as Paolo got in, sandwiching me in the middle.

"Let me out," I said, trying to dive for freedom.

Paolo shoved me roughly back into the seat as the car started. Headlights from several more cars shone through the back window as they pulled up behind us.

I turned to my father. "What the hell is going on?"

He wouldn't look at me. "Let's go," he said to the driver.

The car eased out onto the street but didn't go far. It slowed outside Cillian's house and, just for a moment, my stupid heart almost believed he was going to let me out. Instead, he pulled over again, and I watched as a small figure behind the gates ran toward them. The other cars sped up, driving up onto the side-walk. Men jumped out, all armed. The gates slid open, and a person dressed in black, a hood pulled up concealing their face, stood there, waving them in.

Oh god.

"Have you figured it out yet?" Paolo said beside me.

I watched in horror as men stormed Cillian's house.

"My uncle's time as the head of the family has come to an end. Cillian fucked with me, and tonight, your father and I will take everything from him. Brennan will take control of both territories, and thanks to our new alliance, we'll run this city together."

I tried to dive for the door again and Paolo shoved me back harder this time.

"Do you really think Cillian will let you get away with this?" I fired at him.

Paolo shrugged. "If he survives tonight, let him come. I'd love nothing more than to put a bullet in his brain myself."

I spun to my father. "You have to know you can't trust him. He'll kill you as soon as you turn your back." Paolo was unstable, twisted. "Dad?"

"Don't question me. I know what I'm doing," he said, still avoiding my stare.

Paolo's clammy hand gripped my chin, forcing me to look at him. "Unlike your soon-to-be ex-husband...your marriage will be nothing but a bad memory by the time you wake up tomorrow, just FYI, I would never murder my father-in-law."

"What?" I whispered, horror stealing my voice. He couldn't be serious. That's why my father wanted me to leave Cillian, because I was part of the deal he'd made with Paolo. "I won't do it." I felt sick to my stomach. The annulment had been a safeguard, in case Cillian survived their attack tonight.

Paolo laughed, and it sent ice through my veins. "It's cute you think you have a choice. I told you, Sophia, I'm taking everything from Cillian O'Rourke, including you."

The car sped away as the sound of gunshots filled the night.

———

Cillian

I strode out into the hall as gunfire came from the floor below. Sophia was gone from our bed. I didn't know what the fuck was going on, where she was, but whoever had the balls to break into my house would leave in a black plastic sack.

A gunman rounded the corner. I aimed for his shoulder and fired. He jerked back, dropping his gun and hit the ground. I strode forward, leaning over him. "Where is my wife?"

He scowled up at me, mouth shut.

I pressed my thumb into his now bleeding, fucked-up shoulder. He screamed. "Where?" I demanded.

"I—I d-don't...know."

His eyes darted behind me. I spun and fired another shot at the guy behind me, hitting him in the chest. He went down. I turned back to the bleeding, writhing fucker on the floor. "Tell me."

"I t-tell you, I'm a...d-dead man."

I pressed my gun to his forehead. "You were a dead man the moment you walked into my home. But you have a choice; die a slow, agonizing death or I keep it simple and just splatter your brains all over my floor. What's it gonna be?"

Tears filled his eyes, his face contorted with fear. "Paolo," he rasped.

I straightened, aimed, and shot him between the eyes, then headed downstairs.

Danny stood in the living room. There were several bodies on the floor, all dead.

"How many?" I asked him.

"Eight, the others are outside. Braiden and Lance are doing another perimeter check. Seamus and Sally are fine, but she's pretty freaked. I told her to stay in her room."

"Sophia?" I asked, while my heart slammed wildly in my chest.

A look slid through his eyes I didn't like. "She's gone. Sally saw Sophia leave and followed her. She jumped the fence and took off before the men stormed the place."

"She look scared? Was someone forcing her?"

Danny shook his head.

Fuck. I wanted to roar, to kill, but we'd already killed everyone.

She said she'd find a way to leave when I first brought her here, that she wouldn't be my wife for long... I'd thought...

I'd actually convinced myself she was finally happy, that she actually liked it here with me.

There are things you should worry about, husband, like if your wife is slowly losing her damned mind with all the ways her world has been thrown on its head, or if I'll do to you what Alto's wife did to him or whether I'll run away in the middle of the night, because sometimes I have to seriously talk myself out of both of those things...

She'd said that to me. She'd made it clear she was unhappy, but I didn't want to see it.

My fingers curled into a tight fist. I didn't like this feeling, the monster roaring inside me, the grip of its claws digging into flesh in the center of my chest.

What she somehow hadn't fully grasped was that when I made something mine, I didn't give it up. Ever.

No, pet. This wasn't happening. You don't get to leave.

You are mine.

Chapter Twenty-Two

Cillian

Alto stood as I strode across the restaurant. It was early, the place closed. His gaze darted behind me, looking for his guards, they were both bleeding on the ground.

"Your men will live, if you move fast."

Vince stood beside Alto and drew his gun. So did Conor and Declan who stood either side of me.

"What is the meaning of this, Cillian?"

"You lied, old man," I said.

He straightened, fury filling his dark eyes. "What is it you accuse me of?"

"Paolo. He never left."

Alto's gaze sliced to Vince. "My word is my bond. I didn't lie. Vince put him on the plane."

I raised a brow. "Did he now? Then how is it that Paolo's men broke into my home last night?"

Alto turned to his second. The asshole was sweating. "Tell him, Vince, that my nephew left the city."

Vince scowled at me, but he was shaking. "O'Rourke lies."

I stared the fucker down, and he shifted uneasily. "He has my wife," I said to Alto without looking away. The fact that

Sophia left willingly was irrelevant. I didn't know why she'd go with Paolo. I had my suspicions and, looking at Vince, I was sure the fucker had the answers.

More of Alto's men rushed into the room, guns raised. Alto shook his head, and they lowered their weapons. His cold gaze slid to Vince. "Did my nephew leave?"

The fucker continued to scowl at me, mouth jammed shut.

"Answer me," Alto demanded. "Or I'll have Carmine get you to talk."

Sweat poured down the fucker's face, even as defiance straightened his spine. "He did not."

"You betrayed me?" Alto said, menace in his eyes.

Vince shook his head. "We did this for you. To strengthen our position, to—"

"No," Alto roared. "You undermined me." One of his men pressed a gun to Vince's head. "You think you can take my place? You think Paolo would let you live once I'm gone." He said something in Italian and Vince flinched. "Speak," Alto demanded.

"Paolo, he did a deal with Brennan. They tie the families together, a marriage, Brennan would take O'Rourke's territory, and Paolo would take your place."

"And you'd be his second?"

"Yes."

"Where is my wife?" I said, interrupting. I'd heard enough.

Vince's gaze slid to me. "She isn't your wife anymore. The annulment went through this morning. Her father arranged it." He smirked. "She wanted this, wanted to get away from you. She wanted an Italian between her thighs, not an Irish piece of shit." He spat on the floor, narrowly missing my shoe.

She said she loved me, but it could easily have been an act. How would I know what real love looked like? I didn't. I'd hurt her when I told her I wasn't capable of returning her feelings. I did feel something for her, what that was, I wasn't sure. The thought of her leaving me willingly—I wanted to tear this room apart. I lifted my gun and shot Vince in the face, blood and brains splattering Alto's men.

Their guns flew back up. Con cursed beside me, but Alto barked for them to lower their weapons.

"We're even," I said.

Alto nodded. "Vince was a treacherous fuck, but he was my brother-in-law." He glanced down at the dead man. "I'm sure you understand the alliance between us can no longer go forward, not now. There will be no wedding between your brother and Gaia."

Declan shifted beside me. "Agreed," I said.

Too much had passed between our families. Any alliance would have to wait until everything died down, and that could take years. We strode out of the restaurant. "Gather the men," I said to Conor.

I was going to get Sophia.

Sophia

I paced my old bedroom in my father's house. Scared out of my mind. Was Cillian okay? Goddammit, I needed to know.

He had to be all right.

Please let Cillian be okay.

My gaze slid to the dress hanging on the wardrobe door. Paolo had chosen it. He wanted a proper wedding. This felt like deja vu, only this time my new husband would make my life a living hell.

The annulment would have gone through this morning. I was no longer married to Cillian O'Rourke, and it felt as though a part of me had been ripped from my chest and set ablaze.

Cillian may not know what it was to love, but he'd made me feel more loved than I had in my whole life. I didn't want to leave him. I wanted to stay. I wanted to keep shining light on the shadows inside him. I wanted to keep bringing to life parts of him that he only shared with me. I just wanted him. I didn't need him to love me, not when whatever it was he did feel for me was more than enough.

I'd been locked in my room since we got here last night. I would find a way to escape, though. I had to, and I was taking Tommy with me.

There was a tap on the door, then the sound of the lock. I scrambled back as the door opened.

Paolo walked in, a wide smile on his face. "Soph." His gaze slid over me. "You look a little rough, sweetheart. I hope you're going to clean yourself up for our big day tomorrow. If you embarrass me in front of my men, looking like dog shit, I won't be happy."

"I don't give a fuck if you're happy. I'm not marrying you, I will never marry you—"

He backhanded me, sending me across the room. I hit the floor, and he strode over, straddling my hips and fisted my hair. "You do not speak to me that way, ever, understand?"

I stared up at him in shock. I could taste blood, the inside of my lip split, and pain radiated through my cheek and jaw.

"Nod if you understand," he said and used his grip on my hair to force me to do as he said. He leaned closer, swiping blood from my lip with his thumb and sucked it off, then grinned, flashing me his bloody teeth. "I can't wait for our honeymoon, Soph. The things I'm going to do to you." He shook his head. "Poor thing. You won't like it, any of it." He dragged his mouth over mine, then bit my lip, making me cry out. He fisted my hair tighter and looked into my eyes. "But the thought of you screaming in pain makes me hard as fuck."

He shoved away from me, stood, and straightened his jacket, an obvious tent in his trousers now. I shrunk away, and he chuckled.

"Shame I have some things to organize or I might give you a little taste of what's to come," he said, staring down at me.

He was breathing hard, the look in his eyes sending a shiver down my spine.

"Fuck it," he said and took a step toward me. "I should make time, right? I deserve some fun after everything I did to get you here."

I scrambled back.

"Paolo," someone said from the door. "You're needed downstairs. Now."

He turned to the guy standing there. "It'll have to wait."

The other guy shook his head. "This can't wait."

Paolo cursed and turned back to me, his gaze moving over me. "Clean yourself up," he said, then strode to the door. Just before walking out, he turned back. "And if you think O'Rourke is coming to save you, don't hold your breath. Turns out if the annulment hadn't gone through, you would've been a widow, anyway."

He smirked, then shut the door, locking me in.

Chapter Twenty-Three

Cillian

Brennan's house was mostly dark, only a couple lights shining from inside.

I signaled Declan and he moved forward, then nodded to Conor. He whistled to the guard, and when the guy turned, I ran up behind him, smashed the butt of my gun into his head, and knocked him out cold. He was one of Brennan's men, and though Sophia's father was trying to fuck us over, we knew a lot of them, had known them for a long time. Some of them were good men, loyal men; they didn't deserve to die because of Brennan's fucked-up decisions.

Paolo, on the other hand, would fucking choke to death on his own blood, after I made him scream.

We made it to the house, and I quickly picked the lock and slid inside. The alarm was off because his men were supposed to be coming and going while they patrolled the house and the grounds. My men had seen to them, most were currently lights out.

The downstairs was dimly lit, except for Brennan's office, where the light shone from beneath the closed door. I waved Danny and two other men toward it. There was no sign of Paolo yet. I headed upstairs, Declan and Conor behind me. All was dark and quiet up here. Paolo had to be up here somewhere, but getting Sophia out of this house was priority.

I rounded the corner, and one of Paolo's men sat in a chair outside what was obviously my wife's bedroom. He was slumped, fast asleep. Fucking useless. I turned to Dec and he nodded, then he and Conor carried on down the hall. I moved in behind Sophia's guard, hooked my arm around his throat, and squeezed. He thrashed awake, gripping my arm. I squeezed tighter until he went limp.

Taking the key from his pocket, I unlocked the door and eased it open.

———

Sophia

I startled awake when I was roughly hauled out of bed. I tried to scream, to kick and fight, but a strong hand held me in a bruising grip, another clamped over my mouth.

"Quiet," a familiar voice growled against my ear.

Cillian.

He was alive. I'd cried until I'd passed out from exhaustion. Paolo said he was dead. But he was alive, and he'd come for me. I tried to turn in his arms, to reach for him so I could tell him I loved him, but he threw me back on the bed, one hand still over my mouth while he undid his tie with the other. I nodded, telling him I'd be quiet, that I knew it was him, that he could take away his hand.

He did.

When I opened my mouth to talk, he jammed his tie across

my lips, flipped me to my front, and secured it around my head, gagging me. I heard the clink of his belt, then my hands were gripped behind my back, where he secured them tightly with the thick leather.

Oh god, he thought I'd betrayed him. He thought I was here willingly. He wasn't saving me, he was abducting me. I didn't struggle when he lifted me again and tossed me over his shoulder. With an arm wrapped around the backs of my thighs, he strode from the room. I thumped his back when we hit the hall and flailed, trying to motion to Tommy's room.

"Nothing will happen to your brother," he said, reading my mind, his voice pure ice.

A shiver slid through me at how cold and devoid of all emotion he sounded. He carried me through the house and down the stairs.

"Any sign of Paolo?" Cillian asked someone.

I didn't hear their response.

"Clean house. None of that fucker's men are left breathing, understand?" Cillian said.

"Got it."

That was Danny's voice.

Cillian strode outside. The sound of a car came next. I was jostled and tossed into the back seat. I scrambled to sit up, but it was hard with my hands behind my back—

A shot rang out, and Cillian jerked to the side. I screamed behind my gag as Paolo walked out, fury in his wild eyes, gun in his hand raised.

"Get her out of here," Cillian said, slamming the door closed as gunshots rang out.

The car sped off, leaving him behind, while I screamed.

―――――

I lay on my side in Cillian's bed, the gag in my mouth and my hands still bound with his belt. My feet were tied as well now, and I could do nothing but lie here terrified for him, and for Tommy. Cillian said he wouldn't get hurt, but what if he got caught in the crossfire. He must be so scared.

I don't know how long I'd been lying here, but my hands and feet were numb, and the room was slowly growing lighter. It had to be the early hours of the morning.

The door opened suddenly and Cillian walked in.

His shirt was off. His bicep was bandaged. He'd been hit, but it can't have been bad. Relief flooded me as he shut the door behind him. His gaze sliced down me, bound and gagged and helpless on his bed, and he said nothing. He kicked off his shoes and socks, then his hands dropped to the front of his pants and he undid them, shucking them so he was only in a pair of black boxer briefs, then closed the space between us.

He took my chin in his hand and leaned in close, staring into my eyes. "You had me fooled, pet. That won't happen again. I don't care if you hate me, if you want to run from me, because, wife or not, you are mine, and I will never let you leave me again."

He meant it as a threat, but the terror I felt wasn't from fear, it was from the thought that he'd never believe me. That he thought I didn't love him anymore or never did. He had it wrong. He thought I'd betrayed him, yes, but he still wanted me, that's all that mattered. I'd make him listen. I'd make him hear the truth. I had to.

He scooped me up, and the heat of his skin, his scent, calmed the terror inside me—then he tossed me to the other side of the bed, got under the covers, and closed his eyes.

I lay there staring at his profile. He didn't look at me again, then finally his breathing evened out as he fell asleep.

The next thing I was aware of, was pain radiating through my hands and feet.

It was full light now. My restraints had been removed, but the gag was still in place.

Cillian was up and dressed, and he stared down at me dispassionately while I writhed in pain.

"You'll be fine once the blood gets flowing again," he said as he finished doing up his tie, then started for the door.

My hands were hot with pins and needles, and extremely weak, but I managed to drag the gag from my dry mouth. "Cillian, wait," I choked, my voice nothing but a husky rasp.

He paused but didn't turn back.

"P-please, I need you to..." I coughed. "I—I—"

"Drink, Sophia," he growled out, finally turning back to me.

There was a glass on the bedside table, and I snatched it up, chugging it, water dripping down my chin in my haste. "I d-didn't leave you, not willingly, you have to believe me. I—"

"How did you know your father would be outside?" he asked.

I scrambled out of bed, nearly falling over, and was forced to lean against the wall. "When I went to see Tommy, he said he was going to have our marriage annulled, that he knew someone that could do it, that he—"

"When I came home, after you'd seen Brennan, why didn't you tell me?" he asked. There was no emotion in his tone, not even anger.

"Because..." I felt sick to my stomach. I didn't want to say it. *I didn't want to know the truth.* "Because he said you were going to kill him, that you'd come after Celeste and Tommy, that you'd...kill them too—"

"And you believed him," he said, not an ounce of surprise on his face.

I hated it. After watching him slowly become more

animated—smile, laugh, stare at me in a way that made my heart race—seeing that cold, emotionless expression again was unbearable. Guilt hit me. "He seemed genuinely afraid. I'd never seen him like that. He said he betrayed you, that he was doing deals in your territory again. That you'd kill him. You said yourself, that first night in his office, that you'd take his life for an offence like that." I shook my head. "But the more I thought about it, the more I doubted him. Something seemed off."

"Yet you chose not to tell me about it, left our bed and went to your father anyway. You were seen running off into the night, without anyone's gun to your head, pet, right before my house was invaded. You truly expect me to believe you had no idea what was about to happen?"

"I didn't. I just wanted to talk to him. I wanted proof of what he said. I wanted to find a way to stop all of this, to find out what he really had planned. And if I had told you he was trying to annul our marriage, you would've gone after him. I just wanted to try to talk sense into him, to defuse the situation before it got out of hand. I never planned to leave with him, and then Paolo came and forced me into the car..." I stumbled toward him on shaky legs. "I didn't want to leave, Cillian, I promise. I just wanted—"

"Proof. Proof that the O'Rourke monster planned to murder your traitorous father, that I was capable of putting a bullet in your baby brother's skull?"

"I knew you wouldn't hurt Tommy, I never believed—"

"And if I did kill your father, what then, pet?" His lips curled up in an awful imitation of a smile. "You may have told yourself that you never planned to leave, but the fact you needed proof says it all, doesn't it, Sophia? Or maybe everything you just said to me was a bunch of lies, maybe you're not so different than me. Maybe you're good at pretending as well and the only true version I've seen of you was when I first brought you here. You said you'd find a way to leave me, remember, whatever it took?"

I stumbled forward and grabbed his jacket. "I wanted proof of what my father did, what he had planned, not what he said about you. I just, I wanted to show him I wasn't his to control, that I wouldn't blindly do what he said anymore. That's all. I never lied to you. I told you how I felt and I meant it. I lo—"

He pressed his thumb against my lips and shook his head. "I am not a good man, pet. I don't like lies, and your pretty words and fake declarations won't work on me."

My head jerked back. "I'm not lying, please, you have to listen to me—"

"I had planned to kill your father, right after we were married." His frigid green gaze held mine. "He's weak and pathetic and not fit to be our ally. As for Celeste..." He shrugged. "I didn't care one way or the other. Tommy, I would bring here. A gift for you, for my wife. Your father mistreated you, he didn't deserve to live."

I blinked up at him, stunned, but saw the truth in his eyes.

God, he was so incredibly broken. I'd been getting through to him, but he'd pulled back. He had retreated to the shadows. "But you didn't go through with it...you changed your mind." Horror at what he said filled me, but this was Cillian, he could be monstrous but not to me. If I'd known before, if I'd asked him not to do it, I knew with everything in me that he wouldn't have. Now? I wasn't so sure. "Did you kill him last night?"

"No."

"Are you going to?"

"He's not worth wasting a bullet."

"Is Paolo dead?"

"Yes."

"What are you going to do with me?" I asked. He wouldn't hurt me, even now, after everything that happened, even though he believed I'd betrayed him. But if he sent me away, if he cut me out of his life, I wasn't sure I'd ever find a way back. Whatever came next, I'd accept it. As long as I was here, I could try to get through to him.

"It appears you are no longer my wife, Sophia."

Pain sliced me through my chest. Tears filled my eyes, there was no holding them back, spilling over and running down my cheeks.

Cillian gripped my chin, watching my tears flow. "You're afraid," he said, mistaking them for something else.

I shook my head. "I'm not crying because I'm afraid. I'm sad."

"Why?"

"Because I loved being your wife."

He flinched. It was subtle, but I didn't miss it. "You can't help yourself, can you? The lies fall from your mouth so easily."

"It's the truth. What are you going to do with me, Cillian?"

He dragged his thumb over my lips. "I told you, I don't give up what's mine."

He wasn't going to send me away, that was a start.

"But if you're no longer my wife, pet, the only position for you here..." He gripped my chin. "...is whore."

I tried to jerk back, but he held me fast. "You don't mean that."

"Your things will be moved to the room next door, where you belong. Only my wife shares this room with me."

"Cillian..."

He released me and walked away, shutting and locking the door after him.

Jesus, that hurt, so damn much, but I refused to believe he didn't care about me anymore. He was angry. He thought I'd betrayed him. He said he didn't have a heart, but he did. He'd just let it bleed in front of me and he didn't even know it.

He was hurt. I'd hurt him.

He was a man who didn't understand his own emotions, shutting them down as a neglected and abused child had kept him alive, it was a defense mechanism, and he was doing it again now. He didn't know how to deal with what he was feeling, so he was lashing out, trying to cause me pain in return. Not because he hated me, but because he loved me.

He just hadn't realized it yet.

But he would.

I'd do whatever it took to make him realize just how much he loved me.

Chapter Twenty-Four

Cillian

Declan walked into my office and sat opposite me. I carried on with what I was doing, and he didn't say anything, just sat and waited for me to acknowledge him.

I didn't feel like talking.

I didn't feel like much of anything.

The last two days I'd wandered this house like a fucking ghost, making Danny take Sophia her food, trying to get this... this grip in my gut and in the center of my chest to fucking go away.

Sophia was the cause of it. She was the reason I was sitting here reading the same thing over and over again and getting nothing done.

She was so close, just down the hall, her bedroom right beside mine.

Only a matter of days ago, she'd shared my room with me. Every morning I had to force myself to leave my sleeping wife alone in our bed, and every evening I anticipated coming home to her. I snatched up my glass and downed the contents, pouring another glass as it burned its way down my throat.

I wanted to go to her now, so badly. My skin was hot, drawn

tight over my muscles. I craved her vanilla-and-cinnamon scent, the taste of her, the sound of her moans while I ate her, or fucked her.

She may have lied about the rest, but that she couldn't fake. Not the way her pussy gripped me when she came or the way she soaked my fingers, her cries for more. She'd wanted me, and if that was all we could have now, then so be it. Maybe I should toss her out, forget she exists, but I couldn't bring myself to do it.

"You shaved," Declan finally said, sick of waiting for me to speak.

"Aye." I hadn't been without the beard for over a year, not since Seamus asked me to follow Sophia and find out everything there was to know about her. I don't know why I'd kept it once she was mine.

Yes, you do. You were afraid without a trace of Dean, she wouldn't want you. That she'd see you for what you are—that she'd be afraid of you.

That was it, wasn't it? I may be emotionally stunted, but I'd read enough psychology books to understand the truth of my actions. And today I shaved because I wasn't sure I was strong enough to resist her. I feared I might cave and let her back in, even after what she'd done, but if she saw me like this, all traces of Dean completely gone, she'd make it easy on me and tell me she hated me, that she was scared of me. That she'd see the fucked-up monster Seamus turned me into and make it easier for me to end this for both of us.

"Are you ever going to let her out of that room, brother?" Dec asked when I said no more.

"Sophia isn't any of your business." I frowned at the way her name caught in the back of my throat. "Did you find Sally?"

"Not yet. Got a lead, though."

She'd taken off into the night. It could be that she was

scared after what happened…or it could be something else, and I wouldn't be satisfied until I spoke to her.

Dec sat back. "You can't keep Sophia up there forever," he said, ignoring me.

"I can do whatever the fuck I like." I knew he was right, of course, but I wasn't sure what else to do.

"What did she say happened?"

I took another sip of my drink. "That Paolo forced her into the car, that she didn't want to leave. But no one forced her at gunpoint to leave my bed, to leave this house. None of it adds up. She lied to me." I squeezed my glass tighter. "She says she loves me." The words felt strange in my mouth. I don't think I'd ever said the word love out loud in my life.

Dec's brow lifted, his head tilting to the side. "Do you believe her?"

"No," I said, and my stomach tightened.

"Why?" he asked.

I didn't understand the concept of love; how would I know if she meant it or not? Logically, it should be an impossibility. I'd stalked her, forced her to marry me. I'd held her against her will, then and now. I never bothered to hide what and who I was. "I've given her no reason to."

"How would you know?" he asked.

There was no sarcasm in his voice, he was genuinely curious. "Do I need to list the reasons?" I answered, surprised he'd need to ask.

"Do you want it to be true?" Again, there was nothing but curiosity there. My brother was as confounded by the concept of love as I was.

I sipped my drink again, feeling exposed in a way I couldn't ever remember feeling in front of my brother, and that was saying a lot after the shit we'd been through, especially as children. Yes, when she'd said those words to me, it pleased me, I couldn't deny it. But if Sophia loved me, then she never would have left that night. I wouldn't have to lock her away to keep her because she would have chosen me. "What I want doesn't matter."

"You obviously want her or she wouldn't be locked in one of your rooms."

"Why are we talking about this?" I said, frustration filling me.

"What if she's telling the truth, Cillian? What if she never wanted to leave you, what if she loves you and you have her locked up like a prisoner? Way I see it, you have two choices... you'll either have to leave her locked up for the rest of her life, or figure out a way to trust her." Declan stood. "If she does love you and you insist on treating her like a prisoner, I'm not sure how much longer she'll feel that way. You'll have her, but you would have lost her as well."

"And what do you know about it?" I asked and sat back.

"Fuck all." He shook his head. "Just the idea that someone could love one of us...I don't know, I find it...interesting. I guess I'd like to see it." He shrugged. "Whatever. Listen to me, or don't."

Yeah, my brother was as fucked up as I was.

I got what he was saying, but if I let her out of the room and she ran, I'd lose her anyway. This way she was still mine. She belonged to me.

No, I couldn't let her out of that room. I'd convinced myself that Sophia saw me differently than everyone else. But I'd been wrong.

Yes, I'd thought about killing Brennan, but I'd decided quickly not to act on it. There was no need, he was weak. It had only been a matter of time before his men chose to follow me. I'd never expected him to try anything like he had.

He hadn't realized who he was up against, though. He saw

me like Seamus did. As if the only thing I had to offer of any value was my ability to kill without conscience.

Apparently, Sophia felt the same way.

She didn't see me, she saw the things I'd done. She saw the monster.

A monster she enjoyed fucking and nothing more.

Declan left, and I headed upstairs, undoing my tie as I walked.

If that's what she wanted, if that's who she saw when she looked at me, then that's who she'd get—

Sophia screamed and the fear in her voice lifted the hair on the back of my neck.

I ran for her room, shoved open the door—and I stopped in my tracks, my heart smacking against the back of my ribs. Sophia was arched against the mattress, her legs squeezed together. Her hands over her head as if held there, her nipples tight and straining against her top.

She moaned, the same way she did when I touched her, my name tumbling from her lips, then her body started moving, like it did when I fucked her. I'd seen only a little of this, once when I'd visited her at her apartment, but it was nothing like this.

Because before, she'd been a virgin. Now her body, and her dreams, knew exactly what it was like to be fucked.

"Yes," she whimpered as her legs thrusted wide as if by invisible hands. "Yes, please..." she moaned. "Please...please, fuck me."

I stalked to the bed, eating up the sight of her. I hadn't seen her in days, avoiding her like a fucking coward, and now, seeing her like this as she rocked against the mattress, as if being taken by the monster, *by me*, I felt like an addict getting a hit of my favorite drug.

She'd told me her fantasy, what she wanted me to do the next time I saw her like this. Did she still? She was my prisoner now, maybe I should walk away, but I couldn't. I wanted her despite her traitorous actions, and by the way my name kept falling from her lips, she still wanted me as well.

Dragging back the sheet, I looked down at her, finding it hard to breathe. Jesus fucking Christ, she was straining, her hips moving as if I was already between her thighs.

I quickly undressed and carefully climbed onto the bed.

She was in her usual pj's, and I bunched the shirt and lifted it, revealing her nipples, darker now and tight as fuck. Then hooking my fingers down the sides of her shorts and panties, I slid them down, moving her legs carefully so as not to wake her, and tossed them aside. Her legs instantly parted again, and I groaned at the sight of her pussy, fucking dripping and swollen, her clit begging for attention.

I moved between her spread thighs and almost came when she cried out, her pussy spasming, her juices sliding out and down the crack of her ass. She was coming.

Jealousy slammed through me, and I covered her with my body, gripping her wrists already crossed and pinned over her head, then taking my cock in hand, I pressed the head to her slick-as-fuck opening and slid inside.

I growled as the aftershocks of her orgasm had her clutching me. She was feverish, hair damp at her temples, cheeks dark, lips parted with her cries, with her begging for more. I started fucking her, deep, long strokes, in time with the way her hips were already moving. Giving her the monster, being the monster in her dreams but taking her back, taking what was mine, what would always be mine no matter what.

Sophia started rocking faster, begging and crying for more, for harder, faster, and I gave it to her, slamming into her like the monster she was seeing in her dream.

Her lids snapped open suddenly and she gasped, jerking against my hold, eyes wide with alarm—but just for a split second, then her gaze sliced down my face, my chest, to what I was doing to her, then back up to me.

"*Oh fuck*," she rasped, her eyes rolling back.

"That's right, pet, the monster fucked you awake like you wanted, because you are mine, you belong to *this* monster, not the fucker in your dreams."

"Don't stop," she groaned.

I fucked her harder. "Dirty fucking girl. Sheets soaked from that pussy. Begging me to fuck you in your sleep."

"Y-yes, only you. I only want you." She arched under me, straining, and came again, calling my name.

I kept up the pace, not slowing, grunting and growling, utterly lost as I came hard, pumping her full and claiming her again, like I did every time I fucked my wife.

She's not your wife anymore.

I growled, angry with Sophia, with myself for trusting her, for letting her get under my skin like I had.

I didn't release her wrists, not while I fought to catch my breath. I didn't want her to touch me, not then. Maybe that made me weak, but if I let her touch me, I don't know if I'd be able to walk back out of this room.

As soon as I got my shit together, I did what I had to, I got out of bed and walked out.

Chapter Twenty-Five

Sophia

It was late, and I'd been fighting sleep for hours.

Cillian finally came to me last night, after several days of nothing, and I wanted him to come to me again. My body still ached in the best way. It'd been amazing, everything I'd fantasized about...except for that part where he got up afterward and left. I'd wanted him to stay, to hold me like he used to.

God, I missed him so much.

My lids grew heavier, I tried to fight it, but it was impossible.

But even when I did fall asleep, it wasn't deeply. I tossed and turned. One dream after another, most of them nightmares.

The monster chased me, running faster and faster, its snarls getting closer. I screamed again as he swiped his clawed hand, barely missing me. I spun back and its glowing green eyes bore into me, watching, always watching. My heart pounded harder in my chest.

"Stop," he snarled. "Don't you dare fucking run from me."

I did as he said, as if my feet were encased in concrete, and he stepped out of the shadows. Cillian. His eyes were bright, burning into me. He was naked and covered in blood.

"What are you going to do to me?" I said, breathing hard.

"Exactly what my beauty wants me to do." He reached down, wrapping clawed fingers around his cock that jutted from him, so long and hard. Then he was there, grabbing me roughly and forcing me down on the ground. He shoved my legs wide, and his eyes flashed as he slammed inside me.

I woke, a cry of pleasure still falling from my lips as I blinked into the darkness, but this time I wasn't alone.

Rough hands slid up the front of my top and I stilled, until I smelled Cillian's soap, the deodorant he used. He was breathing heavily, his cock hard against my ass.

"Another dirty dream?" he growled against my ear. "Who were you dreaming about?"

"You," I whispered, trembling, still trapped between this room and the dream.

"I was fucking you again," he said, not a question. "The monster was fucking you."

"Yes," I gasped, squeezing my thighs together.

"That's what you want from me, isn't it, pet?" he growled against my ear.

I didn't answer. He was talking to me, but I wasn't sure what he wanted me to say? If he thought I was going to fight him this time, to tell him to stop, he was wrong. I wanted him to touch me so badly I was slick and achy. He squeezed my breast, and I whimpered.

"Answer me," he said in a hard, detached voice.

He wasn't going to let me hide in the darkness and pretend what happened between us last night hadn't, or what was about to happen between us now was out of my control. And he wasn't going to let me forget that he thought I'd betrayed him, or that he'd made me his prisoner, his whore.

It hurt, even knowing how Cillian was, this fucking hurt. But he was right, I did want him.

"Yes," I whispered.

In the next breath, he yanked my shirt up and off, tossing it aside. His other hand thrust down the front of my panties and he grazed my clit, sliding lower.

"Always fucking desperate for it," he said and shoved me to my back.

"Your beard," I whispered. I'd noticed it was gone last night, but everything had been so out of control, waking to him inside me, then it was over and he'd gotten up and left. The beard had softened him a little, I realized as I looked up at him, but now he was brutally handsome, all sharp angles, a raw fierceness about him that stole my breath.

He pushed my thighs wide and stared down at me as he thrust two fingers inside me. He flashed his teeth, not a smile, not even close. "Is it like being finger-fucked by a stranger?" he asked and thrust in deep, then back out.

No, because the man I loved shone from his gorgeous green eyes. "Cillian," I groaned, reaching for him, touching his smooth jaw.

He grabbed my hand and held it over my head, not letting me touch him, and continued his torture, working me with those long, thick fingers, over and over, until I was a shuddering panting mess.

"Cunt's always drenched and ready for my cock, like a good little whore."

His words should make me feel worthless, but they just told me how much I'd hurt him. I whimpered, so close to coming that my hips lifted, needing more, needing him. "P-please..."

"Please what?" His fingers moved faster.

"I need you," I panted.

"Tell me exactly what you want, Sophia. What was I doing to you in your dream? Say it."

My stomach trembled and my thighs shook. He swiped his

thumb over my clit, and I cried out. "Chasing me...h-holding me down. Please, Cillian, please fuck me."

He pulled his fingers from me, shoved my thighs wide, and pressed the fat head of his cock at my opening, pushing it in. "Fucking take it," he said, then slammed inside me.

I came instantly, arching and screaming, my pussy clamping down on him again and again as stars danced in my eyes. He held me down and fucked me hard and deep. I clung to him, needing something to ground me, needing him to anchor me when I was spiraling out of control. My eyes opened when he took my chin in his hand and stared down at me, teeth gritted, eyes glittering in the shadows. His eyes weren't cold now, they were hot, burning into me.

"You did this," he snarled. "You did this to me."

I gripped the side of his throat and shook my head. "I lov—"

He covered my mouth with his hand and slammed into me, grunting, those eyes still blazing down at me, stopping me from saying the words, even as I felt the smooth metal of his wedding ring against my lips. He hadn't taken it off. He pulsed thickly inside me and groaned, and with how deep he was fucking me, hitting me exactly where I needed him, I came with him, moaning against his hand still clamped over my mouth.

He finally collapsed, his ragged breaths against my throat. I wrapped my arms around him, and he instantly rolled away. He lay on his back, his arm over his eyes, still catching his breath. His rejection hurt, but I refused to let it get to me. He was confused and hurt, and the only way he knew how to deal with that was to punish me.

My gaze moved over his now smooth jaw, down his throat, to the white bandage wrapped around his bicep, then to his hand resting on his stomach, and down to his wedding ring, still where I'd put it. He told me he didn't care, but that ring told me otherwise. God, he was beautiful. "How's your arm?"

He didn't answer.

I edged closer, and this time, he didn't move. "I started to think you'd never come. That you'd forget about me."

Again, no answer.

I eased over the rest of the way and wrapped my arm around his waist, desperate for him to hold me. "I missed you," I whispered.

———

Cillian

I needed to get the hell up and leave this room, but I couldn't bring myself to push her away. I liked her there, pressed against me, too fucking much. Seamus would say I was weak, and he'd be right. When I was a kid, he would have beaten my ass for letting emotion get the better of me, because that's what this was. My breathing had calmed, but it'd started growing choppy again. Fuck, I felt as if something were pressing against my windpipe.

My heart raced faster, a feeling that I did not fucking like almost had me gasping. I felt...out of control. All logic, all common sense vanished when Sophia wrapped her arms around me and pressed close.

She was my prisoner, but right then it was her that held me captive. Whatever it was that had me breaking into her apartment, watching her sleep, obsessing over her, wanting her for a full year, was the same thing that had me lying here now, unable to move. She didn't even know it, but she was the one with all the power.

Why the fuck was she doing this, why was she pressed against me like this?

Because she knew just how weak she made me. Somehow, she knew.

Declan asked me if I wanted her to love me, and the truth was, I did. I wanted that badly. But I couldn't trust her, and I couldn't trust this. Not anymore.

I sure as fuck didn't want her pretending she had feelings for me because she was scared, because I had her locked in my house, in this room, like the psycho I was.

What the fuck was I doing?

I pulled away from her and got the fuck out of the bed. She sat up, her blond hair mussed around her beautiful face, her cheeks still flushed. "Cillian? What are you doing?"

If I didn't do this now, I'd change my mind. I'd keep her locked in here for the rest of her life and never let her go. "Be ready to leave in an hour."

"Leave? Where are we going?"

"We're not going anywhere," I said.

Silence filled the room, and her wide blue eyes filled with hurt.

"You promised me...you promised that you'd never let me go," she whispered.

Her words fucking pierced something inside me. I choked it down. "I lied."

———

Sophia

There was a knock, and the door to my room opened exactly one hour later.

Conor gave my body a sweep, making sure I was ready. "Time to leave."

"Where am I going?"

His gaze actually softened. "I have instructions to take you wherever you want to go."

I didn't understand what was going on here. "Go?"

"Everything's packed, what we couldn't fit in the car will be sent to your new address."

Pain and disbelief had me shaking. This couldn't be happening. Cillian was throwing me out, throwing me away? "I want to speak to Cillian."

"He's busy right now."

"My phone, do you have it?"

He pulled it from his pocket and handed it to me. I quickly opened my contacts.

"He won't answer," Conor said.

I tapped his number anyway. It rang and rang, and then his deep voice echoed down the line telling me to leave a message.

"Sorry, darlin', but it's over," Conor said and closed the space between us, ushering me out of the room and down the hall. The house was silent, felt empty. I looked into my office as we passed, everything except the heavy furniture was gone.

I walked down the stairs, and Conor strode to the door. He opened it, and I turned back, looking up when movement caught my eye. Cillian stood at the top of the stairs, looking down at me. He said nothing. I wanted to run to him, to make him talk to me, to make him believe me, but the look on his face told me he wasn't going to listen.

My legs shook, and my heart broke, but I forced myself to turn away—

Thunder exploded beside me, blood spraying from Conor's

shoulder, hitting my face. I screamed and spun around. Seamus stood in his pajamas, the gun in his shaky hand aimed at Cillian. "No!" I ran at Seamus without thought, colliding with him as more shots exploded around me. We hit the ground. My ears rang, my hip and arm throbbing from the way I hit the tiled floor. Seamus was utterly still beneath me. I scrambled back and my hand slipped. Blood, so much of it.

He was dead, a shot through the head.

I spun around to check that Cillian was okay. He was striding toward us as Danny and several of his men ran in.

"Are you hit?" Cillian snapped.

I looked down at myself. I was covered in blood but none of it was mine. "No."

His jaw was tight as hell. "Get Conor to the hospital." He turned to Danny. "And get Sophia cleaned up and out of here."

What? "No. Cillian..."

"You can't be here," he said through gritted teeth, his gaze slicing back to Danny. "Get her out of here, now."

Danny grabbed my arm and dragged me from the room. We went out to the pool area, and he ushered me into the small bathroom out there. Then ordered one of the other guys to grab me a change of clothes from my bags before giving me another light shove toward the bathroom. He turned his back to me but didn't leave.

I dragged off my blood-slicked clothes and numbly got into the shower. I didn't remember any of it. I dried myself and took the clothes Danny had set on the counter. No underwear, a pair of pants that I'd only worn once to a funeral, and my pajama top. I pulled them on, wrung out my hair as best I could, and let Danny guide me around the side of the house.

There was no sign of Cillian now, but I guess he had a body to deal with. He'd just shot and killed his father.

"Take me to Cillian," I said to Danny.

He shook his head. "He wants you off the property."

"When can I come back?" I asked when he opened the door for me.

"You can't, Soph. I'm sorry," he said, the same look of pity on his face that Conor had given me.

"Are you going to kill me now?" I asked.

"You gonna tell anyone what happened?"

"No." I didn't want to think about it, there was no way I'd tell anyone about it.

"Then, no," he said.

I wasn't really afraid for my life. Cillian may be kicking me out, but he'd never let anyone hurt me. "Will you let me know how Conor is?"

"Yeah," he said and shut the door after me. He got in and turned to me. "There any place you can go?"

I wasn't going home. My father was dead to me. "No."

"What about your friend, the loud, flirty one?"

Fiona's was an option, but if she saw me now, I'd fall apart. I quickly searched my phone and found an Airbnb close by that had a couple weeks available. I booked it for the next day. "Just take me to a hotel, any will do, I have something arranged for tomorrow. I'll text you the address and you can have my stuff delivered there tomorrow, if that's okay?"

Danny nodded, started the car, and we drove away.

It was hard, but I managed to hold my emotions in check as I said goodbye, as I walked away and checked in to my room for the night. I took the elevator to the fifth floor, found my room, and shut the door, and even then, I refused to let the pain and fear overwhelm me. Because despite what had happened, or what Danny said, or Cillian sending me away, this wasn't over—Cillian and I weren't done.

I could be as stubborn as he was.

Chapter Twenty-Six

Cillian

"She's back," Conor said, his lips curled up.

I walked to the balcony and looked out to the front gate.

"What does she want?" I asked, my chest so fucking tight I could hardly breathe.

Conor chuckled behind me. "To talk to you."

I rubbed my forehead, a headache building behind my eyes. Why was she doing this? Fuck, this was torture. Because of me, she'd almost been fucking shot the last time she was here. Watching Danny lead her away covered in Seamus's blood—Jesus, for long seconds I thought that blood was hers—I gripped the railing. My fucking heart had stopped in my chest.

We'd found Sally, and she'd fallen apart, terrified, spilling the truth of what really happened that night. Seamus had been using her as a go-between to make deals with Brennan and Paolo. She'd been the one to open the gates and let him in, not Sophia. She said Sophia didn't know Paolo would be there, that she'd been scared when she'd seen him, and he'd forced her into the car. Sophia had known nothing about her father's plans for her. They'd been feeding Seamus's ego, had used him to get to me, to get into my house, but they had no intention of letting him live.

I realized now, when I'd carried Sophia inside my house after we'd been shot at and found Sally standing there, the shock on her face hadn't been about the shooting but that I was still alive.

I'd failed Sophia, in every possible way. She'd said she loved me, but still, the idea that she could truly feel that way, that she could truly *want me*, be *in love* with me, the O'Rourke monster, was so fucking...foreign, seemed so truly impossible, that believing she'd betrayed me was the more logical choice.

But she hadn't. She hadn't betrayed me. I rubbed the ache in the center of my chest.

Sophia lifted her hand, shading her eyes from the sun, spotting me standing here. What did she want to say to me? She should be afraid. I'd accused her of betraying me, locked her up, called her a whore, then fucked her like one. Then she'd almost been shot and I'd thrown her out of my house like she was nothing.

Yet she'd shown up for the third day in a row, demanding to speak with me. Didn't she know I was trying to protect her? From the violence of this world, from me.

"What do you want me to do?" Conor asked.

I should tell him to send her away, like I had the last two days, but after the shit I did to her, if she came here to cuss me out or take a swing, maybe I should let her in. I owed her that much. Christ, I owed her an apology, but letting her back in this house was dangerous. She made me feel things, do things—want things, I never had before. "Let her in," I said before I realized I was going to say it.

Conor smirked. "You might wanna get the Kevlar out." He huffed a laugh. "Though, the way she went for Seamus when she realized he was aiming for you, I don't think you have anything to worry about." Then he walked out.

She had done that, hadn't she? She'd seen him turn his gun on me and she'd run at him. She'd tried to *protect me*. I gripped the railing tighter as the memory flooded my mind. She could have been killed for fuck's sake. Why would she do that?

I watched as Conor strode toward the gates, then I turned away, not sure how to deal with the storm raging in my gut, the way my heart was suddenly pounding in my chest. I squeezed my fists tight and tried to even out my breathing. I was still trying to pull it the fuck together when the door opened. Conor walked in first, then stepped aside letting Sophia in.

Christ, she was beautiful.

Conor, the fucker, winked at me from behind Sophia before walking back out and shutting the door behind him.

"Sally admitted everything," I said before she could speak. "I know you had nothing to do with what happened that night."

She nodded. "No, I didn't."

We stared at each other across the room, the seconds stretching out.

"Why are you here?" I asked, breaking the silence.

At the same time, she said, "You let me in."

"You seemed determined to talk to me," I said.

She took a step closer. "You don't know why I'm here? Really?"

I studied her beautiful face. "I thought perhaps you'd like to hit me."

She flashed me a smile. "Not only that."

My gaze moved over her arms, seeing the dark bruises there. I'd been worried that without me there to stop her, she'd injure herself while she slept. "You hurt yourself."

"I've been having a lot of nightmares since you sent me

away." She shook her head. "And you aren't there to hold me down."

Fuck. The pull toward her was intense. I'd been in the same room as her a matter of minutes and I was already close to snapping, to snatching her up and not letting her leave. "You need to be more careful." I hadn't meant my voice to come out harsh, but it did. Seeing her hurt was fucking with me.

"Until you, I got hurt all the time, Cillian."

I flinched, the action taking me by surprise. "It's not wise for you to be here."

"No?" She took another step closer. "Why is that?"

"You know the kind of man I am, pet," I said, and my voice shook in a way it never had before. "You shouldn't have come back here."

"Why?" she whispered.

I wasn't sure what to say. I just knew I couldn't force her to be here against her will a moment longer. "Say what you came to, quickly, then you need to leave. I told you, Sophia, what happens when I make something mine. It's...it's dangerous for you to be here."

"You said you don't let go of what's yours." Her head tilted to the side. "So why did you let me go?" she asked again, not letting me off the hook.

I studied her face, the look in her eyes. There was something like triumph there, and I wasn't sure why. "Because I...I didn't want to..." *What?*

"You didn't want to force me to be here against my will," she said as if she'd read my mind.

"No."

"Why do you think that is?"

I was breathing harder, and my fucking hands shook. "Sophia," I growled. I didn't know what she was saying, what she wanted from me, but the longer she was here, the harder this was.

She took another step, so she was standing right in front of me. "You let me go because you wanted me to be with you of my own free will. You wanted me to be here with you because I wanted to be, not because you forced me." She tilted her head back and stared up at me. "And the reason you wanted that, Cillian, is because you're in love with me."

I blinked down at her, fighting the urge to snatch her off her feet and crush her to me, while every muscle in my body seized at what she'd just said. Was that what I was feeling? Was this tangled knot in my gut and this fist in the center of my chest love? I hadn't been able to think of anything but her since I sent her away. I walked around the house fucking lost. Found myself in her office, or her closet, or fuck, sniffing her shampoo that had been left in my bathroom or the vanilla-and-cinnamon lotion I couldn't bring myself to throw away. I hadn't even changed the sheets and woke gripping her fucking pillow every morning.

I still wore my wedding ring. I looked at her hand, and she still wore hers.

"Have you ever heard that saying 'if you love something, set it free, if it comes backs it's yours, if it doesn't, it never was' or something like that?" She placed her hands on my chest. "I came back, Cillian, because despite how we came together, I'm in love with you too."

I actually rocked back. "You still love me?"

"I never stopped."

I slid my hand up the side of her throat and curled my fingers, holding her in place. "You ran at Seamus. You tried to protect me."

"That's what you do when you love someone," she whispered.

She'd walked back into the lion's den and now there was no escape. "I let you go, and you came back to me," I said.

"Yes," she whispered.

"Because you knew I was in love with you," I said roughly. "Even though I didn't realize it myself?"

"Yes," she said again, a small, gorgeous fucking smile curling her lips.

"You know what that means, don't you, pet?"

"What does that mean, Cillian?"

"That you are mine, and I will never let you go again." I snatched her off her feet and thrust my fingers in her hair.

She pressed her curves into me, and I groaned.

"And you are mine." She curled her arms around my neck.

Yes, I fucking was.

I slammed my mouth down on hers and headed for the stairs.

Epilogue

Cillian

I flicked off the lights, rechecked the security system, and headed upstairs. Sophia had moved her office to another room, and we'd converted the room next to us, complete with a connecting door that we kept open, into a nursery for Fia.

My daughter hadn't made a peep, still curled against me as I walked into our room. It wasn't completely dark, a night-light glowed from the wall by the adjoining door.

Soph was still sleeping when I walked back into our room. She was exhausted, needing more sleep than usual, which was normal for any new mother, but with her sleep disorder, she needed even more rest. She was managing well, though, with a little help.

She jolted awake suddenly, instantly searching the bed.

"It's okay, pet. I've got her," I said.

She collapsed back, her breath bursting from her. "I could've hurt her. Oh god, I could have really hurt her."

She'd been feeding Fia and they'd both fallen asleep, but I'd been right there, and I'd scooped her up before I went to lock up. "I promised I'd stay awake, pet, and you're always still when she's beside you. I took her just to be safe, but you never moved once."

Her gaze took me in, cradling our daughter. "I can't do that again," she said, her voice breaking. "If I hurt her, I'd never forgive myself."

I strode over and sat on the side of the bed. "You won't."

"How can you be so sure?"

"Because I know you." I leaned in and kissed her softly. "Even when you sleep, when you dream, you know she exists."

"I won't risk it," she said.

"And you aren't, because I'm here. I'll always be here to make sure both my girls are safe and happy."

She leaned in, resting her head against my thigh. "We are," she said and took my hand, brushing her thumb over my wedding band. "I've never been this happy...or this terrified of losing it all."

"You will never lose me, Soph, or our daughter. I'll make sure of that."

She blinked up at me. "I knew that underneath it all you were this man, at least for me, and our daughter, and Tommy." She pressed a kiss to my hand. "With all the love and care I knew in my heart you were capable of, even if you weren't as sure."

She was right, this part of me only existed for them. "I am because of you."

Sophia pressed a gentle kiss to Fia's little head and smiled up at me. "It was there all the time, you just needed an incentive."

I pressed a kiss to the top of her head and carried Fia to her nursery, placing her carefully in her bassinet.

After Sophia's father was exposed for the traitor he was, he'd emptied his bank accounts and ran, leaving Celeste, Tommy, and Sophia behind without a second glance. What my wife didn't know, was that he didn't get far, he'd never be coming back, and Tommy now had a trust fund waiting for him when he came of age. I'd hired a full-time nanny for Tommy to make sure he was well taken care of when he was with his mother. Celeste was there for him when she wanted to be, but more often than not Tommy was here with us. He was taking it all in stride, and he seemed to like me, but not as much as he liked Declan.

I tucked the covers around our daughter and walked back to my wife, climbing in beside her and pulling her close.

"I miss you," she said.

I tightened my hold on her. "Right here, beauty."

"I miss having you inside me."

My breath punched from my lungs. "Only a little longer, pet," I said, my voice rough as hell.

Fia had been born only a month ago, so we still had a couple weeks before we could have sex again. She said she missed being connected to me that way, and I had to agree. People said her sex drive might be less, that the tiredness would definitely affect it, but she was used to being tired, and I made sure she wasn't doing this alone.

"I've been thinking about something lately," she said.

"What's that?" I asked, while I traced the tattoo she'd gotten after she moved back in here with me.

It was a monster on her arm, her monster. She said it was me, watching, always watching, always keeping her safe. If you looked closely, you could see my name hidden in the design. She'd surprised me with it, and I fucking loved it.

"After the six weeks is up and I'm fully healed...the next time you see me having one of my dreams...about you...would you..." I bit my lip.

"What?" I was breathing harder now. I knew what she was

going to say. "What do you want me to do, pet? I need to hear you say it."

"I want you to fuck me awake."

"Fuck," I said, sounding needy as fuck. I hadn't done it again, not since that first time.

"You like that idea?" she said and reached down between us, wrapping her hand around my achingly hard cock.

"You know I do," I said roughly.

"I think about it a lot, that night when you woke me, the way you felt inside me, over me, the look in your eyes." She shivered.

We talked about it while we fucked all the time, but I wasn't going to do it again until she asked me to. I groaned when she stroked me more firmly and then rolled to my back.

She straddled my hips and ground her clit against my cock trapped between our bodies, so we were dry humping through our underwear like horny teenagers.

It didn't take long before we were both coming hard.

She fell against me, clinging to me. I banded my arms around her, and she rubbed her face against my chest. "I love you, my beautiful monster," she said.

I cupped her face and made her look up at me. "Love you, too, my precious sleeping beauty."

Also by Sherilee Gray

Blood Moon Brides:

Blood Moon Bound

The Thornheart Trials:

A Curse in Darkness

A Vow of Ruin

A Trial by Blood

An Oath at Midnight

A Promise of Ashes

A Bond in Flames

Knights of Hell:

Knight's Seduction

Knight's Redemption

Knight's Salvation

Demon's Temptation

Knight's Dominion

Knight's Absolution

Knight's Retribution

Rocktown Ink:

Beg For You

Sin For You

Meant For you

Bad For You

All For You

Just for You

The Smith Brothers:

Mountain Man

Wild Man

Solitary Man

Lawless Kings:

Shattered King

Broken Rebel

Beautiful Killer

Ruthless Protector

Glorious Sinner

Merciless King

Boosted Hearts:

Swerve

Spin

Slide

Spark

Axle Alley Vipers:

Crashed

Revved

Wrecked

Black Hills Pack:

Lone Wolf's Captive

A Wolf's Deception

Stand Alone Novels:

Breaking Him

While You Sleep

About the Author

Sherilee Gray is a kiwi girl and lives in beautiful New Zealand with her husband and their two children. When she isn't writing sexy contemporary or paranormal romance, searching for her next alpha hero on Pinterest, or fueling her voracious book addiction, she can be found dreaming of far off places with a mug of tea in one hand and a bar of chocolate in the other.

To find out about new releases, giveaways, events and other cool stuff, sign up for my newsletter!

www.sherileegray.com

www.ingramcontent.com/pod-product-compliance
Lightning Source LLC
Chambersburg PA
CBHW031258120726
47906CB00003B/800